Betrayed

Betrayed

Patricia Haley

www.urbanchristianonline.com

Urban Books, LLC
78 East Industry Court
Deer Park, NY 11729

ISBN 13: 978-1-60162-755-1
ISBN 10: 1-60162-755-6

First Printing May 2013
Printed in the United States of America

10 9 8 7 6 5 4 3 2 1

This is a work of fiction. Any references or similarities to actual events, real people, living or dead, or to real locales are intended to give the novel a sense of reality. Any similarity in other names, characters, places, and incidents is entirely coincidental.

Distributed by Kensington Corp.
Submit Wholesale Orders to:
Kensington Publishing Corp.
C/O Penguin Group (USA) Inc.
Attention: Order Processing
405 Murray Hill Parkway
East Rutherford, NJ 07073-2316
Phone: 1-800-526-0275
Fax: 1-800-227-9604

Betrayed

Patricia Haley

"Haley has hit the mark yet again! I couldn't put this book down—the characters are believable and compelling."
—*Maurice M. Gray, Jr., author of All Things Work Together*

"The story grabs the reader from the beginning, drawing you in . . . and keeping you on the edge of your seat as the plot takes unexpected twists and turns."
—*RT Book Reviews on Let Sleeping Dogs Lie*

"The perfect blend of faith and romance."
—*Gospel Book Review*

"Haley's writing and visualization skills are to be reckoned with. . . . This story is full-bodied. . . . Great prose, excellent execution!"
—*RAWSISTAZ™ on Still Waters*

"A deeply moving novel. The characters and the story line remind us that forgiveness and unconditional love are crucial to any relationship."
—*Good Girl Book Club*

"*No Regrets* offered me a different way, a healthier way based in faith and hope, to look at trying situations."
—*Montgomery Newspapers*

Also by **Patricia Haley**

Mitchell Family Drama Series
Anointed
Betrayed
Chosen
Destined
Broken

Other Titles
Let Sleeping Dogs Lie
Still Waters
No Regrets
Blind Faith
Nobody's Perfect

Betrayed is dedicated to the dynamic sisters of

Delta Sigma Theta Sorority, Inc.,
Founded on January 13, 1913,
By twenty-two incredible, young, college-educated
women who believed that they could make a difference in the world by pooling their talents, energy, and
resources together. They were united by a single vision of bettering the lives of others.

One hundred years later, their vision and impact on
the world are a living reality. I'm proud to be a member of such an illustrious international sisterhood.
Blessings and much Delta love to all my beautiful sis-
ters/sorors as we move into the next hundred years of
service, wrapped in the loving arms of sisterhood.

Special recognition to chapters that I've been privi-
leged to be a member of:
Epsilon Nu–San Francisco City Wide (initiated 1982)
Omicron Chi–Stanford (charter member 1983)
Schaumburg-Hoffman Estates Alumnae
(charter member 1991)

Rockford (IL) Alumnae
Valley Forge (PA) Alumnae
Pontiac (MI) Alumnae

For if you forgive men when they sin against you,
your heavenly Father will also forgive you.
But if you do not forgive men their sins, your Father
will not forgive your sins.

Matthew 6:14–15

Chapter 1

Summer was still a few weeks away, but the blistering heat didn't wait for the official notification. It was present today, right now, blanketing Detroit with no regard for those who were sure to get burned.

"We're loaded and ready to go, Mrs. Mitchell," the driver said as Madeline stood in the driveway with her ex-husband, four children, and some of the house staff.

"I don't want to go. You can't make me go," the little girl screamed, clinging to her dad. Her three brothers were visibly unhappy but didn't make a scene.

"I can make you, and I will, young lady," Madeline told her daughter.

"I'd rather die than leave Daddy here by himself. He's going to be super sad."

Madeline snatched up her seven-year-old daughter and shook her frantically. "Don't you ever say that again," Madeline demanded before pulling her daughter in for a tight embrace. The thought of her children dying or being hurt was more than she could bear. "Dave, I need you to help me here." She wanted to scream out for him to do something. He could see how upset the child was. Why was he just standing there with his hands in his pockets? She wanted to yell at him to help, but she didn't want to appear angry in front of her babies. They were already too miserable. Instead she calmly asked, "Dave, how did it come to this?" She pressed hard to keep her emotions in check.

Dave slid his hands out of his pockets and let his gaze slump. "I guess we lost sight of what was important. If it helps, I want you to know that I'm sorry."

Sorry, she thought. That wasn't enough ointment to soothe her aching pain and humiliation. A billion rosy words weren't going to fix their broken relationship. Honesty and respect were what she needed, something she hadn't gotten.

Madeline was snapped back into the moment when Tamara began badgering her father to go with them. Madeline's heart wanted to crumble into tiny little pieces.

"Tamara, Daddy needs you to be a big girl. We might not live in the same house any more, but I'll see you all the time," her father uttered.

She wrapped her little arms around his neck. "You promise?"

"I promise."

Listening to Dave made Madeline cringe. Why was he lying to their child? Even when they lived together, he wasn't home much. Work was his first priority—always had been, always would be. "Can we talk?" she asked him.

"Sure," Dave said, continuing to hug their daughter.

"Wait out here, guys. Mommy and Daddy will be right back." Madeline turned toward the nanny and housekeeper. "Please watch the children while we go inside for a few minutes." They both agreed. She told the driver they'd be right back too.

Madeline and Dave went inside. Despite the twelve-foot-tall solid wood door, the heat had infiltrated the foyer, where Madeline stood with her husband. Tension had a choke hold on the room.

"I can't believe you stood there and lied to that child. How dare you treat us like this?"

"What else do you want from me?" Dave Mitchell asked.

"I want some respect. That's what I want," Madeline barked at him. "Don't ask silly questions, Dave. I don't have time for this." He smirked, which irritated her. "I guess you think this is funny, but then, the joke has apparently always been on me."

His gaze dipped. "Madeline, I'm not going to stand here and rehash our divorce. It won't help either of us."

"You can't dictate anything to me. If I want to discuss the divorce, I'll discuss the divorce. Fourteen years of marriage gives me the right to say whatever I want to."

Dave didn't object, which irritated her further. She wanted him to say something inappropriate and justify the lashing she wanted to give him. He didn't accommodate, but it didn't stop Madeline from commanding center stage.

"Really, tell me what I can do to make our relationship more cordial," he said.

"We're divorced now. It's too late to be concerned about what you can do. I gave you a year to step up and fix your mistake."

Dave sighed. "Come on, Madeline, you know that's not true. I begged you not to get divorced. I pleaded with you to save the marriage, and you wouldn't hear of it. Once your mind was set, there was no turning back."

"So you gave up without a fight?" she hurled at him.

"I accepted reality."

"Humph. Call it whatever you'd like," she said, letting her words pierce like darts. "The truth is, you were too weak to stand up for us." As smart as Dave was, he sounded stupid to her. Didn't he know that she'd wanted his heart? She'd wanted him to woo her back to the marriage.

He hadn't, and it was driving her crazy. "You let that tramp destroy our marriage."

Dave sighed again and tightened his lips but didn't respond.

"Well, what do you have to say? I'm not talking to myself."

"There is nothing to say. Between court and you telling me how you feel every opportunity you get, it's all been said. I made a mistake."

"Humph. You made more than a mistake. You cheated on our marriage. You betrayed my trust and defiled our bed. You ruined us," she said, getting overly emotional, almost like a radiator preparing to explode.

"Fine. I cheated. I'm sorry. I've told you that a million times."

"Maybe I need a million and one."

Dave gently grabbed Madeline's arms. "What are we doing here? Are we fighting to save the marriage, or are we fighting because it's over? Which one is it, because I'm honestly confused about what you want."

Truthfully, Madeline didn't know what she wanted, either. The only thing she knew for sure was that Dave would not have a moment of peace so long as her world was in turmoil. If she was confused and hurt, he was going to have a slice of the same trauma. His selfishness had earned him a sizable slice, and she was intent on making sure he got it, at least that was what her heart said as the hurt rose within her. But the touch of his hands ignited a spark that didn't seem as easily suppressed. A mixture of emotions flooded her, but she refused to let Dave see her as vulnerable. She clung to her anger like an anchor as he spoke.

"I've tried to do right by you. I was very generous with the divorce settlement. You wanted the estate. I gave it to you. Didn't I, even though you decided at the last minute not to keep the house. That was your do-ing—not mine," he said pointing his finger at her.

Madeline didn't want to acknowledge that he was correct. Agreeing might diminish her anger, and she didn't want to let him off so easily. She struggled to maintain her disenchanted attitude.

He went on. "I gave you a permanent position in DMI. I put it in writing so that no one could ever challenge your role in DMI, not even me. I did that for you, didn't I?" Madeline tried looking away, but Dave's gaze followed her, refusing to let go as he let his hands continue to gently grip her arms. "Didn't I?" he asked again.

"Yes, yes, okay," she said, pulling away from his grip as pride took over. "But you didn't do me any favors. You owed me that much after the humiliation you put me through. I earned every dime of the seven million dollars you gave me. We built our company together. I was there from day one." She crossed her arms. "So don't make it seem like you did something special. You just did what was right. The house, the money, the company, and the children are as much mine as yours."

"I agree, which is why you didn't get any resistance from me."

Madeline fought to regain her composure. She handed a cluster of keys to Dave. "Here, take these," she said, closing his fingers around the keys.

"You don't have to do this. This is your house. It's the only house the children know." Dave clutched her hand and peered into her gaze. "They didn't create this situation. They don't deserve to be uprooted. Don't make them move out," he pleaded.

The deal was done. They had to move on. She had to move on. There were too many memories on May-weather Lane for Madeline to stay and have any shot at happiness without Dave. If she changed her mind later, so be it. But for right now Madeline had to walk away to maintain her sanity. "It's yours," she said, opening the door.

Tamara and their youngest son darted toward the door. Tamara latched on to her father's leg and refused to let go. Madeline's heart was breaking, but she had to maintain order. She kept fighting desperately to keep her emotions contained. Madeline and Dave literally had to pry their daughter's fingers to loosen the grip she had on his leg. She was inconsolable, but they managed to get her in the car with the other children before Madeline pulled away, leaving Dave standing alone on the front doorstep.

Forty minutes later Madeline and her four children entered a town near Rochester Hills, a place where modest homes were over four thousand square feet. Madeline had searched intensely for a secluded neighborhood where her family could grow up protected from public scrutiny. The limousine eased up to the wrought-iron security gate surrounding the home, which was nearly a block long. The whimpering of her children, coupled with a heaviness saturating the car, drained Madeline. She didn't want to move. Why bother? It didn't feel like she had anything left except her pride. When the driver opened the door, Madeline got out.

The children climbed out behind her.

"No, no, stay in the car. I'm just getting out to program the new code."

"But we want to get out too," one of the children said.

"Fine. Get out," Madeline told them, too tired to fight with her six-, seven-, nine-, and twelve year-old children. The day had worn her down.

She watched as the children stood next to the daunting security gate, crying their eyes out. Their misery pierced her soul, hacking at the core of her motherhood. In that moment, Madeline didn't know if she'd made the right decision in leaving Dave or the Mitchell estate. Her greatest fear was the impact on her children. Was her decision to leave the right one? She just didn't know. After what seemed like hours, she finally acknowledged that the decision was made, and whatever happened now, she'd just have to live with.

"Get back in the car, children. We have to go," she said, keying in the security code. As the massive gate opened, she felt her heart closing. She wanted to cry but wouldn't, not yet, not until they were safely inside their new home and her bedroom door was locked. Then she'd release the depth of her pain and sob privately until either her tear ducts dried up or sleep swept in and had mercy on her.

Chapter 2

"Good morning, Mr. Mitchell," the security guard called as Dave strolled through the lobby of DMI.

Dave replied with a pleasant greeting. Indeed it was a good morning. For the first time in over a year, he'd slept at home, in his own bed, instead of in the leased unit. Night after night of lying down and getting up in the leased penthouse suite had been agonizing, more than he'd realized until this morning. Waking up and setting his feet on the rug he and Madeline had purchased in Spain many years ago, had given him an extra charge. He was reminded of how happy they once were as a couple.

Rising at 5:00 A.M. to be in the office by 6:00 A.M. didn't feel as daunting, not today. He was alive. Now that he was at DMI, his place of refuge, he experienced a renewed sense of purpose, which strengthened with each step.

"You have a good day, sir," Dave told the guard as he approached the elevators. On second thought, he had enough energy to climb the stairs to the sixth floor. He could use the time to clear out any lingering thoughts of the fiasco that had happened with Madeline and the kids when they left the estate yesterday. His feelings wanted to be heavy, but his mind wouldn't take the guilt trip. He knew better. Fretting over areas that he couldn't control was dangerous. One thought would lead to regret, with the next stops sure to be guilt and resentment, ending at bitterness and unforgiveness. That wasn't a path he chose to travel. He'd repented for his infidelity, and as much as failure wanted to press him, there was no regressing. He'd keep stepping.

Dave took two stairs at a time, reaching the executive floor rather quickly. He didn't want to spend an extra second dwelling on the past if there was nothing to be gained. He went into his office, mentally preparing his agenda for the day. The photo with former President Jimmy Carter and current President Ronald Reagan was prominently displayed on his wall. It was taken a few years ago during the 1980 election campaign and served as the only greeting he got this morning.

Dave prayed for direction and strength as he shunned the negative thoughts. Separation from his kids and divorce from his wife could have killed his spirit, but he'd fought hard not to let despair take residency. He delved into the handful of contracts on his desk prepared to submerge his energy and loneliness into his work.

Time slipped by. By 8:30 A.M. his secretary, Sharon, was poking her head inside his office. The door was open. "Mr. Mitchell. I just wanted to let you know that I'm in."

"Good. Can you do me a favor and have Frank come up to my office? I need to see him."

Dave returned his attention to the Eastern Lutheran Group contract after she left. Something wasn't right. The numbers weren't adding up. He tapped at the calculator for a while, each time netting the same results.

The eldest Mitchell brother walked in. "You looking for me?" Frank asked.

"Have a seat," Dave said, pointing to one of the chairs at his conference table. He got up from the desk and went to the table too. "I can't figure out what's going on with the Eastern Lutheran Group (ELG) account," he said, sliding the stapled cluster of papers toward Frank. "This should be four hundred fifty thousand. Based on this quote, all I can come up with is two hundred seventy-five thousand. There's a mistake somewhere, but for the life of me, I don't see it."

Frank breathed a sigh and exhaled loudly. "There's no mistake," he said, leaning on the table. Dave looked perplexed. "The numbers don't lie."

"Well, somebody's lying if you're telling me this is correct. What changed?" Dave asked. "Did they decide to cut down on the number of people they had originally registered to take our leadership training program?"

"Nope. No changes with the assumptions."

"Then what's going on?" Dave said emphatically. Frank knew something. Dave could tell. He wasn't up for games. He needed his brother to start talking. "What is it?"

"We had to give ELG a sizable cut."

"Why? I'm okay with giving discounts to make a deal work for a client, but this is about forty percent off. That's steep, especially this early into the East Coast expansion project. At this rate, we'll burn through our surplus and have little to no funds left to subsidize other churches that need financial support."

"Had no choice."

"Of course we had a choice."

"Trust me, we didn't."

"What's so special about the Eastern Lutheran Group that they need this kind of a break? You know I've dealt with the group before. They're always looking for a ridiculous discount, which we don't give." Dave trusted his brother with managing the corporate finances and running the operation, but no deal was fully complete unless he had some level of involvement and gave his blessing. That was Dave's strength, being able to influence clients and get them to understand why they needed the same financial and leadership services that DMI provided to a long list of satisfied churches and religious organizations.

"It's different in this case. We have no option based on the situation you've put us in."

"Me?" Dave said raising his voice slightly.

"Yes, you."

Dave heard the tone in Frank's response but didn't comment.

"I told you last year that your indiscretion was going to affect all of us, including your beloved DMI. Now it has." Dave was silent. He let Frank continue. His tone became increasingly agitated. "I told you that the relationship with your former secretary was going to ruin your reputation along with the company," Frank said, slapping his hand on the tabletop.

"We can't blame Sherry for this."

"Maybe you can't, but I sure can. You better blame somebody, unless you're prepared to keep seeing the kind of numbers you have here," Frank said, poking his finger at the page.

"It's not that bad."

"Look at the numbers, man. We have to give the services away in order to keep the doors open. The pathetic part is that we had to twist their arms to keep the deal going, period."

"I don't know why. This is their second contract expansion. Obviously, they're pleased with our services," Dave said.

"They can read the newspaper like the rest of us. Face it. You left Madeline and your kids for a secretary young enough to be your daughter. Nobody, except a fool, is going to pay you to give them lessons on integrity and leadership. Who's giving you lessons?" Frank's fury appeared to ease slightly. "Take my advice. Go back to your wife if you want better numbers."

Dave's gaze slumped as he toyed with a pen. "I can't. It's over. Madeline and the children moved out of the estate yesterday. There's no chance of reconciling now. She's made it clear that we're history." The reality rolled off his tongue, refusing to be delayed by wishful thinking.

"Wow," Frank said, shaking his head. "You really blew it, little brother. How could you mess up in such a major way? And you're supposed to be the godly one in the bunch." Frank snickered.

"I'm not proud of what I did, but I honestly believe in my spirit that God's plan for my life hasn't vanished because of my big mistake."

"Oh, come on. Cut the crap, Dave. It's me, Frank, your brother, your chief financial officer," he said, poking his index finger in his chest. "I'm your chief operations manager, your right-hand man, the one who knows everything around here."

"What's done is done." Dave didn't bother telling his brother how hard he'd tried reconciling with Madeline, how much he yearned to be with his family. He didn't bother telling Frank, because it wouldn't make a difference. There were times when people didn't want to know the truth. Sitting in the seat of judgment was sometimes preferred. "I can choose to dwell on what I can't change, or I can opt to direct my energy toward the future." Dave had chosen to move on. Frank had to get over it too.

"You can lay that cavalier mumbo jumbo on someone who's willing to listen. That's not for me. Two years ago you were someone who seemed to practice what you preached, but this is a new day," Frank said, staring at Dave. "Now it sounds like a bunch of self-righteous hogwash. Brother, things have definitely changed."

"Not between us," Dave said.

Frank shrugged his shoulders. "Everything has changed. I've backed you all this time because you were different. You were for real. I honestly thought you were an honorable man who knew how to keep his eye on the prize. Now I see you're common like the rest of us who sit at home on Sundays instead of running up in the church."

"I'm sorry you feel that way, but I don't need to justify myself to you. I can apologize for how my actions have affected you, but what else can I do to make this right with you? I'm at a loss here."

"Then I guess there's nothing left to say," Frank said.

"I guess not."

The meeting ended abruptly with neither willing to continue with the conversation. Dave sat numb, fumbling with his pen, while guilt hovered. Frank wasn't budging on his position. Dave didn't plan to grovel for his brother's validation, but the undeniable fact was that they had to work together. They had to figure out how to get past their discord so that DMI didn't suffer a double dose of failure.

Chapter 3

Frank stormed down the hallway, passing one office after the next. Frustration blinded him, causing his charge down the executive row to be a blur. Images of Dave and Sherry being intimately involved while he was married to Madeline further clouded the vision. They were messing with Frank's livelihood and a career he'd made sacrifices to build. He couldn't think straight. Frank wanted to shake some sense into his brother. What was Dave thinking? To be so smart, he was making such dumb choices, Frank thought.

"Hello, Mr. Mitchell," one of the secretaries greeted as he stood at the elevators.

"Oh, uh, hello," he said, oblivious to his surroundings. Frank didn't want to be any meaner than necessary. So he eased into the stairwell and sighed. Rubbing his head, he let his eyelids close to catch a moment of control.

Frank couldn't believe how caught up he'd gotten into Dave's drama. The word *selfish* played repeatedly in his mind, like a record on a turntable. With no regard to the damage he'd caused everybody else, Dave had selfishly let his careless act of passion bring down an entire company. Frank continued scratching his head as he descended the steps one at a time.

Disappointment and blame took turns holding his hand as he continued going downstairs. There was so much to go around that maybe Dave shouldn't get the total brunt of Frank's attitude. After all, Sherry had played a major role in destroying a family. She'd boldly inserted her single self into a well-established marriage. She definitely deserved a piece of the blame.

He paused on the landing between the third and fourth floors, pretending to be adjusting his watch, as a couple of employees ascended the stairs. Frank gave them a nod, hoping they'd get out of there quickly so he could return to his thoughts, unhindered. Once the employees were gone, Frank's assessment of who had ruined his professional life picked up right where he'd paused.

As much as he adored Madeline, he was angry at her too. She might have been a victim in the beginning, but playing the pity role wasn't the answer. The more he thought about it, the madder he became at Madeline for being so stubborn and refusing to consider the notion of reconciliation. She knew what was at stake with DMI. She knew better than anyone, but it wasn't enough to get her head on right.

Frank reached his floor and opened the door, but not before thinking about God. Perhaps He was the most significant culprit in this fiasco. He was the one who'd let Dave slip, especially when everybody knew how spiritually motivated Dave was and how much he walked in some kind of special grace and favor. Standing in the stairwell, Frank chalked the religious zeal up to a bunch of foolishness. Heck, he didn't claim to believe in or worship anyone. He could freely admit that there wasn't any special power or blessings lining his path. But Frank could also say that he wasn't an adulterer, a fraud, or a front. With that said, who needed religion? If it hadn't kept the special man of God from falling into one of the biggest traps in the world, then there was no hope for slobs like him.

Frank grabbed the doorknob. By the time Dave, Madeline, Sherry, and God split the pie of blame, Frank had only a sliver left. There was no way around choking down his cut for putting too much faith and trust into somebody. Wherever the anger ended up residing, there was plenty to share, enabling him to stay frustrated for quite a while. Frank stepped into the hallway, but wisdom chipped at him, small pecks at first. As he approached his office, the pecks of wisdom were more like slashes. His frustration hadn't dissipated, but the venom oozed out with each slash, providing a gentle reminder that the brothers had to work together as members of DMI's senior staff. Frank had to find a way to get the job done despite his personal disappointment. He pushed his pride aside and decided to go back and talk with Dave to figure it out. He had too much invested in both DMI and his own career not to work this out.

Chapter 4

Dave remained at the table in his office long after Frank had stormed out. Fretting didn't get the work done, so he didn't waste the energy. He sighed, peering over the Georgia Evangelical documents.

"Knock, knock," he heard someone say, looking up and seeing Sherry Henderson standing in his doorway. His reaction was unfiltered as joy leapt within him. "Thought I'd stop by and say hello," she said with a hint of a smile.

He was glad to see her. The mental illness hospital had served as a literal lifesaver for Sherry. "You look well," he said, getting up and approaching the door.

"I feel good."

"Yeah?" he said.

"Yes, really, I do," she said, coming closer.

His natural instinct would be to give her a big hug, demonstrating how pleased he was to see her healthy again. After delivering their stillborn baby last year, Sherry had suffered a mental breakdown. She had worked diligently to regain her strength and had come such a long ways.

"Have a seat," he said, directing her to his conference table. She went to close the door. "Oh no," he said, jumping to his feet. Every compassionate cell in his body reached for her, but decorum instantly erected a brick wall between them. He intentionally sat on opposite sides and told her to leave the door open. "So when did you go home?"

"Last week, and I'm ready to come back to work, but they don't have a job for me."

Dave wasn't exactly sure how he should respond. He was the chief executive officer, the ultimate decision maker at DMI. He had the power to hire and fire whoever, whenever, and for whatever reason. Yet her situation was a tad more complex. Before Sherry took the medical leave, she was working as an administrative assistant in Human Resources. He had had no choice but to move her to another department after Madeline found out about Sherry and the baby. Continuing as his administrative assistant hadn't been an option back then. He was pretty sure it wasn't one now. Even though he was divorced, he still had to consider the DMI staff. No one on his team was going to approach him about the former indiscretion, but he recognized that rumors and distractions didn't require his permission.

"I'm not fully aware of which positions are open."

"Could you maybe find out for me?" she asked in such a pitiful tone that it clutched his attention.

He reared back in his chair. "I thought you were on medical leave and getting paid."

"I am, but they want to give me a severance package instead of a job."

"I see."

Dave hadn't personally structured Sherry's employment plan. Madeline had given him an ultimatum of firing Sherry before the divorce was finalized. He hadn't done so due to her illness. Months ago he reluctantly agreed to a generous severance package for Sherry to calm the concerns of his executive team, mostly Madeline and Frank. Now that he was in a strained relationship with both, it didn't much matter to him whether Sherry kept her job or not. He just didn't want to be the one hammering out the details of her return.

"I don't want to give up my job. DMI gives me something to do every day. When I was working for you, I always had so much work to do." She giggled.

"I did work you pretty hard around here, didn't I?" Dave said, chuckling too and rearing back a little farther.

"Sure did," she replied.

As the two talked, Frank walked in. It was surprising to Dave as he wasn't expecting to see Frank for at least a day based on their earlier disagreement. Before Dave could acknowledge his brother's presence, he watched the enthusiasm drain from Frank's face. Frank turned to walk out without speaking.

"Where are you going?" Dave asked. "Please stay."

Sherry's gaze dropped, and it seemed like she was avoiding eye contact with Frank.

"That's okay. I'm going to my office," Frank mumbled.

"You don't have to leave," Dave pleaded. "Let's talk."

"There's no point," Frank said, hurling a dagger-like look at Sherry.

Dave stood. "You came up here for a reason. Please don't leave until you get what you came for."

"I have a job to do, and you can't help me with it," Frank told him.

"What do you mean by that? How do you know what I can and can't do?" Dave replied.

Frank glanced at Sherry. "Because you can't help yourself. So how can you help me or anyone else?"

"Excuse me, Dave. I'm going to leave," Sherry said. "Thank you for meeting with me. It was nice seeing you."

Dave was about to tell her it was okay to stay, but Frank beat him to it. "Please don't leave on my account.

Whatever you and Dave are doing is your business. Keep me out of it."

Sherry continued fidgeting without speaking to Frank. The tension was thick. Dave, once again, was feeling the effects of his circumstances.

Frank hustled out.

Dave didn't move. He didn't know exactly what had just happened.

"I'm so sorry, Dave. I didn't mean to cause you any trouble," Sherry said, appearing frantic. "The last thing I wanted to do is upset you or anyone else here." She grabbed her purse. "I'm going. Please accept my apology."

"You don't owe me an apology," he said, standing in the same spot, rubbing the back side of his neck.

"But—"

"There is no but," he said, placing his index finger across his lips. Dave didn't blame Sherry, and he wasn't in favor of letting others do it, either. He needed a breath of fresh air. "Have you eaten?"

"What?"

"I'm asking if you've eaten."

"N-no, I haven't," she stammered.

"Good. Because I'd like for you to join me for lunch," Dave said, going to his desk and pulling out a small roll of cash, which he slid into his pocket. "I could stand a break and would love some company." He could tell she was interested. "We can go to the Summit. I know how much you love it." He'd taken Sherry to the upscale restaurant, situated at the top of Detroit's tallest skyscraper, several times when she was his personal secretary.

"How can I say no to the Summit?" Sherry said, appearing to cheer up. "But I don't want to go that far today. How about that café we used to go to around the corner for lunch?"

"You got it. Let's go."

He ushered her out of his office, through the lobby doors, and a few blocks down the street. The two were whisked to a table and had menus in hand before they had to ask.

The waiter he normally got at lunchtime approached the table. "Mr. Mitchell, are you ready to place your order?"

"Ah, not yet," Dave said.

"No problem. Just wave for me when you're ready."

Dave spent the next fifteen minutes perusing the menu.

"Are you sure you're up for lunch?" Sherry asked. "Because we don't have to stay. I understand how busy you are and how much is on your mind. You don't have to tell me. I already know."

"Are you in a hurry?" he asked.

"No, not really."

"Then we're going to have lunch. Forget about me. There may be a few things on my mind but nothing that should destroy our lunch."

Her concern was unsolicited, but the words, softly spoken, were as satisfying as a cool glass of water in the middle of a scorching heat wave. Admittedly, the break from DMI, Frank's disappointment, Madeline's anger, and the probing eyes in the office were making for a tranquil lunch, and Sherry's words helped shave away his melancholy mood. Finally their orders were placed.

"Thank you for joining me," he said once the waiter left the table. "I'm truly glad that we came to lunch together."

It wasn't long before Sherry and Dave were laughing and talking about positive DMI memories. He soaked up the camaraderie. The companionship was a treat he hadn't experienced in a long time, probably a year or so. The conversation flowed. One o'clock came and went, along with two o'clock, three o'clock, and eventually three thirty. He beckoned for the waiter to bring their bill.

"Well, Mr. Mitchell, I'm going to let you get back to work. Thank you so much for inviting me. Please allow me to pay for lunch," Sherry said.

"Absolutely not. This is one hundred percent on me. You've made my day," he said, more chipper than he'd been since Madeline finalized the divorce papers a few days ago and moved out yesterday.

"Then we'll just have to fight over it," she said.

As Sherry reached for the check, Dave did too. Their hands touched, and there was a moment of unspoken connection, one they'd shared previously. He felt it and was sure she did too. Words weren't inserted into the mood.

Outside the restaurant, Dave hugged Sherry. She was hesitant in responding but didn't pull away too quickly.

Sherry prepared to go in the other direction as Dave was about to make his way to DMI. Just as she was walking away, Dave asked, "Do you have dinner plans tonight?"

"No, I don't."

"Great. Then you're coming with me." If Sherry was harboring feelings of guilt about their brief past together, then she was most likely going to find an excuse to get out of his offer. He was determined not to let her. He suspected that Sherry valued his companionship just as much as he did hers. "Seven thirty at the Summit. I'll pick you up."

"No need. I'll meet you there," she said, walking away.

Chapter 5

The long dark curtains remained tightly drawn, preventing a ray of light from penetrating the fortress Madeline had purchased for her and the children. She lay across the bed, on top of the covers, not wanting to get up. Depression was the only blanket she seemed to want. The two younger Mitchell's, Don and Tamara, lay with her. Misery was generously distributed among the bunch, with Madeline getting a slightly larger helping.

Their whimpers were becoming annoying. Actually, most noises, smells, and thoughts were annoying.

"Mommy, please let us go see Daddy," cried Tamara, who was rolled up in a ball and pressed against her mother's stomach. "I really want to go, Mommy."

"Me too, Mommy. I really want to go too," six-year-old Don said, mimicking his big sister. They were only one year apart, but Madeline knew that Tamara was the leader in that duo. Having two children whining and crying was too much. She was barely hanging on as it was without their constant reminder of how awful everyone was feeling about moving to the new house.

She could blame Dave and probably would, but it wasn't going to brighten her den of doom.

Tamara began tapping on Madeline's shoulder. "Mommy, are you awake? Can you hear me? You didn't answer me."

The questions began coming rapid fire. Madeline wanted to cover her ears and block out the entire inquisition. It wasn't that she found joy in ignoring her daughter, but the child's intensity was more than she could bear. Tamara was too young to understand what had happened a few days ago. She couldn't appreciate the brave act of unselfishness that Madeline had committed in walking away from a marriage that didn't put her and the children first. Tamara couldn't see the long-term damage their father had inflicted in allowing another woman to enter their lives when the one they had was already super fragile due to his excessive commitment to DMI. Their family had already been third in line after DMI and his God. With Sherry in the picture, their family had slid to number four.

"I want to see Daddy, and you can't stop us from seeing him," Tamara said, increasing the force of her shoulder taps, causing Madeline to sit up.

"Tamara," Madeline said with such frustration that her daughter instantly stopped hitting her. "First of all, what did I tell you yesterday, young lady?"

Tamara shrugged her shoulders.

"Don't act like you've forgotten. What did I tell you?" she said, raising her voice slightly.

Tamara buried her head in the pillow. "That you have to make arrangements with Daddy later in the week."

"That's right. So why are you asking me again today when I answered you last night?"

"I don't know," Tamara said, totally dejected, which made Madeline feel worse. She didn't want to be a tyrant with her children. It wasn't their fault that their world had fallen apart.

Madeline was convinced, at least at the moment, that Dave didn't deserve a family. He was the one who'd cast them frivolously aside for a one-night traipse with his floozy. Yet his two little ones wanted their dad. They didn't understand that he was the one who had orchestrated their gloom.

Tamara didn't protest any further, which again zapped the dab of peace Madeline had in reserve. Seeing her children so miserable depleted her. She had to set aside her resentment and let the children visit their father. It wasn't her preference, but not much seemed to be these days.

"Okay, you win. I'll call your father and see when you can go for a visit."

Screams sailed through the bedroom, reverberating against each wall and slapping Madeline across the face. She might have divorced Dave, but the ongoing persecution hadn't evaporated. Hearing her son and daughter was a reminder that she couldn't escape from Dave's clutches. She winced subtly, as her heart was more honest about how she really felt.

"When can we go? Huh? When?" Tamara asked.

"Yeah, I want to go too," Don said.

"Don't worry, Don. You can go with me," Tamara told him.

"Let me find out if Sam and Andre want to go too. Then I'll call your dad."

Madeline got up to find the other boys, leaving the young ones behind. The celebration continued as they bounced on her bed as if it were a trampoline. She didn't mind, so long as they were happy.

In search of her two oldest sons, she went into Sam's room and found him tinkering with a model car. "Here you are," she said. "Tamara and Don want to go to your father's house for a visit. Do you want to go too?"

"Do I have to go?" he said without taking his gaze off the car.

Madeline leaned against the door frame and crossed her arms. "No, you don't have to go. I'm not going to make you, but I'm sure your father would be glad to see you."

"Nah, I don't want to go."

"Okay, but can you tell me why?"

"I just don't want to go," he said, briefly glancing at her.

"Well, that's your choice," she said and walked away. Madeline didn't quite know how to react to the host of extreme emotions operating under one roof. Two of the children were overly persistent about seeing Dave, whereas one didn't care. If Dave only knew what she was dealing with. Her hope was that he'd get a taste of it when the children were with him.

Madeline went to Andre's room next. He wasn't there. She descended the stairs, figuring he was in the family room. Madeline heard the TV blaring as she approached the room. Andre was sprawled across the sofa.

"Why do you have the TV up so loud?" she asked, reaching for the remote control, which was lying next to him.

"Stop it," he yelled, snatching the remote from her loose grip.

"Andre, what is wrong with you?" she snapped back, shocked at his behavior.

"Nothing. I just don't want you messing with the TV."

"Listen, little boy, you don't get to talk to me like that," Madeline said. She appreciated the trauma her children had suffered from the divorce and the subsequent move. Everybody was out of sorts, but combative behavior wasn't going to be tolerated, period. She snatched the remote from him and turned the TV off. Andre popped up and pushed past her. "Sit down," she said.

"Ah, man," he mumbled, adding a huge sigh before plopping down on the sofa.

Madeline stared at him, letting the silence calm the tension. "Don and Tamara want to see your dad." She paused, allowing extra time for him to calm down. She didn't want to fight with her eldest son, but disrespect was not to be tolerated. "Would you like to go with them to see your dad?"

"Why do I want to see him?"

"Because he's your father, that's why," she said, tightly monitoring each word.

"He's not my father. Not my real one," he said.

Madeline wasn't prepared for his response. She hadn't realized how much rejection he had absorbed as a result of being separated from Dave. She felt awful, which boosted her patience in the face of his outburst, but her concern was heightened by his aggressive behavior.

"He's your father, and you know it. Dave loves you as if you were his own son." She took a seat next to him. "I know that Jonathan was your real father." Madeline didn't like using that phrase, but she opted to use Andre's language in an effort to keep him engaged in a meaningful conversation.

He showed no reaction. It didn't deflate her resolve. She was intent on diffusing his hostility. "I don't know if you were told this, but Jonathan and Dave were best friends. They were like brothers. After your mother died, your father decided that if something happened to him, the only person in the world that he trusted to take care of you was Dave. That's how special you were to him. He made sure that you'd live with people who loved you and cared about you. When he died, Dave didn't hesitate to come and get you, not for a second. At that time, you were the most important priority to him. So, young man, Dave is your father because he loves you dearly."

"Then why isn't he here with us?"

Madeline didn't want to get into the details with a child, but he was obviously going to require more explanation than the younger ones. "Your dad and I had some adult problems that we couldn't fix." She placed her hand on his. Andre pulled away. "What happened to our family is not your fault. I'm sorry that you children have been hurt. It's not what we wanted to happen, but we will get through this together."

"It doesn't matter. I don't care about anybody anymore."

"You don't mean that."

"Yes, I do!" he shouted. "Everybody that I care about leaves me. So I'm not going to care about anybody ever again."

"It hurts now. Trust me, you'll feel differently in a little while."

"No, I won't," Andre said and ran off.

She didn't attempt to stop him. There was no point. Madeline's limbs were logs preventing her from rising. She sat quietly for nearly an hour as her world rotated without her. Finally, she mustered the energy to get up and call Dave.

Several rings and she reached him at DMI. The basic greetings were bypassed as she jumped right in. "Your children are begging to see you. Will you have time over the next couple of days to see them?"

"Are you kidding? Of course I'll make time."

He hadn't made time when they were married, but that wasn't an argument she was starting today. Her children needed him, and she wouldn't stand in the way. Her babies needed the time with him.

"When can you get them?"

"I can stop by this evening."

"Good. Then we'll see you around seven thirty."

"That works for me. I can swing by and pick them up, or you can drop the four of them off at the office. Whatever works best for you."

"Oh, I meant to tell you that it's only going to be Don and Tamara. Sam and Andre aren't ready to see you."

"I'm disappointed, because I wanted to have all my children this evening."

"Well, it's not going to happen tonight. As a matter of fact, we need to have a serious discussion about Andre. He's very angry, to the point of being borderline disrespectful."

"Do you want me to speak with him tonight?"

"It doesn't have to be tonight, but we'll need to have the conversation soon. He's struggling more than I realized."

"Just let me know what I can do to help."

"For now you can pick up Don and Tamara. We'll figure out the rest later."

They ended the call. Madeline didn't want to dwell on the fact that she was going to spend the next few nights practically alone. It was going to be crushing, but it was the nature of their family now. She'd have to learn how to live with disappointment.

Chapter 6

The last couple of hours in the office sprinted to a close. Dave was overwhelmed with the notion that his kids had asked to see him. He packed up his briefcase, preparing to leave DMI for the evening. He couldn't be happier having some of his kids to spend the night with him. He hustled on out of there, determined not to be a minute later than he'd told Madeline. About halfway down to the lobby he stopped abruptly and groaned. *Sherry*. He'd forgotten about their dinner date that fast. The kids and Madeline had distracted him completely.

He set his briefcase on a desk belonging to one of the administrative assistants. He considered returning to his office and placing a call. Since the executive floor was empty, as far as he could tell, Dave decided to call Sherry from the closest phone. He picked up the receiver, and then it hit him. She'd never given him her new home phone number. He had no way to reach her, and Dave definitely wasn't going to tell Madeline about his schedule conflict. No way. He'd rather pick up the kids and hope that Sherry would wait for him. He placed the receiver back on its base, snatched his briefcase, and flew to the stairwell.

A quick thirty-minute ride up I-75 and down Rochester Road had him rolling up to the gate at Madeline's new home. It was his good fortune to have driven by the estate a week ago, after Madeline told him she was planning to make settlement on the place. He pressed the security intercom and told Madeline it was him, and she let him enter. He punched the gas pedal on his trusty Cadillac and reduced the quarter-mile drive to less than a minute. He skidded up to the front door and popped the gearshift into park. Dave left the car running and hopped out. He took a quick peek at his watch before knocking. Seven twenty eight. He sighed with relief and rang the bell. His plan was to scoop up the kids and whizz downtown by eight o'clock. That was wishful thinking, as he estimated the ride to be about forty minutes from Madeline's house if he did at least ten miles an hour above the speed limit.

Andre opened the door.

"Hey, buddy," Dave said.

Andre offered no more than a grunt and a wave.

"Is that the best you can do for your old man?" Dave asked, desperately wanting to lighten the mood.

"Hello," Andre uttered, making zero eye contact.

"How about a hug or a high five or something?" Andre turned around and gave his father a high five. "I wish you were coming with me tonight."

"There's nothing to do at your hotel. It's boring."

"Ah, but remember that I'm not at the hotel anymore. I'm at our house."

"Oh yeah, okay," Andre said, sounding either unconvinced or disinterested. "Can I go watch TV?" he asked, already walking away.

"Sure, but I want you to consider coming with the other kids next time."

Andre didn't respond.

"Did you hear me?" Dave said with more bass in his tone.

"Yeah, I heard you," he said.

Dave glanced at his watch again. Minutes were ticking by. He wanted to pursue the conversation with Andre, but there wasn't time. "Where's Sam?" he asked while Andre was within earshot.

"I don't know."

"How about your mom?"

"I don't know," Andre said, sounding increasingly agitated.

"Come back here," Dave said. Andre didn't react immediately. "I said to come back here, son," Dave said with boldness.

Andre obeyed. He returned to the foyer, leaving noticeable distance between himself and Dave.

"Your mom told me that you've been disrespectful." Andre used his right hand to brush his hair forward, letting his gaze sweep along the floor. "What do you have to say for yourself, young man?"

"Nothing," Andre said. He kept brushing his hair.

"We'll need to talk about this as a family."

"Whatever."

Dave was about to deal with the attitude when Tamara and Don came flying down the stairs. Madeline was at the top of the stairs.

"Daddy, Daddy, you're here already," Tamara said, in such a hurry that she slipped on the last steps. Dave lunged to catch her.

Dave needed only a few more minutes with Andre, but based on Tamara's enthusiasm and the dinner date with Sherry, he'd have to continue the discussion later. "Andre, I plan to pick up on this conversation again very soon," he said as Tamara clung to him.

"Yeah, sure, right, whatever," Andre said and eased out of the foyer disengaged. Tamara was demanding Dave's full attention, and unconsciously he obliged.

Don descended the stairs with his mother. There was no surprise there. He figured Don was coming along only because of Tamara. She was always glad to see her dad. His heart warmed.

"Ready to go?" he asked the kids, peering at Madeline.

"We didn't realize you were here," she said.

"I said seven thirty, and I was right on time."

"Humph. You've made other promises that didn't pan out," Madeline replied.

No way was Dave going to respond. Right or wrong, Madeline could gladly have the last word. He was focused on snatching up the kids and getting out of there before drama struck.

"Where's Sam? I want to say hello to him," Dave said.

"He's probably in his room. Somebody get your brother." When Madeline didn't get a volunteer she said, "Tamara, go get him."

"Why do I have to go?" she protested.

Dave jumped in to avoid discord. "Don't worry about it. I'll see him when I bring the kids home. Just tell him I said hello and that his dad loves him."

Madeline didn't appear content with his response, but finally she said, "I'll tell him."

Dave was thrilled that he'd managed to spend ten minutes under the same roof with Madeline without arguing. Miracles were possible in their relationship. "Everybody ready?" he asked again, this time directing his question to the kids.

"Yes." "

Let's go," he said, reaching for their suitcases and then moving toward the door.

"Dave, take care of my babies," Madeline called out as they exited the house.

"You know I will," he said, checking his watch again. Seven-fifty. Thank goodness he had a full tank of gas, with the car running as long as it had.

Tamara climbed into the front seat.

"Don't you want to sit in the back with Don?" Dave asked her.

"No. I'm sitting in the front because I'm the oldest," she said and closed the door.

Dave poked his head into the backseat. "Don, are you okay sitting in the backseat by yourself?"

Don nodded yes.

"Okay," Dave said and closed the door. He knew it was pointless asking Don that question. Whatever made his big sister, Tamara, happy, Don was going to do.

Dave ran around to the driver's side and jumped in. With any grace, he could get to the restaurant by eight thirty. He winced. An hour late was a bit much, but the delay couldn't be avoided.

Chapter 7

Tamara chattered every second of the ride. Dave hopped onto the expressway, soon reaching a cruising speed of seventy-five. At a quarter past eight he was at least twenty minutes away from downtown. He pressed the gas pedal until the speedometer read eighty five. He was certain the extra speed would shave off five minutes.

The Cadillac purred down the highway until Don said, "Daddy, the car behind us has on Christmas lights."

Dave glanced into the rearview mirror and saw a highway patrol car rolling up behind them. He winced in his seat. Defeated, he slowed down and gradually maneuvered to the shoulder.

"Why are we stopping, Daddy?" Tamara asked, seeming excited.

Don continued being intrigued by the flashing lights. "Who is he?" his son asked as Dave fumbled with his papers.

"Excuse me, kids, but Daddy has to get out for a minute. I'll be right back."

"Ooh, it's a policeman," Tamara said. "What is he going to do? Are you going to jail?" she asked, sounding frightened.

"I have to talk to him for a few minutes. Don't worry. I'll be fine," Dave said, trying hard to gather his registration from the glove compartment and get out of the car before the officer approached his door. Dave couldn't dare let Tamara get a whiff of the conversation if he wanted to keep a distorted version from getting back to Madeline. Their mother wouldn't care what the reason was. He'd be toast, which caused him to open the car door and practically leap out with his hands raised.

"Daddy, don't go. I'm scared!" Don screamed as his father let the door close.

Dave was crushed as he digested the fright in their voices. He prayed silently for mercy. That was the most Dave could do, recognizing he was in the wrong.

He approached the policeman slowly with arms raised.

"Stop right there," the officer demanded, with his hand latched on to his gun.

"Officer, I'm not armed. I just didn't want my kids to be frightened by seeing you."

"Sir, you should never approach an officer during a traffic stop. Please place your hands on the car."

"Here's my registration papers and ID," Dave said, extracting his license from his wallet.

"Hands on the car, sir."

Dave did as he was told and said no more.

"Do you know why I stopped you?"

"Speeding?"

"Yes, you were doing eighty-five in a seventy-mile-an-hour speed zone."

Dave didn't protest. How could he when the officer was telling the truth? The officer took the materials and went to his car. Don stared at Dave through the back window. Tamara climbed into the driver's seat and poked her head out the window. Dave was mortified.

"Daddy, what are you doing? Are you going to jail?" Tamara asked.

"Get back in the car, young lady."

"But—"

"No buts. Put your head in the car right this second, young lady," he said with enough force to get her out of harm's way.

"Is that your daughter?" the officer asked.

"Yes, she's my little princess," Dave said.

Dave heard the officer laugh softly. "I have a little girl about her age. What is she? Six?"

"Seven going on thirty."

"I understand exactly what you mean," the officer said, handing Dave his registration and ID back. "I have a six-year-old," he said, laughing openly, allowing Dave to relax some. "Mr. Mitchell, I don't want your children to be frightened, either. So I'm going to give you a warning if you promise to slow down."

"I can do that," Dave said, relieved.

"Then you're free to go, but slow down." The officer started walking away. "Take care of that beautiful family of yours."

Dave got into his car, grateful. Tamara was asking questions rapid fire. Don was too quiet.

"I told you we'd be fine. Nobody's going to jail," Dave told his daughter.

"Where are we going, then?" Tamara asked.

"We have to make a stop. Are you hungry?" he asked.

"No," Tamara and Don said simultaneously.

Dave took one more glance at his watch. Eight-forty. He hung his head. He was an hour late, with another twenty to thirty minutes of driving at the speed limit remaining. He sighed and eased onto the highway. He considered pulling over and using his car phone to call the restaurant. They should be able to get a message to

Sherry if she was still waiting. He set the cruise control and decided to keep moving. He'd get there and deal with the situation then.

Arriving at 9:00 P.M., Dave took the glass elevators to the seventy-second floor. It was like an amusement ride to the kids.

"Can we go down and then come back up?" Don asked.

"No, son. We have to hurry," Dave said, combing the lobby as they meandered to the dining room. Much to his surprise, he saw Sherry sitting in a dimly lit corner of the adjoining reception area. He was fully prepared for her to have bailed on him by now.

"Sherry," he called out. "I'm very sorry for showing up so late."

"Are you all right?" she asked with a tone of concern.

Dave wasn't prepared for her sincere reaction, and it caused him to take notice. "You won't believe how much has happened since we spoke this morning."

Tamara chimed in, but Dave didn't answer. He was focused on Sherry.

"Dave, it's all right. I didn't mind waiting. Are these your children?" she asked.

Dave had forgotten that she had never met his children in person. Sherry had seen plenty of photos during her reign as his administrative assistant. During his separation from Madeline he'd get the kids for weekends, but Sherry hadn't met them.

"Yes, these are my two youngest, Don and Tamara."

"Are they joining us for dinner?"

"I really am truly sorry, but we can't stay." He couldn't possibly hang out with Sherry and ever hope to see his kids again without a court order and federal marshals. "I am truly sorry." He couldn't help but feel badly about inviting Sherry to dinner and then canceling.

Tamara tried interrupting again, but Dave couldn't speak with her and Sherry simultaneously. He'd conclude this conversation, leave, and let Tamara have his sole attention.

"It's okay. I understand," Sherry responded.

She accepted Dave's apology and showed no sign of excessive disappointment, although it was there. It didn't feel good being placed on the bottom rung of his priority list. She knew his children were important, and they would rank higher than a casual date with her. Deep within, she wanted to understand and not lodge a complaint. Sherry would have to accept his reality if she wanted to have her friend back. It didn't mean she had to like his set of priorities, especially when she was excluded.

Tamara wasn't keeping quiet. "What's your name?" she asked, too loud to ignore.

"Sherry."

Dave coughed as they remained in the reception area.

"Are you my auntie?" Don asked.

"No."

"Then who are you?" Tamara quizzed.

"A friend of your dad's."

"And my mom too?" Don added.

Sherry hesitated. "Not really."

"Oh," Dave's son said, sporting a look of confusion.

Tamara didn't ask any more questions.

"It's time for us to go," Dave said moving toward the elevator. Don and Tamara followed.

"Maybe I can join you and your children for dinner one day?" Sherry said.

"Maybe," he said, punctuating his answer with a slight grin. "Since it's after nine, can I give you a ride home?"

"No, thank you. I'll take the bus."

"My dad had to talk with the policeman," Don blurted.

Dave was even more embarrassed, as Sherry appeared perplexed. "It's a long story for another night," he said as they exchanged glances. "Seriously, let me give you a ride home."

"Trust me, it's not necessary."

"Maybe not, but I'd feel a whole lot better about it since I had you waiting here for almost two hours. Please let me take you home."

She finally acquiesced. When they got to the car, Tamara climbed into the front seat. Dave didn't say anything to his daughter, so Sherry didn't, either. Sherry sat in the back with Don as he asked question after question. The bittersweet ride would be over in a half hour, but the possible effects might last long after. Sherry knew at least one of the children would tell their mother about her being with them. She hoped for the best, but knowing Madeline, that wish was a stretch.

Chapter 8

A year later . . .

Dinners, dancing, and dating had landed Dave at the Summit, gazing at Sherry. "You're an incredible woman," he said, unprompted, causing her to blush.

"Why, thank you," she said, sipping from the water glass.

The dining room turned slowly as Dave's thoughts gelled. He wanted to maximize the setting without seeming overdramatic. "I'm glad that you're here with me," he said, taking her hand.

Sherry let her gaze dance around the room. He knew she was downplaying his compliments, and didn't mind. There would be plenty more to come.

"No matter how many times we come here, this is such an awesome view of downtown Detroit and Windsor. It never gets old for me," she said.

"That's one of the many characteristics I love about you. You're very positive and appreciate the simple beauties in life." He pressed his palm against hers, letting their fingers latch. "Sherry Henderson, what would I do without you? You've been a good friend and confidante at a time when I craved a friendship."

She had no idea just how much. After losing his brother's friendship last year, Dave was in somewhat of a drought when it came to relationships. He and Madeline were cordial for the sake of their kids. He and Frank were basically coworkers with no interaction outside of DMI meetings. The loss of both Madeline and Frank cut deeply, but he couldn't dwell on disappointment. He was still breathing, which meant that there was more life to live and more purpose to fulfill. He wasn't going to waste another precious second. He was going to make his feelings known and get on with the business of enjoying each day. "You've become very special to me."

"You've been a good friend to me too," Sherry said.

"Friend, huh? That's it?"

"Oh, Dave, you know what I mean," she said as the palm of her hand began sweating against his.

Without causing her to be too embarrassed, he continued with his probing. "Actually, I don't know." She looked away. This time he took the index finger on his other hand and gently lifted her chin. Her gaze wandered like a trapped kitten trying to escape danger. Dave chased her gaze until he finally caught it. "Really, I'd like to know how you feel about me." Her reluctance to respond didn't vanish with his gentle touch and coaxing. "Would it help for you to know that I love you?"

Her gaze shot up to meet his. She nodded in affirmation.

"Well, it's true. Miss Sherry Henderson, I love you."

"Dave, I don't know what to say."

"Hopefully, you can say that you love me too."

"I do," she blurted, showing the first sign of unbridled emotion. "Yes, I do. You know that I do. I've loved you for the past three years. When I was your assistant, I loved you," she said, tightening her fingers around his. "When I got pregnant with our baby, I loved you even more. Even though our baby died, it didn't change my love for you. Actually, it made me more connected with you, because you were the father of my first child."

Thinking back, Dave was glad when Madeline had hired Sherry at DMI. The two had connected on a purely professional level. He'd valued her. No excuses about problems in his marriage could justify what happened between him and Sherry several years ago. That he accepted. The way his relationship had evolved with Sherry didn't represent a proud moment for him, but time and circumstances had brought them together again.

Dave relaxed as Sherry continued expressing her feelings. They'd spent enough time together for him to believe she felt a certain way about him, but it was imperative that he had confirmation. With each word, he was more convinced about what to do next.

"Sherry, I'm glad to know how you feel."

He delicately unlatched his right hand from hers and reached into the inner pocket of his suit coat and pulled out a small box. Her eyelids widened to the point where silver dollars couldn't cover her eyes.

"Miss Sherry Henderson," he said, "will you marry me?" He opened the box so she could see the three-carat, round-cut diamond ring selected especially for her. He would have gotten a larger diamond but didn't want the ring to overpower her tiny hand.

She gasped, covering her mouth with both hands. "Yes, yes!" she practically screamed as Dave eased the ring onto her finger. She jumped up and embraced him. At least for those few seconds, her shy tendencies were cast aside.

Dave was pleased to see her so joyful. Her girlish exuberance fueled his enthusiasm, reminding him of his youth. Yet Dave was careful not to make the same mistake twice by reading too much into the scene. He'd experienced a similar reaction from Madeline fifteen years ago, when they'd gotten engaged. Madeline had eagerly agreed to his terms, and then reality had a way of converting joy into resentment several years into the marriage.

Dave had so much to say, but the words wouldn't come out. As he caressed her hand, she trembled. Sherry felt like such an idiot, sitting there with her mouth gaping. Sherry wanted to pour out her heart and tell him she'd never been happier—never, not even when she was engaged to Edward, her ex, two and a half years ago. Dave was like no other man in the world.

"Is the ring to your liking?"

"Yes, of course. It's beautiful."

"Because we can replace it with whatever ring you'd like."

"No, no," she retorted, extending her arm as far as it would go. "It's perfect, just like you are for me." There, whew, she'd said it. Finally, her words were getting beyond her jumbled mind.

"Great. So long as you're satisfied, I am too." He reclaimed her hand and gazed into her eyes. "There is something we need to discuss."

Sherry tensed, not sure what was coming next.

"You know how much time and energy I have to pour into DMI. It's my calling. It's my ministry," he told her.

"I know."

"Well, not so fast," he said, stroking her hand. "This will mean that there are days and nights where you'll see very little of me."

"I understand."

"Do you really? Because it's important that I'm up front with you. I need to know that you understand what kind of relationship you're getting into."

She knew too well. She'd seen firsthand as his administrative assistant how much of his life was dedicated to DMI and how much pressure it put on his marriage to

Madeline. But that didn't discourage her. Dave was her dream come true. She was willing to take him on whatever terms he offered. Her answer was going to remain yes to marriage, regardless of what truths he revealed. He would soon be her husband, and it was the only thing she cared about from that moment on. Whatever happened after that would have to be accepted.

"Dave Mitchell, there's nothing that I want more in this world than to marry you."

He kept quiet, gazing at her. Finally, while still holding her hand, he said, "Okay, then let's get married. We can go to Cancun next week."

"Where is that?" she asked.

"It's known to be a popular wedding destination in Mexico."

She was ready to burst. "I've never been out of the country. Don't I have to get a passport?"

"No, not for Mexico. It's just like crossing into Canada from Detroit. Your birth certificate will be sufficient. I'll book the plane tickets, and we can get the marriage license once we're there. From what I've been told, it's an easy process. What do you think? Can we do this next week?" he asked with such sweetness that she melted inside.

"Yes, yes," she said, gleeful and ready to explode. Her dream was actually coming true, and she couldn't be happier, regardless of the sacrifices that would have to come later.

Chapter 9

Dave fumbled with his second cuff link while standing in front of the master bathroom mirror. A new chapter had begun with him proposing to Sherry last night at their favorite restaurant. Her faithful companionship over the past year had gotten him through a rough patch following the divorce. Living without his family had proved to be much more difficult than he'd dreamed.

Speaking of family, he had to break the news of his upcoming nuptials to Madeline, a deed Dave was not eager to do. He adjusted his tie and gave thought on how best to approach her, releasing a slight chuckle. He reflected on how far his perspective had evolved. There was a time when he sought God for direction on every decision. Once he'd created the tense situation between Madeline and Sherry, some prayers just didn't feel right. For a man who yearned for the active presence of God daily, Dave had admittedly been out of sorts on several occasions in the past couple of years. He prayed that would change, because he was keenly aware of the miracle that was going to be required for Madeline to embrace his decision. He wasn't delusional in thinking the women would become friends. His only concern was maintaining contact with his kids. Madeline had the control, and he prayed she wouldn't abuse it.

Dave finished dressing and made his way to DMI. The drive prepared him only slightly for the inevitable. Tossing procrastination aside, Dave picked up the phone receiver and made his call. Madeline was on the phone fairly quickly.

"How are the children?" he asked, checking her attitude before diving in.

"Okay, I guess, except for Andre. The separation has taken its toll on him, and now it's been another year since we've been in this house without you. The poor child . . . I feel for him. We were together only one year out of the three that Andre has been with us. The first year you worked all the time and got tangled up with Sherry. The second year we were separated, and this past year we've been divorced."

Dave hadn't considered the full impact on Andre. Memories of his beloved friend Jonathan rushed in. Andre's father had trusted Dave with his son. He had to honor Jonathan's memory by helping Andre navigate along this bumpy road. Dave would see to it, but one step at a time. He had to break the news to Madeline about his plans to remarry and then fight for continued visitation. No sense stalling. He leaned against his desk and prayed silently for the right words. Grace was his new favorite plea.

"Madeline, I'm getting married." Silence choked the line, causing him to wonder if she was still on the other end. "Are you there?"

"I'm here."

"Did you hear me? I'm getting married."

"Sure, and I'm the queen of England," she said, punctuating her statement with mockery.

"Seriously, I'm getting married."

"Dave Mitchell, you better not tell me that you're marrying that woman," she said, raising her voice.

"Sherry and I are getting married next week in Cancun."

"Humph, you can't possibly be serious."

"We're having a very small private ceremony, and I'd love it if the kids could come with me."

Madeline began cackling uncontrollably on the phone, and in a blink, she was yelling obscenities. "You have lost your mind if you think any of my children are going to Cancun, macaroon, or any other 'roon' with that floozy."

"I was hoping we could discuss this in a civil manner."

"Looks like you guessed wrong. You have some nerve telling me that you're marrying the woman who broke up our marriage. You have to be kidding me. The ink is barely dry on the divorce papers, and you're already rushing to the altar with your home wrecker! Are you expecting some kind of gift from me?" Dave didn't know if she wanted him to answer. Just when he was about to, Madeline went on. "Ha, I have a gift for you, all right . . . for you and her."

Dave took a seat at his desk. He recognized the call might take a while. He'd experienced Madeline's tirades before. If left alone, she'd fizzle out in another minute or two. He was patient. After all, he'd created the situation. Waiting for the storm to pass wasn't too bad.

"You can't stop me from wanting my kids to be with me," he finally said.

"You're right. I can't stop you from *wanting* anything," she said, barking louder. "For that matter, people in hell want ice water, which they aren't getting, either. So what's your point?"

"Come on, Madeline. Let's not start."

"You started this mess when you decided to marry that thing."

He had messed up, but had she forgotten the rest? "Madeline, *you* put me out. I pleaded with you to consider reconciling, and you wanted no parts of it. You told me, in no uncertain terms, that we'd never get back together."

"And you believed me?"

Dave paused, unsure of where she was headed with the conversation. He'd follow for as long as he could. He meandered to the windows and peered into the distant sky as the long phone cord stretched with him. "Yes, I believed you. What else was I supposed to do?"

"You were supposed to love me!" she shouted. He wasn't prepared to hear her voice cracking. "And cherish me. And respect me. You were supposed to be here with our family. That's what you were supposed to do."

He let the words simmer. Nothing he could add or subtract would mend her soul. Only God had that ability, and Dave was pretty sure she wasn't speaking to Him. Finally, when it seemed that it was safe to speak, he did. "You're mad at me. I get it. And most of the time you want nothing to do with me. I get it."

"So what! I didn't mean for you to marry your mistress." For Dave to clarify that Sherry wasn't his mistress, that they'd had a one-night stand during his marriage to Madeline several years ago, was a total waste of breath. Madeline would forever see Sherry as the DMI temptress. He wasn't going to change her opinion in this call or any other. "Where are you going to live after you get married? And it better not be the estate."

"Madeline, where else am I going to live?"

"Anywhere else, but not in my house."

"But you didn't want to stay in the house. I begged you to let the kids stay in the only home they've known. You turned me down cold."

"So what! I don't want her to live there."

There was no winning this battle, which was why Dave pleaded the fifth and shut up. There was more stormy weather to endure.

"Do you love her?"

"Yes, I do."

"There was a time when you loved me too. How can you all of a sudden love her now?"

Dave didn't owe Madeline an explanation about Sherry, not after the divorce. Besides, he'd never be able to give one that sufficiently covered her loss. Dave couldn't tell her how much he'd missed his family after they moved out last year. Loneliness had plagued his evenings before Sherry came back into his life. It was true. They had a history, but there was a mutual love between them. It might not be the intense sense of purpose he'd shared with Madeline for fourteen years, but their feelings were real, and the relationship was sustainable.

"I'd like for you to consider letting the kids come to the wedding,'" he said. "I think they'll have fun. If you want, I can let them stay at a hotel during the wedding. They don't have to attend the actual ceremony, if it makes you feel better."

Sherry eased into his office. He acknowledged her presence, motioning for her to take a seat.

"Let me be very clear so there's no confusion. My kids aren't coming to your wedding with her."

"They're my kids too."

"And is that supposed to justify your wanting to take them down to Cancun to watch you pledge some twisted love to the woman who stole their dad? As far as I'm concerned, she's a common thief. Come on, Dave, you're a highly intelligent man. Exactly what part of this scenario seems crazy to you? You marrying that tramp, you asking my kids to witness that farce, or you even thinking that I'd consider such foolishness? Well, which is it, Dave?"

"So I guess that's a no, they can't come."

"I guess that would be a no."

"Madeline, you know I could push for this in family court and get my kids on the plane."

"Yes, you probably could, and go ahead if you want your children to hate you and Sherry more than they already do."

"My children don't hate me."

"Really? Now, that is news to me."

Chapter 10

Sherry couldn't sit still and listen to Dave pleading with Madeline. He ended the call as she became increasingly terrified. Her dream was slipping away at the hands of Madeline. Her happy day was quickly turning into one of her worst.

"That was rough," he said, scooping Sherry into his embrace and then giving her a peck on the cheek.

"Sounds like Madeline doesn't want the children to come with us," Sherry said, afraid of what was coming next.

Dave returned to the windows and peered out. "No, I guess she doesn't."

Sherry felt numb watching the disappointment looming around Dave. He wanted his kids with him. If they couldn't come, he probably didn't want to go either. He didn't have to tell her what was coming next. She already knew. Maybe if she ignored the obvious, her joy could rise again. She fought with her fear and finally gave in. "So, I guess this means you'll need time to think this over," she said, speaking loudly to keep her emotions from taking over. "I understand if you need to postpone the wedding," she said, desperately working to maintain control. She was doing okay for the moment, but she felt shaky. Her world was shaking. It was best for her to be quiet until she could deal with what was happening.

He rushed to Sherry and grabbed her hands. "Oh no, we're not postponing the wedding."

His assurance should have eased her concern, but it didn't. Having his children upset about him marrying a woman that their mother didn't like was a bigger deal than he was letting on. Sherry was aware of how much Dave adored his children. If they were unhappy, eventually he would be too.

"I think we should postpone the wedding, at least until you give Madeline a chance to change her mind."

Dave chuckled.

"What's so funny?"

He stroked her hair. "You're sweet. You know that?" She melted as she stood close to him. "I'm laughing because there is no amount of time on earth that would be sufficient for Madeline to change her mind." He chuckled again, louder. "She's tough, and this, my dear, is one of those times when Madeline has dug in her heels and refuses to budge."

"I know. I get it, but we can wait a few weeks or even a month to see if something good happens."

"Like what? What would you like to happen?"

"I don't know. Maybe the children will tell you that it's okay to marry me. Maybe Madeline will accept the fact that we're getting married. Right now she might just be operating out of shock. Who knows what can change in a month?"

"Thank you for the encouragement," he said, stroking her hair again, "but we can't wait for Madeline or anyone else to endorse our marriage. Maybe her heart will soften toward me, and maybe not. I can only pray and hope for the best, but I won't let her manipulate me by restricting my time with my kids."

"What are you going to do? Fight for custody or visitation?"

"Absolutely not. I plan on doing nothing. I'm not about to fight her. I choose to focus on the future and restoring my place of leadership with DMI."

"This doesn't bother you?"

"Of course it does, but there are circumstances when you have to make a decision and see it through, regardless of how much encouragement or discouragement you get from others. They don't know your heart," he said, placing his palm on the center of her chest. "They don't know mine," he added, guiding her palm to the center of his chest. She calmed, feeling his heartbeat in rhythm with hers. "Only God truly knows our hearts."

They stood quietly for a bit and then caressed each other.

He pulled away to say, "When I asked you to marry me, I asked you and you alone."

"But—"

"No. Let me finish," he said. "I've apologized to Madeline many times for what happened between us, but the past is gone and buried. I asked the Lord to forgive me, and He did. That's going to have to be good enough for me."

"It doesn't seem to be good enough for Madeline."

"Honestly, I get where Madeline is coming from. I did her wrong. That's a fact. I'm not proud of it. I wasn't then, and I'm not now. Even though I messed up, I wanted to save my marriage with Madeline, but it wasn't what she wanted. Madeline hasn't forgiven me yet. I don't know if she ever will. That's why I seek redemption from God and not from a man or woman. He loves me beyond my mistakes. So, here I am, a free man to love and live freely." He took a step back. "I'm not saying that as an uncaring person."

"I know," she said reaching for him.

"No, please listen," he insisted. "I can't change the past. If I could, honestly, I would have."

She remained slightly uncomfortable. She knew how much of a partnership Dave and Madeline had. She suspected some kind of love remained between them, but hopefully not the "get back together" kind.

"Hear me good when I tell you that Madeline doesn't want to reconcile with me. She's made it clear that our time is over. What we had is gone and my future is with you," he said drawing her close to him.

Her tiny bit of concern vanished once Dave confessed his loyalty and love to her again. Nothing else seemed to matter. Madeline couldn't shatter her dream. Dave wasn't going to let her. Sherry leaned into Dave's chest and found total comfort. Her world was spinning slowly again, in control.

"I love you," she whispered.

Dave dropped to one knee and peered up at her. She was too giddy to speak. "Miss Sherry Henderson, will you marry me?" he said with enough charm to melt the largest iceberg in Alaska.

Her heart melted under his power.

"Dave what are you doing? You already proposed to me at the restaurant."

"But not on one knee," he said grinning.

"That's true."

"So what's your answer?" he asked laughing.

"Yes, yes, I will!" she screamed as he rose and lifted her slightly off the floor in a tight hug. She said yes again and again.

"Then that's what we're going to do, get married. We're the only people that have to be there, plus one witness. It would be nice if certain people came with us, but their participation isn't required," he said, giving her another glimpse of his signature grin. She'd seen his confidence oozing from him countless times in meetings and in side conversations, and she saw it again today, when their future depended on him.

Sherry was overjoyed. She didn't believe there could be any greater joy than what she was feeling at this moment. Dave had made it clear that she was his priority. Neither his children, former wife, nor even God was going to stop their marriage. As he was about to let her go, she gripped him as tightly as she could. Sherry was determined to hang on regardless of what challenges came their way.

Madeline was fuming. She plopped onto her bed, pulling the covers over her head in one instance and flinging them off the next second. Despite her sincere efforts, she couldn't get situated. The sound of the air conditioner irritated her, and the silence did too. The smell of furniture polish was giving her a headache. She toyed with the bedcovers again. She'd make a mental note to tell the new housekeeper to ease up on the polish. They weren't in a stable. This was her home, the one she was building from scratch. Madeline wanted the same respect and cleaning quality that she'd grown accustomed to on Mayweather Lane.

The more she dwelled on her failed marriage, the angrier Madeline became. Dave had gotten everything. How did he end up with the housekeeper and the cook? He was the one who should have been left destitute and been forced to start over from scratch. Instead, he was lying in the estate, next to Miss Sherry. The image was painfully piercing.

"Mom, I'm going out to shoot a few hoops," Sam said. She should have been thrilled with his interest in getting out of the house, but there wasn't any joy to be found in her room.

"Good. Take Don with you."

"I don't want him tagging along with me," he retorted.

"I'm not going to argue with you. Just take him with you," she said, massaging her temples.

"Huh, I don't get to do anything that I want to around here," he said, stomping off.

Madeline craved silence, but not too much of it. She didn't want it to be so quiet that her thoughts were the loudest sound in the room. She couldn't stand that, not when Sherry and Dave were consuming her space. They were everywhere, choking the life out of her.

"Tell Tamara to go outside too," she called, loud enough for Sam to hear her.

"Come on! Why does she have to come? She doesn't even like basketball," he yelled from the hallway.

"Don't you back sass me, young man! Do what I told you to do," she said, unable to yell. Her headache was intensifying with each word, forcing Madeline to reflect on her circumstances.

"How dare him?" she moaned. She was stuck in bed with a nagging headache in the middle of the day. Madeline envisioned Dave and his mistress enjoying lunch in the park or strolling along the Detroit waterfront, while she waddled in a funk, becoming increasingly tired of thinking about him. That was it. No more.

Madeline gently pulled the covers back and eased off the bed. The pain in her head hadn't diminished, but it didn't keep her from reaching the floor-to-ceiling drapes and snatching them open. Dave wasn't the only one who was going to live happily ever after. She'd sulked too long, waiting on what? For Dave to come back on bended knee? Her days of being in a funk were over. She'd shake off the gloom and work on getting her life back. She returned to the bed and sat on the edge. Sherry crossed her mind again, but this time Madeline had a plan. It was only fair that Miss Home Wrecker made payment in full for her actions. Dave had paid the price of losing his family and his credibility. Madeline couldn't list everything she'd lost. *Her dignity and a long-term friendship for starters,* she thought. The children had lost their father. Everyone had suffered except for Sherry.

Madeline lay back on the bed and stared at the ceiling. She exhaled. Finally, after two years, she was poised and ready to fight back. Sherry had better get ready, because payback was on the way—a nice huge chunk.

Chapter 11

Frank trudged to his brother's office, having been summoned by the chief executive officer. The way the past couple of years had gone between them, he didn't know what to expect. Ever since Sherry had entered the doors of DMI, his tight-knit relationship with his brother had been compromised. Frank saw his brother as a religious hypocrite who'd recklessly put the company at risk. With that belief came a loss of trust and respect which Dave couldn't seem to regain.

"Can I go in?" Frank asked Dave's secretary, who was sitting out front.

"Yes, Mr. Mitchell. He's waiting for you."

Frank reached the doorway, not sure if he was entering a peace or a war zone. He braced for both. "Were you looking for me?" he asked in a guarded tone.

"Sure was," Dave said, beckoning for Frank to come in. "Close the door behind you," he added, getting up with a cup in his hand and walking to the table. Frank met him there, and they took seats across from one another. "Have you eaten breakfast yet?"

"No, but I don't normally eat breakfast."

"You know breakfast is the most important meal of the day."

"And so what?" Frank responded, not trying to hide his irritation. "I'm sure you didn't call me in here to talk about my dietary habits, because if you did, we'll have to resume this chat later. Right now I have way too much on my plate to sit around and chitchat like a bunch of schoolgirls."

"You're right."

Dave scratched underneath his eyelid, as if he was stalling. Frank ignored the gesture. Before the distractions, Frank knew his brother to be decisive and fearless when it came to tackling big and small issues. Stalling wasn't in his makeup. Dave was known for tackling opposition head-on. And once he dashed in with heavy reliance on God, problems that seemed impossible were often solved. Frank would have considered his brother's actions a hoax had he not personally witnessed the numerous victories in civil suits and in closing million-dollar deals. There was no denying that Dave had something unique going on, or at least he used to. It appeared that some of his favor and those victories had gone south in the past six months. Frank was actually earning his pay these days by putting out fires related to the company's reputation.

"So what's going on?" Frank said, hunching his shoulders, eager to get out of there.

Dave stared at Frank and said, "I'm marrying Sherry next week in Cancun."

Frank didn't speak immediately, causing Dave to prod him.

"You have anything to say?"

"Oh, I have plenty to say, but I'm sure it's nothing you want to hear," Frank snarled.

"I know you're not fond of Sherry—"

"Let's just say she's no Madeline," Frank interrupted. "You need a strong woman who can stand on her own in tough situations, a woman who knows what it takes to make this place run. There's only one woman, probably on earth, who fits that bill, and it is not Sherry."

"She's a good woman."

"'A young and inexperienced woman' is the part you left out."

"Okay, yes, she's young."

"Young enough to be your daughter. You're close to twenty years older than she is."

"Regardless, she's twenty-seven years old. She's a grown woman, fully capable of making her own decisions."

"If you say so, but it sounds like you're trying to convince either me or yourself."

"I don't need to be convinced. I love her. She loves me, and I've asked her to marry me. That's the bottom line," Dave said, slicing his hands through the air like an umpire calling a runner safe.

"You wish it was that easy."

"It is."

"I guess it is if you don't care about your reputation. DMI has already taken a noticeable hit in revenues over the past six months."

"You can't irrefutably tie the slight drop in revenue to my personal life."

"Are you serious?" Frank slapped his hand across his thigh. "Man, please. You can't possibly believe what you're saying. You've been in this game long enough to know better. A company is only as strong as the reputation of those running it. How many times have you told me that? And I agree, so for you to sit there like nothing you're doing is impacting DMI is just silly," he said, snickering.

"DMI is just as viable as it's always been. The hand of God was on this place from the beginning, and no matter what personal failures I have, His plan will succeed whether I'm here or not."

"Blah, blah, blah. I don't want to hear that religious mumbo jumbo. I'm talking cold, hard facts." In the past, Frank wouldn't have challenged Dave's reliance on religion to fix their problems. Dave had changed. Times had changed. Frank had to change too, just to keep up. "Look, little brother, do I have to remind you that we're in the business of helping churches learn how to operate ethically and with integrity?"

"No, you don't have to remind me," Dave said with an edge. "I know my purpose for creating DMI better than anyone big brother," he added, sounding angry.

"Then you can understand my point. Who's going to listen to anything we're peddling if the head of DMI leaves his wife and four children to marry his mistress, a woman he got pregnant while he was still married"

"You know that's not how this went down. You know Madeline wanted the divorce, not me. I tried, but I couldn't stop her from finalizing the divorce last year. Her mind was set."

"Maybe you should have tried harder before picking up with the mistress."

"We were finished long before I considered marrying Sherry."

"That might be a fact, but know that's not what people on the outside will believe. Between the media and your long list of jealous adversaries, they'll make a big deal out of this."

"Perhaps, but I'm willing to take the chance."

Frank chuckled. "You used to be unbeatable when it came to DMI business, but I'm waiting to see how this turns out. I just don't see you winning this round." He rose from his seat. "I think you've lost your touch."

Dave's secretary brushed against Frank on his way out of his brother's office. "Excuse me, Mr. Mitchell," she said, causing both brothers to respond, since they were not sure which one she meant. "Mr. Dave," she added, smiling.

"Well, I'm out," Frank said.

"Mr. Morgan Davis's office from the Midwest Association of Bible Scholars just called, and they've requested an urgent meeting with you this afternoon."

Frank paused mid step and backtracked into the office. "MABS? What do they want?"

"Their secretary is holding on the line. Can I schedule him for two o'clock?" she asked, directing the question to Dave.

"What's the meeting for?" Frank asked, knowing this was the largest new account they'd signed for the Midwest expansion. After taking a hit on revenues over the better part of six months, DMI couldn't afford to lose new business. They had to nurse each account like a newborn.

"His secretary just said that he wants to fly in and meet this afternoon, and that it was important based on a chain of recent events."

"Go ahead and schedule him for this afternoon," Dave said.

The secretary darted from her boss's office to finish the call that was on hold. That left Frank with Dave.

"What do you think he wants?" Dave asked Frank.

"I can't read a crystal ball, but if I had to put money on it, I'd say they've gotten wind of your upcoming marriage and a taste of the rumors and gossip that are hitting the airwaves."

Dave scrunched his face and shook off Frank's pessimism. "No, I doubt that. MABS is too large of a ministry to be swayed by media innuendos."

"Get real, little brother. Religious folks read the papers too. Look at how much damage the divorce did to DMI. Can you imagine what's going to happen when everybody finds out more specifics about the affair, Sherry's age, and the baby? I bet Davis has gotten wind of the story and wants to distance his organization from the fallout."

"No, it has to be something else. Hopefully, he's just coming to touch base."

"He's flying from Chicago to Detroit in the middle of the day just to say hello? I don't think so."

"Frank, don't be ridiculous. I know the man isn't showing up here to say hello. Give me some credit. I've run this place for fifteen years. I know how DMI works and how our clients think. That's why we've realized unprecedented growth every year," he said and meandered toward the windows.

"Maybe that was true before."

"Before what? My divorce or my engagement to Sherry?" Dave asked, snapping at Frank.

"Either one. You pick, because they're both nails in DMI's coffin. How did the media find out so quickly, anyway?"

"Good question. Nobody has spoken to me or to Sherry directly, other than the travel agency and the dress shop that she's using."

"Who knows how your business got out there? Just goes to show that you can't hide. End this train wreck now and save yourself. Save the rest of us."

Dave faced the windows and flung his hand in the air. "I'm not rehashing this conversation with you. I have to get to work. I need to review their contract and be ready for Mr. Davis."

"If it was only that simple. Read a contract, meet with a disgruntled client, and walk away with your so-called unprecedented growth record intact. Well, not this time."

Dave turned to face Frank. "What do you suggest I do, since you have all the answers?"

"I don't know, but you'd better figure it out soon, before we lose the new business and the old."

Dave sat at his desk. "I have to get to work."

Frank knew that meant Dave was tired of talking about this matter. He would gladly exit, but not before adding one more comment. "Oh, and, Dave, where is your faith now? I suggest you bring it for this meeting, because you're going to need all the help you can get on this one. See you later," he said and actually left this time.

Chapter 12

The morning scampered along. Dave volleyed repeatedly between reviewing the contract on his desk and revisiting the conversation he'd had earlier with Frank. It was a few minutes before one o'clock in the afternoon. He shoved Frank out of his head and saturated his thoughts with MABS.

There was a knock on the door, which irritated him slightly. He had to get focused if there was any chance of getting ready for the impromptu meeting that Davis had requested. He didn't respond until the second series of knocks, which seemed louder. "Come in," he yelled, loud enough to be heard.

"Excuse me, Mr., Mitchell, but Mr. Davis from the Midwest Association of Bible Scholars is here," Dave's secretary said, poking her head inside.

"I thought we had him down for two o'clock?" Dave stammered.

She stepped into the office. Yes. He's early."

Dave glanced at his watch. "Very early." He thought for a minute. "Is he alone?"

"Yes, it's just him."

"Did we find out why Mr. Davis wanted to meet with me?"

"His secretary said Mr. Davis had a concern about recent events and needed to speak with you right away. That was it."

"Hmmm, I wonder what this is about." He thought some more, scratching his head. "Okay, give me twenty minutes. Offer him coffee, tea, a soft drink, or something from the cafeteria. Make him comfortable until I get these papers organized," he said, shuffling the stack on his desk.

The secretary didn't move.

"Well, is there a reason why you're still standing there?" The secretary seemed reluctant to speak. "Sharon, what is it?" He needed her to speak up and then leave. Time was scarce, and he couldn't squander the little he had.

"I'm sorry, Mr. Mitchell, but I don't normally see you this rushed. It seems like you're always in control, and I mean that in a good way."

"Then that's how I'll receive your comment. In a good way," he said.

He hadn't realized there'd been a change in his behavior, but apparently others had, which had to be corrected. Every step of his DMI journey had been taken with wisdom, peace, boldness, and confidence. Whatever he undertook in the name of the Lord worked. Success was his trademark. Frank had reminded him about that time and time again. Whatever project or business he'd pursued in the past fifteen years was successful.

"Thank you," he told Sharon. She probably thought it was for the compliment. Actually, it was for the reminder of who he was. He was a man who walked in faith—faith in God's ability, not his own. Perhaps he was anxiously scrambling to get organized before Sharon came in. But she was right. That wasn't Dave Mitchell. He wouldn't dare worry and stress while at the same time confessing his faith in God's plan. Faith and fear were opposites, unable to operate simultaneously. He had to choose one or the other, but not both.

"Should I tell him you'll be free in twenty minutes, thirty, or longer?"

"No, just give me five minutes, and he can come in."

"Five minutes?" she questioned, seeing the pile of papers spread across the folder on his desk.

"Don't worry. Five minutes is more than enough."

"All right, if you insist, but please let me know if there's anything I can do to help."

"Will do," he said, ushering her from his office.

After the door closed, he moved to the center of the room and collected his thoughts. "He desired guidance and favor with Morgan Davis. Most importantly, Dave didn't want his personal shortcomings to become a stumbling block for others. His prayer was that they would see the good in him, the godly part and discount the rest." With that, Dave was ready for Mr. Davis.

He called Sharon on the line that went directly to her desk. "You can send him in."

"So soon? Are you sure?" she practically whispered into the phone.

"I'm sure," he said.

Dave greeted his client when he entered the office.

"Mr. Mitchell, thank you for seeing me on such short notice," Davis said.

"The pleasure is mine. Anytime we can help, we're here. Why don't you take a seat at my conference table? We'll be more comfortable here than sitting around my desk," Dave said, chuckling.

Davis walked over to the table.

"So, tell me, what can I do for you?" Dave asked, discarding the small talk.

Davis sat and immediately began speaking. "Well, since you're being direct with me, I owe you the same courtesy." Dave was extremely curious. "Our ministry is based on stability. We have to stand on a solid foundation if we want others to take our lead."

Dave was waiting to see where Davis was headed. Nothing he'd said so far warranted an impromptu meeting. "I understand, but what does this have to do with DMI?"

Davis sat up tall in his seat. "The divorce from your DMI partner last year was concerning, but we stuck with you. Now we've recently been informed that you're engaged to the former employee linked to the failure of your marriage."

"What?" Dave asked, stunned that the leader of a multimillion-dollar ministry had actually got on a plane in Chicago and had flown for an hour to tell him this nonsense.

"We have a reputation to uphold. I'm afraid if we continue working with you, it sends the wrong message."

"I don't see how. My track record speaks for itself."

"You're absolutely correct, which is why I'm meeting you in person. I needed to look into your eyes and have you give me your word that DMI is solid."

"I assure you that we are. Nothing has changed. My personal life doesn't affect DMI. When I'm here in this office, I'm the chief executive officer, which I take very seriously. When I'm in this seat, I'm working for you. And I do a heck of a job. So if you want to use the services of DMI to get your staff trained, DMI is the place for you. If you're seeking a perfect man beyond these walls, then you'll have to keep walking past this building." He peered directly into Davis's eyes and said, "Because we don't have anyone here that meets that description." He stopped talking, wanting to let his comments marinate. He could see the concern diminish on Davis's face.

"Well, Mr. Mitchell, you raise a fair point."

"Does that mean we still have a deal?"

Davis hesitated. Finally, he shook Dave's hand and said, "We most certainly do."

Dave was relieved. Frank's words had tried to chip at his confidence, but it was too deeply rooted in years of success to be erased by a few harsh words from his brother. It was going to take a lot more for him to back down from his role as head of the company. Frank and Madeline better beware. Dave Mitchell was back and ready for business.

Chapter 13

Dave wrapped up a few notes from the meeting, and the savor of success remained until Frank popped in.

"How did the meeting go with MABS?" Frank said, easing into a seat and grinning.

"It was difficult at first. You were right. He'd heard about certain events."

"You mean your divorce and remarriage?"

"Yes. Okay, are you satisfied?"

"Don't get mad at me. I'm just telling the truth."

"Fine, but did you come here to talk or to listen?"

"Go ahead. Tell me what happened," Frank said, locking his hands behind his head and rearing back.

Dave continued. "Davis was concerned that my circumstances would affect my ability to run DMI."

"How did you answer that?" Frank asked, as if he agreed with Davis.

"How do you think I answered?" Frank hunched his shoulders. "I basically told him that my personal challenges are not a factor when it comes to handling DMI business."

"I don't believe that, and I doubt if he did, either," Frank responded.

"He believed me after I reminded him of my lengthy and successful track record. Apparently, I have to remind you of the same record, since you seem to have lost confidence in my ability to run this place."

"I'm just calling it like I see it."

"Well, you don't have to worry about MABS. The deal is ironclad. They're on board, and your worries are pointless."

"Maybe, but you know how I feel about Sherry."

"Yes, I do, and that's your problem," Dave told his brother. He'd heard enough about Sherry. There was no need to continue. Frank could feel the way he wanted so long as he kept it out of DMI and away from Dave.

"I suspect you don't want to hear this, but you have to do the right thing."

Dave sighed loudly. "And what is that, Frank?" he asked, unwilling to bridle his aggravation.

"The smartest decision you can make is to get Madeline back in this office before DMI goes down as a result of the divorce."

"Our divorce was final a year ago. That's old news."

"It was old until you added a fresh young woman to the mix," Frank said, chuckling. Dave didn't laugh.

"Excuse me, Mr. Mitchell," his secretary said, entering the office and appearing distressed. "Oh, I didn't know you were meeting with Mr. Mitchell. I can come back after you're finished."

"It's okay, Sharon. Come on in. Tell me what's going on, because you look worried."

"I got a call from the legal department. Tri-State and the Eastern Lutheran Group are opting out of their maintenance contracts, and two new clients are canceling their deals."

"What?" Frank blurted. "Why didn't I get those messages?"

"I don't know, sir. Maybe they didn't know you were up here. I don't know, but the chief counsel told me to tell you that he's reviewing the contracts."

Dave did a quick calculation and realized the news equated to roughly one and a half million dollars in revenue. "Get him up here in my office, pronto," he said.

Sharon hustled from the office.

"We must have stiff language and penalties in the contract surrounding early terminations," Frank said.

"Not really. We've never had an early termination."

Frank slapped the table. "My point exactly. You have to face it. We're treading in uncharted waters. You're accustomed to dictating to clients what we're going to do. Now that your reputation is compromised, those vultures are going to pick the bones of DMI if we don't get a plan in place."

"And you have the perfect plan, right?"

"You betcha I do. In one word, the answer is Madeline. Get her in here. Show the clients that it's business as usual between the two of you."

"You have a good point. The only problem is that Madeline doesn't want anything to do with me or Sherry. Can you imagine the two of them working here together? Because I certainly can't."

"True, that is a small technicality," Frank said, letting his gaze dip.

"But I think her passion for DMI might outweigh her contempt for me and for Sherry."

"I'm betting on it," Frank said. "If I was a religious man, which we know I'm not, this would be a good time to say a prayer," he added, laughing and prompting a reaction from Dave. "But we'll leave that business to you. I'll rely on my good old-fashioned instincts. DMI is in Madeline's bones. She might have been gone for two or three years, but nobody can replace her around here, and I hope Madeline knows it."

"You have a point," Dave told his brother. Frank was right. Madeline had always been a solid partner at DMI. She was with him from the beginning. Truth was, he needed her then and he needed her now. Dave had to acknowledge the other side of the predicament—his bride-to-be. Sherry wouldn't be pleased, but he had to save the company.

"You want me to call Madeline and tell her what's going on here? It might sway her decision," Frank said.

"Thanks for the offer, but I'll call her. She needs to hear the request from me. I owe her that much."

Chapter 14

"Stop hitting me," Sam shouted as he ran through the family room. Tamara was hot on his trail, and Don came around the corner, trying to keep up.

"Stop that running in here," Madeline shouted, loud enough for everyone in the house to hear. Madeline opened the magazine again in search of the spot where she'd paused. Finally, she found it, just as the children were taking another turn running through the room. "Didn't I say stop running in here?" she said, slamming the magazine down on the sofa. The telephone rang. "Cut it out," she yelled. The phone rang and rang. "Is anyone going to get the phone?" she shouted.

The children were so hyped that they probably didn't hear her. It was the middle of summer. They were out of school, and Madeline was overwhelmed with all four children being home with no real plans. She felt awful seeing them stuck in the house, but it was their choice. She was accustomed to them playing with their neighborhood friends when they lived on Mayweather Lane. Despite her sincere efforts, no one seemed interested in making friends in their new neighborhood. Her children had waged a major protest against her decision to leave their father. Over a year had elapsed, and not much had improved. She went back to flipping the magazine pages.

The phone rang again, prompting Madeline to go to the kitchen and answer the call.

"Madeline, did I catch you at a bad time?" Dave asked.

Having the children running around like madmen should have forced her to answer with a resounding yes, but Dave was even less equipped to handle the family chaos than she was. He'd struggled when they lived together. No way could he be of any value, living thirty minutes away.

"What do you want, Dave?" Between the children's rambunctious energy and her being worn out, there was no sanity left to handle an argument.

"I need your help."

"With what?"

"With DMI business."

"What do you mean?"

"I have several critical accounts that require my full attention."

"What about Frank? Can't he help you?"

"We need you here. I need you," he said. It wasn't what Dave said, but the way he said it, that made her willing to listen. "I need you to come back to the office and help me with marketing and publicity."

Madeline wasn't prepared for Dave's request. They hadn't spoken about DMI for a very long time. She'd decided to take a sabbatical right after Andre came to live with them, refusing to let her children be raised by nannies. That was three years ago. Back then, DMI was considered her fifth child. She had diligently stayed in tune with the company the first six months after stepping down. Soon her dedication to her children took precedence, and she dropped any involvement with DMI. Yet the yearning to be involved in the company had never completely evaporated.

"Why now?"

"I'm going to be completely honest with you. Our divorce and my recent engagement may be affecting business. Several accounts are in jeopardy."

"Really?" she said, genuinely surprised.

The divorce had severely impacted their children and their relationship, but until now she hadn't considered DMI. Hearing that the place was falling apart because of her absence sparked a sense of appreciation. Madeline hadn't felt valued in months, possibly a few years. Her contributions weren't so easily discounted, after all. She felt inspired to know that DMI needed her, and Dave too, but he couldn't know how she really felt about him. Her pride still wouldn't let her open up about her feelings about wanting him back. Instead, she'd keep the distance, confirming to him that she was done with their union.

She could hear the children playing rough and yelling in the family room. Maybe it was time to get out of the house to give her and the children a break. "What time frame were you thinking about? Ideally, I could start when the children go back to school next month."

"We can't wait that long. I need you there tomorrow."

"Tomorrow?" she blurted out. "You're insane. No way. We have to make arrangements for the children," she said and then remembered who she was talking to. "I mean, *I* have to make arrangements."

"Can you just extend the nanny's shift for a few days?" Dave asked.

Madeline felt instant irritation and had to refrain from reacting. Those were almost the same words he'd spoken three years ago. Handing her children over to a bunch of nannies didn't sit well then, and it wasn't generating more acceptance now. But she'd decided at the beginning of the call not to get into an argument with Dave. Instead she said, "I can't start this week, but I should be able to get a plan in place for the children next week and start then, even if it's part time for the first couple of weeks."

"I'll take whatever time I can get from you," he said.

Dave's words stroked Madeline's ego. "I'll be in next week," she told him.

"Madeline, thank you, and I owe you one," he said.

"You're right. You definitely owe me," she replied as they ended the call.

Madeline stood in the kitchen, letting her thoughts swirl, which made her dizzy with excitement. The children's noise faded. It sounded like the birds were chirping and angels were singing a hymn, if only in her world. She savored the sensation. Feeling valued and respected was doing wonders for her.

In a whirlwind, her daydreaming episode ended. Madeline began creating an intense list of activities that had to get done in the next few days. She raced to the junk drawer and opened it in search of a pen and a sheet of paper. After digging past coupons, crayons, and who knows what, she found them. Madeline scribbled, "Register children for day camps and extend Mrs. Jenkins's hours." She'd keep working with one nanny as long as possible before freely tossing her children to a second and third one. There was more to go on the list but first things first. She had to speak with her children and let them know what was going on. She found them in the family room, finally settled down.

"Aren't you tired of being stuck in this house?" she asked them.

No one really said anything. They were watching TV. She had to get their attention. Madeline turned the TV off, which produced all kinds of responses. "Good. Now I have your attention."

"Come on, Mom. We want to see *Batman* before it goes off," Andre said, mad. He was often mad these days, so his response didn't derail her.

She continued, "I have big news to tell you."

"Oh no, not again," Tamara said.

"What now?" Sam asked.

"You've already ruined our lives. What else is there left to do to us?" Andre said.

"Is it that bad," Madeline asked.

"Yes, it is," Sam and Andre said in unison.

"I didn't know you were this miserable." No one seemed to be looking at her. "Then you'll be happy to know that you're going to day camp next week."

"What camp?" Sam asked.

"I don't want to go to any stinking camp with a bunch of kids I don't know," Andre said.

"I'll stay home with you," Tamara said.

"Me too," Don said, finally chiming in.

"You have no choice, because I have to go back to work next week."

"Work? Why? You haven't worked in a long time," Sam said.

Tamara lunged toward her mother and clung to her. "Mommy, don't go to work. If you go, we'll never see you."

"That's not true," Madeline said, bending down to console her daughter, who was now crying. Don fell on the couch and started crying too. "Really, I'm only going to work a few hours each day until you go back to school."

"Who's going to take care of us if you're leaving us too?" Don asked.

"I'm not leaving you. That's number one," she said, raising two fingers, "and number two, Mrs. Jenkins will be here with you."

"Ah, don't believe her, Don. Parents always leave you. I ought to know," Andre warned.

Madeline went to hug Andre, but he resisted. She didn't push.

"Daddy was gone for work a lot, and then he was gone for good. Please don't leave us, Mommy, please," Tamara cried.

"I promise to never leave any of you. I will be here in this house with you every day of my life. Do you understand that?" she said as her heart was being ripped apart. Her children's pain was hers, always had been and always would be. That would never change. They had to know the depths of her love. "Do you understand, Andre?"

He didn't speak.

"Do you understand?" she bellowed.

"Yes, okay," Andre muttered.

"Sam?"

"Yes, yes," Sam answered.

The other two children gave their confirmation too. Madeline was at peace. She opened her arms wide and made each child nestle in for a group hug. They were battling insecurity, but she was convinced the children were going to be all right. They were too young and didn't understand the sacrifice she was making now. Hopefully, one day they could appreciate what she was doing. Their mother had to get back into the office and help save the company she'd built with their father. She couldn't sit on the sidelines and watch Sherry destroy their livelihood. Madeline vowed to personally protect the Mitchell investment, convinced that her children's inheritance depended on her.

Chapter 15

Monday morning had swallowed up any semblance of order in Madeline's household. The nanny was there by 6:30 A.M., which was a help, but it was not quite early enough to get four children dressed, fed, and off to camp in time for Madeline to hit the DMI parking lot by eight. Today she was willing to settle for what she could get. The clock in her Mercedes displayed 9:05 A.M. when she pulled into the lot. Tomorrow she'd set a goal of 8:45 A.M. and keep shaving off five or ten minutes each day.

The lot was already loaded with cars. She crept to the section up front, which was reserved for the executive team: CEO, CFO, general counsel, head of Human Resources, and Mrs. Mitchell. Her reserved spot was sandwiched between Dave's shiny Cadillac and Frank's Chevy pickup truck. Madeline was prepared to pull into her old spot when she had to slam on the brakes to avoid hitting the tiny car already there. Who had the nerve to park in her spot? She was irked but wasn't going to go ballistic as long as the car was moved or towed by tomorrow. Anyone was entitled to one mistake. The owner of this car had just made theirs.

Madeline regrouped and circled the lot until she found a space in the rear, about eight rows away from the building. She killed the ignition, drew in a long-winded sigh, and released the air very slowly, methodically taking in the scene. She extracted a tube of lipstick from her purse. Madeline stretched forward, peering into the rearview mirror as she colored her lips. She used the palm of her hand to flatten any stray strands of hair that had eased from her tightly drawn curly ponytail.

Realizing she couldn't stall any longer, Madeline opened the car door. The July heat was already rising uncontrollably this early in the morning. It smashed against her cheeks, causing her to hustle down the long walkway as fast as her four-inch stilettos allowed. Once the piercing heat, the pressure on her feet, and the weight of her portfolio bag meshed, Madeline couldn't maintain her calm disposition about someone parking in her spot. She wasn't dressed for a hike. She was hot in her Chanel suit and felt disheveled. *Forget about waiting until tomorrow,* she thought. *They need to get out today.* She was too uncomfortable to think straight. Her temper was boiling hotter with each step, especially after remembering the local magazine was coming out to do an article. She'd arranged the interview as a means of publicly announcing that the DMI leadership team was intact and ready for business. Marketing was her strength and she knew what had to be done quickly to repair the corporate image. Finally, she reached the revolving door and stepped inside.

Madeline rushed to the guard desk and set the portfolio bag down. She caught her breath and said, "Someone is in my parking spot, and I want them out now."

She wasn't in the office a lot, but the staff knew who she was. An introduction wasn't necessary.

"Mrs. Mitchell, we'll check into it," one of the guards assured her.

"Don't just check into it. Find out who owns the car that's parked in the slot for Mrs. Mitchell and get it out. I don't care if you announce it over the loudspeaker or have the car towed. I really don't care how you take care of it, so long as it's out of there by lunchtime."

The guards immediately began scrambling.

Madeline wanted to take off her shoe to relieve the pain in her toe, but she feared it wouldn't go back on. She decided to stand there for a while and calm down. Eventually, she tiptoed to the elevators and made it upstairs. She gingerly moved down the hallway, acknowledging the greetings coming from the few administrative assistants on the floor.

"Is that my sister-in-law?" she heard someone say from behind her.

Madeline turned to see Frank approaching, with a grin plastered across his lips. "You mean ex-sister-in-law, don't you?" she said with sprinkles of humor. Frank was family. She relaxed as each shoe was pulled off.

"Never that," Frank said, giving her a friendly hug. Madeline rested the heavy bag on a desk. "It's good to see you. I mean, really good."

"It's good to be back. Honestly, I didn't think anyone noticed that I was gone."

"Are you kidding me? We've missed you around here. I've missed you being here," he said, poking his thumbs in his chest. "Let's just say it hasn't been the same around here without you."

"You mean Sherry didn't fill in for me?" she whispered, barely able to get the words out before bursting into laughter.

"Pleassse," Frank said, joining in the laughter. He whispered in her ear, "There's only one Mrs. Mitchell, and she ain't it."

They continued laughing until Dave came into the hallway. "I thought that was you," he said.

"Showtime," Madeline whispered to Frank and picked up her shoulder bag.

"Got a minute?" Dave asked her and Frank. "I'd like to chat for a few minutes."

"I'm free," Frank said, walking toward Dave's office.

"Let me drop my bag off in my office, and I'll be right in." Madeline thought about it, and when she was in close proximity to Dave, she said, "That is, if I still have an office."

"Of course you do. It's been untouched since you left," Dave said.

Chapter 16

Madeline popped into her office and hurried back to the meeting, eager to get going. When she got there, Sherry had arrived.

"What is she doing here?" Madeline asked.

"I need to get Dave's signature on a Human Resources document. What are you doing here?"

Madeline sashayed past Dave's young fling. "Didn't you know that the executive team is meeting so we can get this place back on track?"

"What does that have to do with you?" Sherry asked.

"Didn't you hear me say the executive team is meeting? I'm part of the executive team," Madeline said, hurling dagger-filled stares at Sherry. "No matter *who* crawls their way into this company, my position is set forever, thanks to my generous divorce clause. Isn't that right, Dave?" Madeline punctuated her statement with a smirk.

Sherry glanced at Dave. "What is she talking about, Dave?"

"I've been so busy that I didn't get a chance to tell you that Madeline has decided to come back to DMI," Dave announced.

Sherry was visibly upset. "Why?"

"This is a critical time for DMI, and Madeline has the expertise that we desperately need to get through this tough spot."

"But what about me?" Sherry replied.

"Let's not get into this here," Dave quickly interjected. "We have work to do. Sherry, why don't you leave the document with me and I'll sign it later?"

Sherry handed it to him.

"Yes, Miss Henderson, drop off the document and run along like a nice assistant." Madeline was egged on by Frank, who was chuckling under his breath, although she didn't need an audience. Actually, Madeline didn't consider dueling with Sherry a fair fight. It was like a lion and a fawn. If Sherry would learn to shut up and stay out of Madeline's way, she might be able to survive in her new role. Madeline crossed her legs, finished with Sherry. Then she remembered her parking spot. "Speaking of having a permanent position here, do you know someone had the nerve to park in my spot?" she told Dave and Frank. "But don't worry. I'm having the security guard take care of it. I told them to page the person and give them fair warning. By this afternoon, they can tow the car if need be—"

Sherry, who had lingered at the doorway, interrupted and said, "That's my car parked in that spot."

Frank wiped his hand across his eyebrows and let his gaze drop.

"Your car? What are you doing in my space?"

"Because—"

"Because nothing," Madeline said, standing up. Frank and Dave stood instantly, as if expecting her to be erratic. Making a public scene and compromising her dignity weren't Madeline's style. Both Frank and Dave knew that, but whatever, she thought. If they felt a need to protect the fawn, fine.

"But I figured since you weren't working here any longer, I could use the space," Sherry explained.

Madeline folded her arms tightly, her neck stiff. "So you did, huh?"

"Yes, I did."

"Well, I'm assuming you can read," Madeline said, drumming her fingers in the air. "The sign clearly says Mrs. Mitchell, doesn't it?"

Sherry didn't answer.

"Doesn't it?" Madeline yelled, locking her right arm to her waist.

"Come on, Madeline. She didn't know you'd be in today," Dave said.

"She doesn't have to know when I'm coming in. That's not the point. The space is reserved for Mrs. Mitchell. There should be no confusion, since she's Miss Henderson."

"We're getting married next week. Then I *will* be Mrs. Mitchell," Sherry said in a seemingly mocking tone.

Madeline was well aware of the upcoming marriage, but until then Sherry was a Henderson. From Madeline's perspective, she always would be.

"By next week I'll have the sign replaced with one that has the full name of Madeline Mitchell, since you seem to be confused about who you are. That way, you can drive right on past the spot and find any space you want in the back. I won't object," Madeline said, relocating to the conference table and taking a seat. "Anyone ready to get down to business? We have a lot to review before the reporter gets here. Are you going to join me, gentlemen?"

"That's what we love about you, speaking your mind. Let's get this train moving," Frank said, joining her at the table.

Dave gave Sherry a peck on the cheek. Madeline pretended not to see it. "We'll take care of your car right after my meeting," he told her.

"Where do we start?" Madeline said, hoping Dave would be forced to break up his romantic interlude.

He did and jumped right into the conversation. "We need to focus on the key accounts first. If we can convince them that DMI is open for business as usual, then the smaller clients will follow suit and be at ease," Dave said.

"I'm working with legal to see what leverage we have with the termination clauses," Frank added.

"Why is that?" Madeline asked.

"If clients know it's going to cost them a few hundred thousand dollars to terminate the contract, they may change their minds without us having to put pressure on them," Dave said.

"We should have Rob at this meeting. He is our new general counsel. He might as well jump into the shark-infested waters with us," Frank said.

"Would you like for me to go get him?" Sherry asked.

Madeline had forgotten she was in the room. Once business was under way, Sherry had virtually been ignored. Madeline imagined that Sherry must have felt dejected, awkward, and in the way. Madeline knew personally how it felt, having been there too often.

"Thanks for the offer," Dave said, "but we'll reach out to Rob later."

"Don't worry, Dave. I'll follow up with Rob," Frank said.

"And I'll get the marketing and publicity plan finalized by the end of the week, and I'll set up a formal press conference for next week. For today, let's concentrate on the message we want to share with the reporter," Madeline said.

"We have to milk this opportunity," Frank said.

"The main message is that you and I are a team. We built this company from scratch, and we may be divorced, but we're still partners here at DMI. That's never going to change," Dave said.

Madeline saw Sherry ease out of the room without being acknowledged. It was a role she'd better get used to, because Madeline wasn't planning on leaving DMI again. She'd done it once, and it had cost her her marriage. Never again.

In the late afternoon Dave caught a glimpse of Madeline walking past his office with her bag on her shoulder. He called out to her, and she stepped inside.

"Are you heading out for the day?" he asked, walking around to the front of his desk and leaning back against it.

"I am. That way I can get home before the children arrive from camp around five. They weren't too pleased with me coming back to work. So I'm going to ease into the hours. I figure somewhere between nine and two should be plenty in the beginning."

"Every minute we have you here is a blessing. Whatever schedule you work out is great with me," he said.

Madeline was about to walk away, but Dave couldn't let her go without asking another favor, a huge one. He wasn't sure how she'd react, but he had to ask, anyway. "What are the kids doing this evening?"

"Nothing special," she answered. "Why?"

Dave braced his palms on the desk. "I was hoping to pick up the kids this evening and spend time with them."

"Where?"

"At the estate," he said.

"With whom?" she snapped.

"Sherry and I."

"Oh no, not with her. I've had a long day. I don't want to start in with Sherry."

"I don't, either, which is why I'm praying that you'll change your mind and let me see the kids. I really miss them."

"I'll think about letting them come over later in the week—without Sherry."

"My schedule is going to be full the rest of the week, which is why it's important that I get them tonight."

"What's the rush?"

Dave hesitated, mustered his resolve, and said, "Because I want to tell them about the wedding, unless you've already told them."

"No, I have not told them," she said, giggling, but she didn't really seem to be amused. "I wasn't about to tell them."

"Then I'd like to share my news with them tonight," he said. Dave had been patient with Madeline for months. It wasn't like their marriage had been problem free, but the pivotal moment was his infidelity with Sherry. So he understood that Madeline's hurt masqueraded as anger. But there were instances when he had to shake her from the web of bitterness she was weaving in order to see his kids. This was one of those times. "Madeline, let me see the kids this evening," he said.

She stared at him with her toes pointed and her arms crossed. He stared right back, not flinching as her stare intensified. This was a battle he wasn't going to lose.

"Fine. You can get the children this evening," she said, looking into her bag. "If you want to crush their hearts and tell them about this marriage, go right ahead."

"I'll pick them up at seven."

"All I can say is good luck, because you're going to need it."

Dave hadn't relied on luck before and wasn't about to cling to it now. He said bye as Madeline left. She wasn't in a huff but her dissatisfaction was obvious. Dave didn't get any satisfaction from Madeline's discomfort, but the marriage was over. He was free to marry Sherry, and he was committed to doing just that.

Chapter 17

Seven o'clock arrived and went as the kids piled out of Dave's car. Tamara and Don were the only ones who had talked during the ride from Madeline's house to his. He wasn't counting on the evening being easy, but he was determined to make the most of their visit.

"Are you hungry?" he asked as he fumbled with his keys at the front door.

"No, we've already eaten," Tamara said.

"What about dessert? Anyone wants ice cream?" he asked, finally getting the door open.

"I want some," Tamara answered.

"Me too," Don said.

Sam and Andre grunted as they walked in the house, practically despondent.

They were headed straight for the family room until Dave said, "Let's get the ice cream, and then I have to talk to you about something."

His brood entered the kitchen and found Sherry sitting at the counter.

"What's she doing here?" Andre asked.

"That's what I wanted to talk to you about," Dave said, embracing Sherry. Tamara walked over and hugged him around his waist. Sherry backed away. He reached for her, but Tamara's grip was tight and she left no room for Sherry. "We've decided to get married."

"Why?"

"When?"

"Oh, boy."

The flurry of mumbling continued. The kids were speaking all at once. It was hard for him to distinguish who was saying what. "Time out," he said, making the letter *T* in the air and loosening Tamara's grip around his waist so he could speak. "I know you have questions, and I plan to answer each one. But you have to give me a chance to hear each of you. Let's get ice cream and sit down in the family room and discuss this like a family."

"We're not a family anymore," Sam said.

"As far as I'm concerned, we are," Dave responded.

"*She's* not our family. She might be yours, but not ours," Andre added.

"We already have a mother. We don't need another one. If our mom died, then we'd have to get another one, like Andre had to. But she's not dead," Tamara said.

"Leave me out of this!" Andre shouted.

"Okay, everybody, let's calm down," Dave ordered and drew Sherry close to him. She was clearly outnumbered and deserved his support. If they were going to make the marriage work, his kids had to find peace with his decision. He didn't know how or when the acceptance of Sherry would come, but he hoped it would soon. Tamara resumed her hug too. This time he gently pushed her away. "I'm hugging Sherry right now."

Tamara looked sad, but what else could he do? He couldn't have the two fighting over his affection even before the marriage was finalized. He couldn't imagine what was in store afterward if it was this bad already. He wiped the scary notion from his thoughts.

"You are still Daddy's little girl and always will be," he told Tamara. "I promise that won't change."

Andre stormed off. Dave made him come back. "I'm not finished talking," Dave told everyone. Andre groaned but stayed, as he was asked to do. "I wanted you to go with us to Mexico next week for the wedding, but your mother thought it best for you to stay in Detroit."

"I want to go to Mexico," Don said.

Sherry tightened her grip on Dave. For the first time she gave a slight smile. "You want to go with us?"

"Sure," Don said, excited.

"No, you don't," Tamara jumped in and said.

"Yes, I do," Don said.

"No, you don't!" Tamara told him again. "Remember what Mommy said about Sherry?" This time she whispered in Don's ear.

"Oh yeah. No, I don't want to go to Mexico with you," Don told Sherry.

Dave could feel Sherry pulling away, but he wouldn't let her go. She finally stopped pulling.

"Even though you're not going to be at the ceremony with us, I want you to know how much I love each of you. My love for you won't change after we get married. That's a promise. I am your father, and I will love you every day," Dave said with as much sincerity as his heart would allow without erupting.

"I know this is going to be new for each of you to have me as a stepmom, but I want you to know that I love your dad," Sherry added.

"Our dad loved our mom first," Sam said.

"And I will always care about your mom, but Sherry and I have decided to live together as husband and wife. I know you're all young. So I don't expect you to understand this, but I do expect you to respect Sherry."

"What does that mean?" Don asked.

"I don't expect you to say or do mean things to her when I'm around or when I'm not. Do you understand that?" No one answered until Dave asked again in a forceful tone.

A bunch of mumbles and shouts was sufficient for now.

"Does anyone want to make cookies?" Sherry asked.

"I do," Don answered immediately.

Dave could tell Sherry had sparked some interest in his daughter too. "Tamara, you love baking cookies."

She was on the brink of saying yes when a sense of loyalty must have kicked in, because she said no.

Andre stormed off. Dave let him go.

Sherry shrugged. "It's okay. I can bake the cookies with Don."

"He doesn't want any, either," Tamara said.

"Yes, I do," Don insisted.

Dave was sure Tamara wanted to nudge him back into the "no" corner, but the thought of fresh-baked cookies was too powerful for his youngest son to resist. Maybe the sweet allure would be too much for Tamara too. Dave could only hope.

Sherry felt invisible. Except for Don, the children virtually ignored her. She thought baking cookies would sway their attitude, but Madeline's children were tough like their mother. They weren't willing to give Sherry a chance to show them how much fun she was and how nice she could be. Thank goodness Don was giving her a chance when Tamara let him.

"The cookies are ready to come out of the oven, Don," Sherry said, watching Tamara pull him into a corner of the kitchen and whisper in his ear again. Sherry was losing her grip on his interest. She could feel it. "Let's get them out while they're warm," she said in a desperate attempt to rescue him from Madeline's advocate. "Um, um, nice and hot," she said, grabbing the oven mitts. He was still being sequestered in the corner by mini-Madeline. Sherry couldn't believe she was battling an eight-year old for the attention of a seven-year-old. Her love for Dave had to endure. Otherwise, living like this would be unbearable for any amount of time. "Don, are you coming?" she asked.

"No, I changed my mind," he said in a pitiful voice as Tamara pulled him toward the family room.

Sherry was hurt and disillusioned. She slammed the tray of cookies on the cooling mat, fighting back the tears. How was she going to survive? She poured a glass of milk from the refrigerator and gulped it down, secretly wishing for her own children one day. Then she wouldn't have to take this kind of treatment from Madeline's kids any longer. Her day was coming. She choked down the warm cookie, balancing the sweet with the heat. Apparently, it was a skill she'd better master quickly in order to survive in that house and in the Mitchell family.

Chapter 18

Dave sat at his desk with his back to Sherry as she stood next to one of the windows in his office.

"It's hard to believe we've been married seven months already."

"They say time flies when you're happy," Dave responded.

"That I am," she said gently hugging him around the neck and laying her head on his shoulder.

"You know tomorrow's Valentine's Day. What would you like to do? It's your choice," Dave told her.

"Anything that's not associated with food," Sherry said.

Dave turned to face her. "You have to eat. The baby has to eat."

"I know, but I just don't have an appetite." She drew a deep breath.

"Well, we'll have to find something," he said, gently placing his palm on her stomach.

His touch put her at ease, at least as much as was possible. She'd been pregnant for five of the seven months they'd been married, and his doting had only intensified. Sherry had exactly what she'd craved, a loving husband who was able to provide for his family and their child. Yet peace escaped her, and she knew why. Dave did too.

Her morning sickness ended almost two months ago but her taste for food must have gone with it. "Give me another month, and maybe this will have passed, and I'll be eating up a storm," she said, both hopeful and saddened.

Dave must have detected the change in her disposition, because he said, "You're thinking about the other baby, aren't you?"

Sherry couldn't lie. "He's all I think about."

He embraced her, and it helped, but not completely. Five months along and she wasn't even showing yet. The baby wasn't growing like it needed to be which caused her great concern.

"You and this baby will be fine."

"How do you know?" she said, feeling her anxiety rising. "We thought the first baby was going to be fine, but look what happened."

Dave took her hand and led her to the seats in front of his desk. "It was different then. You were under a tremendous amount of stress. Remember I was married to Madeline then."

How could she forget?

"You and Edward had just ended your engagement," he added. "It was a tough patch for all of us."

That much pain never died. Those days were etched in her memory forever.

"This is different. We're married," he said, rubbing her stomach. "This baby is going to be healthy. Stop worrying. You're my wife, and I'm going to take care of you. I just have to find a way to get some food into you."

If only she could stop worrying. If only she could believe him. If only she could be sure. He was right about one point. It was better being his wife than the secret woman with no title or valid position in his life. Before, Sherry was invisible to the world. Madeline was his wife, the one in control. She had only been a woman with a heart for Dave and dreams of happiness. Sherry placed her hand on top of his, bonding with him and their baby. For a brief second, she felt validated. She was Mrs. Dave Mitchell, the soon-to-be mother of his youngest child. Joy hovered until Madeline walked in.

Madeline tossed a short stack of stapled papers in Dave's lap. "Read that," she said, waltzing to his table, claiming a seat, and crossing her legs. "That's what a good marketing plan will do for you."

Sherry was silent as Dave flipped through the pages and said with excitement, "Have you shown these to Frank?"

"Not yet. I came to you first."

"This is impressive. We can increase the East Coast market share by twenty-five percent."

"And that's conservative," Madeline noted, wearing a smug look on her face.

Sherry wanted to jump in and say something smart too. She didn't understand marketing or much else about the decisions Dave had to make. He relied on Madeline and Frank mostly. She heard about details only in passing. Watching him and Madeline go back and forth was crushing, especially when Dave walked away from her, joining Madeline at the conference table. There was that feeling of being invisible again. She had to get involved. Otherwise, Madeline would have a major part of him, the business side.

"Did you need me to make copies or follow up on anything for you?" Sherry asked, desperately grasping for any involvement.

Dave must not have heard her, because he didn't answer.

"Did you hear me?" Sherry said raising her voice so loudly that Madeline and Dave stared at her. She was kind of embarrassed but hid it. "Can I make copies or get anything for you?"

"Run along. We have grown folks' business to handle here," Madeline said.

"You can't talk to me like that!" Sherry shouted, hustling toward Madeline. The anger became so overwhelming that Sherry couldn't restrain her legs or lips. She didn't know what the plan was once she reached Madeline, but sitting back and letting the former Mrs. Mitchell treat her like a child wasn't acceptable. She had to stand up for herself.

Madeline popped up. "What are you going to do? Hit me?"

Sherry was angry enough to hit her but wasn't willing to go that far. Plus, she had to think about the baby.

"You're lucky I don't hit you."

"No, you're the lucky one," Madeline said, resting her knuckles on the desk. "Actually, I'm kind of impressed. You're not as crazy as I thought, because if you dared lift a finger to hit me, you'd better be."

Dave rushed in between them. "Let's calm down," he said, grabbing Sherry.

"I'm not the one who needs to calm down," Sherry snapped.

"That's right. Calm down, Sherry," Madeline mocked in a high-pitched, squeaky voice.

Sherry was getting angry again. "Dave, please make her get out."

"You get out," Madeline fired right back. "I'm not going anywhere, *ever,* right, Dave?" she said, digging her hand into her hip. The way she said it caused Sherry's anxiety to peak. This was never going to end. Madeline was determined to make her life miserable. Sherry wanted to fight back, but the baby couldn't stand the pressure. She couldn't either.

"Dave, do something," Sherry pleaded.

"Madeline, can you please leave?" he asked, obviously frustrated too.

"No. I'm not going anywhere."

Sherry didn't know if he was upset with her, with Madeline, or with both of them. The way she figured, Dave was her husband. So she was entitled to the tie-breaker. Madeline should be the one getting kicked out, not her.

"Madeline, please step out for a minute," Dave said.

Madeline stood there stubbornly, like a big old bull, grunting and sighing. "Humph, fine! I'll step out, but I'll be back in fifteen minutes. We need to get this plan reviewed and approved, and the brochures to the printer, by tomorrow morning. We have business to handle here, if we want to keep this place open," she said, brushing past Sherry.

"Please close the door behind you," he said.

Chapter 19

"Dave, I can't take this," Sherry said, breaking down in her husband's arms. "Madeline hates me, and she's determined to make my life painful every single day. When is it going to end?" she said, balling.

Dave sat next to her. "You're right. This has to stop," he said, taking her hand and sitting on the edge of the chair. "You can't keep up this kind of stress without affecting your pregnancy."

"Can't you make her go? Can't she work somewhere else?"

"I can't. She has a job here for the rest of her life."

"You can fire her."

Dave scratched his head and sat back in the chair. "It's not that simple."

"Why isn't it? You're in charge. You can fire her, and that will give me a break from her for a change."

"I can't fire her."

He reached for her hand again, and she snatched it away. "You can't or you won't?"

"I can't."

He sighed, but she didn't care if the conversation about his precious Madeline was uncomfortable. Welcome to her club. It was about time some of the other Mitchells joined her in the private hell she was experiencing at the hands of Dave's first family.

"No one can fire her. She has a permanent position in her contract."

"How did that happen?"

"I gave it to her."

"When?" Sherry asked, becoming more upset.

"When we got divorced. It was included in the divorce settlement."

"How could you do such a thing?" Sherry said, totally frazzled by now. "Now I definitely won't be able to get rid of her." She shook her head. "Just because she asked for a clause like that didn't mean you had to give it to her." The image of Madeline, smug and in charge, at DMI threatened to make Sherry nauseous.

"Madeline didn't ask," he said, letting his voice drop very low. "I offered it to her."

"You what?" she said, leaping to her feet. "What were you thinking?" Sherry couldn't believe he was the one who'd turned DMI into a prison for her. So long as Madeline was in the building, peace was not possible. "I'm shocked that you would do something like that to me."

"Sherry, remember, this was part of my divorce settlement. You weren't in the picture then. We weren't a couple and weren't discussing a future together. This was strictly between me and Madeline."

"You don't get it, do you?"

"Get what?" he asked.

"That you don't seem to be able to let go of Madeline. You're divorced, and she's still your wife."

"That's ridiculous!" he said.

"Is it?" Sherry asked. "You're probably the only person in the world who thinks so."

"What does that mean?"

"Madeline acts like she's your wife. She even gets the parking space next to yours, the spot reserved for Mrs. Mitchell, while I park in the next row."

"I didn't realize that bothered you. We can swap your space with one of the other executives in the front row, no problem."

"No, Dave, no, you're not getting it," she said, shaking his shoulders as he sat there. "I don't want another spot. I want the one reserved for Mrs. Mitchell, the one next to you." He shifted his gaze away from hers. "Can you do that for me?"

He didn't answer, didn't have to.

"Of course not. This is Madeline's company, not mine. How many times has she told me that? A hundred? A million? And thanks to you, she'll tell me a million more times," Sherry said, feeling exhausted.

"Here, sit and calm down," he said, patting the seat next to him.

"I don't need to calm down. I need to get fired up. Maybe that's what it will take to get respect around here."

"Sherry, I know you don't want to hear this, but Madeline deserved a permanent position here at DMI. She helped me build this company. Honestly, she's an invaluable member of the team."

"Right, right," Sherry said, refusing to sit down. "I know, Madeline is Mrs. Wonderful. She tells me constantly, and I guess you're telling me too."

"That's not what I said," Dave responded in a harsh voice, which hurt her feelings. He was making her seem like the disgruntled woman, when Madeline was the troublemaker. Dave couldn't see it, which was painful.

"I'm tired. I'm going home," she said, beyond the point of frustration. She was flat-out boiling.

"Are the part-time hours too much?"

"I don't know. I can't think straight right now."

"Maybe you should take off completely. The tension between you and Madeline isn't going to end, and we can't take a chance with the pregnancy." He rubbed her stomach again. "The doctor is already concerned that you've only gained a few pounds this far along. We have to take precautions for the baby."

"Is this about protecting the baby or Madeline?"

"How can you ask me a question like this?" Dave said. "You're my wife, and you're carrying my child. Shouldn't that answer your question?"

"No, not really," she said, ready to go.

"Wait! Don't rush off mad. We can work this out. Why don't you seriously consider taking the time off and giving you and our baby a rest?" he said grabbing her hand.

Sherry didn't pull away, but she wanted to. Her tired limbs just wouldn't move.

"I pray that the tension in my family will end soon, but in the meantime I believe it will be safer at home for the baby," he added.

Sherry wasn't going to fight. Dave and Madeline were too much for her to battle alone. Maybe once her baby was born, she'd have another person on her side. "You and Madeline win. I quit."

Chapter 20

"You're right. The new marketing plan is aggressive, but I'm willing to consider adding the Southern region," Madeline told Frank, talking to him outside Dave's office. She hadn't gotten very far after being kicked out. "We'll need to run this by Dave, because I got the impression he wanted to concentrate on the Midwest and East Coast."

"We'll see what he says. Since you've been back, business is booming. I say we hit the entire country at once—*bam,* one big media blitz—and ride this gravy train to the bank," Frank said, chuckling.

Sherry came tearing out of Dave's office. "You win. I told Dave that I'm quitting. You won't be able to stress me out anymore. I'm done with this insanity."

Madeline leaned against the wall, crossed her arms, and said, "I guess if it's too hot, then you should get out of the kitchen." She couldn't possibly hide her sense of satisfaction.

"You're very smug, aren't you?" Sherry retorted. Madeline grinned slightly. "If you say so."

Sherry leaned in close to Madeline. "Let me tell you a little secret," she said, rubbing her stomach. "I know you can't tell, because I'm not really showing yet. But I'm pregnant. I'm also quitting because Dave doesn't want me bothering with the stress around here." Madeline slid over a bit. "Like I said, you win Mrs. Madeline, or do you?" Sherry said while gently rubbing her stomach. For once, she was the one with the grin. "See you later, Frank, and take care Madeline."

Madeline grunted. "Frank, do you mind if I meet with Dave separately before we all get together?"

"Sure. Call me when you're ready to meet," he said.

Within a few seconds Madeline was in Dave's office with the door closed and was standing in his face, deflated. "Are you out of your mind? You got that woman pregnant again?"

"That woman is my wife."

"Oh, don't even go there with me about the wife thing. I will never accept her as your wife. Do you understand? Never!" Madeline said, almost sounding like she was humming the words.

"I thought we were making progress. I don't figure the two of you will be friends, but you have to be civil to each other if we're going to make this work."

"I'm not trying to make it work. That's your job."

She struggled to hide the extent of her outrage. Her nightmare was on auto play, repeating over and over, not requiring any prompting. The horror of Sherry entering their lives was never-ending. She reflected on the day Sherry walked into the office, seeking a job. Although she didn't have much experience, Madeline was willing to give her a chance. She saw a passion to succeed in Sherry and brought her on board as Dave's administrative assistant. Knowing Sherry was pregnant slashed Madeline to the core. She paced around the room.

"I can't believe you got her pregnant," she huffed. "Do you know how humiliating it will be for me when the public finds out?"

"Madeline, we're divorced. Why does it matter what people say?"

"It matters to me. Thank goodness she quit and won't have her belly growing for the entire company to see."

"I'm not ashamed of Sherry's pregnancy."

"Then I'm ashamed of you."

Dave cocked his head to the side. "Madeline, when will this end?"

"Probably after you're dead and long gone. Who knows? Maybe not then, either."

"That's too bad," he said.

"Tell me about it. You should have thought about this when you decided to get with that woman. You can't possibly think that your children and I will be a family with you, Sherry, and your new offspring. Accept the fact that we don't like her."

There was a knock on Dave's door.

"Come in," he shouted.

The door opened slowly. Madeline half expected it to be Sherry, coming back to torment her more. Instead Sharon stuck her head inside the small opening.

"Excuse me, Mrs. Mitchell, but there's an important call for you from Cedarbrook Academy."

"Did they say what they wanted?" Madeline asked.

"No, but I can send the call in here or to your office."

"In here," Dave told her.

"Okay, I'll take care of it," Sharon said and pulled the door shut.

"What could the school want?" Dave asked.

"If I have to guess, I'll say it's Andre."

"Why?"

"He keeps getting into trouble. I don't understand what's going on with him. I've been to the school three times in the past month. Thank goodness only one resulted in a suspension."

"Why haven't you told me about this? You know I want to be involved with the children. They are mine too, and you have to stop shutting me out," Dave said.

The phone rang. Madeline answered it.

"Mrs. Mitchell, this is Mr. Cruthers. I wanted you to know that Andre in the office with us."

"What happened?" Madeline asked the headmaster.

"He got into a fight with another student. As you're aware, we have to suspend him for any acts of physical violence."

"Oh no, he's already been out of school once this month. Is there anything we can do to give him consequences without him having to miss school?"

"I'm afraid not, Mrs. Mitchell. The other student suffered a broken nose. We have to suspend Andre. Otherwise, I'm afraid other parents will complain."

"Well, do what you have to do," she said, disgusted mostly at Andre and his recent behavior.

"We'll wait for you to pick him up this afternoon."

Madeline ended the call and peered at Dave, who was standing close by, waiting for the update. "I was right, unfortunately." She clapped her hands together and held them out in front of her. "He broke some other child's nose."

"What?" Dave asked.

"I honestly don't know what to do with our son. I'm at a loss. Since you left, the boy has been difficult to manage. But I think that my coming back to work really did it. He's acting out like crazy now."

"Let me help."

"What can you do that I haven't already done?"

"I'm not sure what I can do, but please let me try."

"For starters, you can pick him up today. Maybe if he sees you at the school, it will spark a positive reaction in him. Pick him up, and then we can discuss how you might be able to help," Madeline said. "Maybe your involvement is exactly what he needs. Clearly, my single parenting isn't working," she added, feeling defeated.

"It's going to be tough for me this afternoon. I'm meeting with Bert Richardson in less than an hour, and you remember how difficult it has been to get the Faith Coalition to extend their contract."

"Of course I remember," she snapped, not caring about her tone. "How could I forget? It was the first account we courted when I came back."

"So you understand why I have to have this meeting?"

"No, I don't. You see, the problem between us is that I'm there for you, with the Faith Coalition, Tri-State, and MABS, but when the children or I need you to step in, you have a long list of excuses." Madeline stomped her way to the door. "I don't have time for excuses. I have a child in crisis. Your grown behind can take care of yourself, including handling the Faith Coalition."

"I'm sorry if I've offended you. It certainly wasn't my intent."

Nothing had changed. Dave was the same self-absorbed man he'd been when they got married. "You're seriously going to put a meeting ahead of your son's needs? Really, Dave?" she said, flailing her hands in the air.

"Madeline, that's not fair. I've tried to spend quality time with my kids for years, and you have not made it easy, but I keep trying."

"Don't try to blame the strained relationship you have with your children on me. You are totally responsible. You've always put work ahead of your family, because of some great spiritual purpose you claim to be fulfilling."

"I'm not going to argue with you about my purpose, but I will say that you, of all people, know how hard we've worked to keep DMI on track."

"And whose fault was it that we were off track?" she said, spewing each syllable at him.

"You're mad again. I understand."

"You bet your behind I'm mad, mad at you, mad at Andre, mad at Sherry, mad at God, you name it. You're right I'm mad, but it doesn't change the facts. You are a hands-off father who has the nerve to allow his pregnant wife to parade down these hallways, and you're excited about your new child when the four you already have are drowning. You can't possibly feel good about yourself as a man, as a CEO, or as a so-called man of God." Madeline was through. She had to go get her son. Obviously, no one else was going to get him.

"There's nothing I can say or do that will please you."

"Maybe not, but you haven't tried," she said, storming out.

Chapter 21

The road to family restoration was getting bumpier by the minute. Dave was naive in believing he, Sherry, and Madeline could find common ground. He stood pondering what Madeline had said about not being involved with his children. She had a good point. Andre needed both parents. Madeline was doing her part, and he had to get involved and do his. He picked up the intercom to reach his secretary.

"Yes, Mr. Mitchell? Can I help you?"

"Sharon, I need to step out for a few hours. Can you juggle my schedule around and get me freed up until about two thirty?" Dave asked.

"Mr. Mitchell, I don't know how I can."

"What do you mean? Just push a few meetings back an hour. This is important," he enunciated. She had to understand the urgency of his request.

"Sir, the driver for the Faith Coalition called a few minutes ago and said the flight landed early. They'll be at our building in about forty-five minutes."

"I see," Dave said.

"Do you want me to make them comfortable in the office until you return?"

"No, that won't be necessary, Sharon. I'll be here when they arrive. Send them right in," he said.

"I'm sorry the schedule isn't working out for you, Mr. Mitchell."

"It's okay, Sharon. It's not your fault. Thanks for offering to help." Dave pushed the intercom button, terminating the conversation. There was nothing Sharon could do, and there didn't appear to be much he could do, either.

He lifted his hands in surrender. "Father, I am just a man trying to do what it is you've called me to do. I don't know what else to do except to follow your lead. You have directed and guided me even when I was unworthy. I'm asking for your guidance this day. My son is in trouble, and I need your help. Help me, Lord, to figure out how to balance my calling here at DMI with my role as a father to Andre, Sam, Tamara, and Don, because I'm lost. I don't know what to do, but my faith is in you," he cried out, shaking off the distress and instantly switching into CEO mode. He tapped the intercom again with boldness.

"Sharon, please bring in the files for the Faith Coalition."

She responded quickly and had the files in his hand within ten minutes, just before the client arrived.

Dave was prepping when there was a knock on the door. "Yes, come in," he said, going to the door as Sharon escorted the client in.

The attorney for Faith Coalition, whom Dave had met several times previously, entered the office a minute later. The greetings were short. Business ensued immediately after Dave directed the president of the Faith Coalition and the attorney to take seats at his conference table. He joined them.

"I was surprised to get your request for a meeting," Dave said. "How can I help you?"

Mr. Richardson peered directly into Dave's eyes and said, "Did we make a wise decision going with you and DMI?"

Dave wanted to ask, "What?" Instead he let Mr. Richardson continue, hoping he made sense.

"You know we have about one hundred leaders slotted for training."

Dave nodded. He wasn't sure of the exact number, but seventy-five to a hundred seemed to be in the range that Dave recalled.

"That's six hundred thousand dollars over three years," Mr. Richardson noted.

Dave nodded again, wondering what Bert Richardson was implying.

"As leader of this organization, I have to ask myself, are we partnering with a company that demonstrates the kind of moral and religious philosophy that we're seeking?"

Now Dave had an inkling of what he was trying to say. "Okay, what do you need to hear in order to make this work?"

"I'm not sure. We've had several conversations about the state of DMI."

"Then you know we're solid, our revenue is up, our client base is strong, and our management team is fully intact, starting with me, Madeline Mitchell as our executive marketing director, and Frank Mitchell as CFO and COO. We also have a general counsel and an officer overseeing Human Resources. As you can see, we've grown by leaps and bounds."

"I personally don't care about your revenues. I'm strictly interested in your reputation."

Dave wasn't prepared for that statement. When Madeline returned last summer, he figured the concerns about DMI's stability were gone. In listening to Mr. Richardson, Dave realized that he had been wrong. Since the Faith Coalition was a sizable account, the comment couldn't be simply discounted. He was forced to address Mr. Richardson's concern.

"We've had a few twists and turns, but I'd say we're on track and strong as ever," Dave declared.

"You don't say. What about your divorce?"

Dave wanted to tell Mr. Richardson the divorce happened nearly two years ago. They'd moved on. He and Sherry had gotten married, and Mr. Richardson needed to move on too. That was what he yearned to say, but he thought wiser.

"The divorce was clearly not God's best for my life. Thank goodness for repentance, redemption, and restoration." Dave picked up a pen from the table and tapped it lightly. "I'm not a perfect man, by no means. But I am a huge recipient of mercy and forgiveness." He set the pen down and peered at Mr. Richardson. "I am saved by grace. I live by grace, and I run this company by grace."

Dave leaned closer to the table. "If you want a company that's run by a leader who has given his life and love completely over to the Lord, then work with us. If you want to work with someone who has been humbled by his shortcomings and now has an even deeper appreciation for life, then work with me. If you're looking for a company that is filled with sinless people, then take your business somewhere else," Dave said, sliding the thick folder across to Mr. Richardson. "If that's what you're looking for, I can't help you at DMI." Dave shut up and let Mr. Richardson ponder his words, determined not to let his shortcomings be used to derail his mission.

"Please give us a few minutes to think this over." Mr. Richardson asked.

"Absolutely, I'll have my secretary move you to the conference room. Take as much time as you need. There are a couple of nice restaurants in the area if you're interested in a late lunch."

"Thanks, but the conference room will be sufficient. Give us about an hour and we'll have an answer for you."

Dave agreed. What choice did he have?

Chapter 22

Madeline sat in the parking lot of Cedarbrook Academy. Her thoughts were jumbled, darting in and out. Many questions rushed in, with no answers following. She wanted to scream, but it was no use. No one who mattered would hear her cry, and no one else cared. In the midst of a megacity like Detroit, she felt incredibly alone, to the point of aching. She rested her forehead on the steering wheel, wishing it was possible to stop time and stay in her claimed space of solitude. The honking horn from a car entering the lot ended her fantasy. Reality had a way of shaking her when she was getting too comfortable. She opened the car door and proceeded to handle the business at hand, Mr. Andre.

"Good afternoon, Mrs. Mitchell," the school secretary said as Madeline entered the main office. "You can go right in. Mr. Cruthers and Andre are waiting inside."

"Andre's in there too? Why isn't he waiting out here?"

"I don't know, Mrs. Mitchell, but you can go in."

Madeline was curious but didn't press the secretary for more information. The secretary obviously didn't know or wasn't saying. Madeline opened the door and found Andre sitting in a chair toward the rear of the room.

"Come in, Mrs. Mitchell," the headmaster said.

"What's Andre doing in here?" For previous incidents, he'd been sitting in the main office, waiting for someone to pick him up, which meant her.

"I decided it is best to keep him away from the other students until Andre is able to gain control of his temper."

"I see," Madeline said, irritated but not sure who most deserved her ire. She truly wanted to vanish. She envied Dave for having the luxury of choosing what he wanted to do and when. He was content in a meeting at this very second, while she was forced to bail their son out of detention, again. Madeline took a seat. "Come out of that corner, and sit up here with me and Mr. Cruthers," she said. Madeline didn't seek the headmaster's approval. She would have preferred it if Andre had been left in the main office, rather than being forced to sit in some isolated nook like a common criminal. She wasn't pleased with the headmaster and would let him know, but her disdain for his judgment in no way compared to how outraged she was with Andre.

Her son took his time moving up front. She turned to him.

"Did you hear me?" she said cynically, enunciating her words, having no regard for what the headmaster might think.

Andre picked up his pace and plopped down into the seat next to her.

"Thank you for coming over so quickly," Mr. Cruthers said.

"No problem," she said, although it was a huge problem. She had a job to do, and so did Andre. He was supposed to take his behind to school and stay out of trouble. How was that asking too much she wondered? "Why am I here again, Andre?"

"I don't know," he said, hunching his shoulders and scooting down in the seat.

"Sit up!" Madeline shouted before catching her tone. "You know why I'm here," she told her son.

"He was fighting again—"

Madeline interrupted. "Excuse me, Mr. Cruthers. I'd like to hear it from Andre."

Her son shut his eyelids and relaxed his head on the back of the chair.

"Did you hear me?" Madeline said, coming close to his ear, enunciating again intentionally conveying the fact that she meant business.

"All right, jeez. I was fighting."

"I see."

"I don't know why you asked me when he's already told you," Andre muttered.

That was it. "Let's go," she said, ready to lift him by his tie and drag his grown behind to the car. Since he had so much lip and wanted to talk back, she'd find a long list of grueling chores for him at home. That should give him something else to do besides getting into trouble.

"Mrs. Mitchell, can I please speak with you alone?"

"Sure," she responded after whispering a set of instructions to Andre about how he should conduct himself in the main office. Madeline didn't have patience for his foolishness. He'd better get his act together and quickly if there was any chance of escaping severe consequences. Turning fourteen in a few months, he was getting too old for this, and she was too tired to be running back and forth to school to deal with his schoolyard brawls. When the divorce was finalized he was only twelve. She'd extended extra grace because he was having a difficult time adjusting from the start. Years were passing without him getting better. Her patience was wearing thin. "Wait outside until I'm finished," she ordered.

When he was out of the room, the headmaster said, "We've had many behavioral challenges with Andre in the past two years. However, it has intensified in the past three months. Are there factors at home that might be adversely affecting Andre's behavior?"

"The only factor I can think of was his father getting remarried this past summer." Madeline had to think. Up until now, she hadn't given too much consideration to the outside factors. Mr. Cruthers had her thinking. She realized the children had suffered abandonment issues with Dave's departure. They each had their bouts with sadness, including her, but the other children were adjusting. Until this second, she'd figured Andre would too.

"Does he interact with his father?"

"He does." "As I mentioned, his father got remarried last year, and I went from being a stay-at-home mom to going into the office every day."

"My, that's quite a few significant changes for Andre that happened in a relatively short time frame."

And that was not counting the fact that his natural father died four years ago and his mother died several years before his dad. Hearing the scenario recited aloud caused her to pause. Madeline's heart went out to Andre. If he was already overwhelmed, how were they going to tell him that his father and Sherry were expecting a child together? She guessed Dave had a tough job to do; one Madeline had no intention of doing for him.

Chapter 23

Madeline glanced at her watch. "Let's go," she snapped at Andre as he sat in the main office. He rubbed his forehead, grumbling incoherently. "Grab your backpack and let's go, I told you." She didn't modify her tone to impress the staff. She had compassion for his situation but firm consistency was what he needed, not coddling.

He got moving.

"Mrs. Mitchell, he'll be out for three days," the headmaster informed her as they neared the front door. Then he turned to Andre and said, "So we'll see you on Monday."

Her son grumbled.

"Did you hear the headmaster talking to you?" Madeline asked, grabbing Andre's arm gently.

He pulled away. "Yes, I heard him."

"Then act like it."

"I'll see you on Monday," he mumbled.

Madeline was satisfied. "Let's go," she said, desperately trying to keep from getting too upset with him. She glanced at her watch again. One thirty. Where had the afternoon gone? She had to get back to the office by three for a prep meeting. She stepped faster, in a big hurry. "Keep up. I'm not going to tell you again."

"Why are you bugging me? I'm right behind you," Andre said.

"You're going to get enough of talking back to me, young man, and I mean it," she said, pausing to get her point across. He was going too far, and she knew it. She was concerned.

Good for him that she didn't have time to address his attitude. They had to keep moving if she had a shot at making the thirty-minute ride home, dropping him off, and traveling another half hour to DMI before her scheduled meeting.

They got in the Mercedes and zoomed off.

"Andre, I don't know what to do with you," she said as he turned his back to her and stared out the window. She wanted to snatch him up and make him listen, but force wasn't the answer. Once again he had narrowly escaped her wrath. He truly was a blessed young man and didn't know it, but Madeline couldn't give any guarantees about when her patience would wear out and allow him to get the hand of discipline he sorely needed.

"Don't do anything. Nobody does for me, anyway."

Madeline wasn't buying into his "poor me" attitude. From the moment he set foot on the estate, he'd been embraced as a Mitchell heir with all the rights and privileges. As a matter of fact, Madeline had made sure he was treated well, going the extra step to personally nurture him.

"Don't even try to sound pitiful and mistreated. You have opportunities most children could only dream of having."

"Let them take my place, then. They can have it."

"Nobody can take your place in this family. Cut the crap, Andre," she said, ramping up the speedometer another ten miles an hour. The traffic was light, and she was capitalizing on there being only a handful of cars on the road. "You can't blame anyone for your actions. You're the one making choices that has you sitting in the chair next to your mother during school hours." She sighed, causing him to take a quick glance at her and immediately look away. "Andre, what's the problem? What's going on with you?"

"Nothing," he whispered.

"It's definitely something. You've been kicked out of school twice this month. How can you tell me nothing? When I get home tonight, we're going to talk about you going to counseling—"

Andre seemed riled up and interrupted. "I don't want counseling. That's for babies and old people."

"Well, you don't get a choice, young man," Madeline said, peering over her left shoulder to see if there was a car in her blind spot. There wasn't, and she scooted into the left lane and pressed the gas a little more. She'd whittled five minutes off the ride home.

"I'm not going."

"If I say you are, then you're going, end of story." She thought over and over about pulling the car over and having it out with him. His willfulness was challenging. If only she could shape his will without breaking his spirit. If only she knew what else to do for Andre.

As Madeline took her exit off I-75, she felt like a total failure as Andre's mom. She'd earnestly tried to fill a hole of love and acceptance in him, but her efforts had fallen short. "When I get back to the office, I'm going to talk with your father and figure out a plan for you."

"He won't have time to talk to you about me. He doesn't have time for anyone except Tamara and Don."

"That's not true," Madeline said, or at least she didn't believe Dave played favorites. Andre was seeing what he wanted to see.

The remaining ride was silent. Madeline zipped up the circular drive and parked in front of the door.

"I'll run in with you to make sure Mrs. Jenkins can stay with you."

"I don't need a kiddie babysitter."

"You need someone here."

"Why don't you just go to work and forget about me? That's what Dad did every day, and now you do it too."

Madeline listened in disbelief. She hadn't considered the real possibility that her children were hurt by her returning to work. She hadn't given the notion any thought but Andre's words took root. Failure clawed its way back into her mind and rested there.

She ran inside the house and went straight to the phone. When her assistant was on the line, she said, "I have a family emergency. I won't be back for several hours."

"What about your East Coast prep meeting that's scheduled to start in a half hour?"

"Call the team and let them know the meeting will be delayed two hours. I'll let you know when I'm on my way." She thanked her assistant and ended the call, not sure what to do next. She had to figure out a plan and soon. She called Dave. Maybe he had some ideas.

Dave was sitting in his office half-heartedly browsing a civil petition when the phone rang. He anxiously answered thinking it was his secretary alerting him that Mr. Richardson was ready to resume their meeting. Instead, it was Madeline on the line.

"We need to talk," she told him.

"Uh-huh," he responded.

She must have sensed his distraction. "Dave, what are you doing? Because you sure aren't paying attention to what I'm saying."

"I heard you say we need to talk. About what?" he asked.

"What do you think? Andre."

"I've been waiting to hear how you made out at the school with him."

"Not good. He has a real problem. As soon as I get into the office, we have to work out a plan. It's that serious."

Dave was concerned, but he couldn't fix the problem until later. One issue at a time was the most he could handle. First up this afternoon was the civil suit filed against DMI. Madeline continued talking. He attempted to pay attention, but it wasn't working.

"Can we finish this conversation in person when you get here? Frank should be here any minute."

"Fine, Dave," she said, disconnecting without saying bye.

He knew what that meant. Hopefully, she'd settle down later in the afternoon. He couldn't dwell on her reaction with other pressing work at hand. Madeline and Andre needed his full attention, and they would have it—just not right now.

Frank knocked on the door as the call ended. "I got a note that you want to see me?"

"I do. Please come in," he said, beckoning to a chair.

"What's going on?" Frank asked, waving off Dave's offer for him to take a seat.

"I called you here to discuss the pending wrongful termination employment case." Dave got up from the desk and went to the table. Frank still wasn't interested in sitting, but Dave was and did. "You remember the older guy who claimed we fired him because of his age?" he said, laughing.

"I kind of remember a little bit about him," Frank said without laughing, which made Dave stop too.

"Well, there's an arbitration meeting scheduled for tomorrow." Normally one of the corporate attorneys or the general counsel would go to court. In prior years, the attorneys had repeatedly quit from the onslaught of DMI legal activity. Dave retained legal services when needed. Six months ago they'd finally landed a strong general counsel.

"Is Rob handling the case?" Frank asked.

"No," Dave said, earning a puzzled expression from Frank. "He's on vacation tomorrow, but I told him not to bother having the arbitration date changed." Dave jotted a few notes.

"Then who's going?"

"Me." Dave felt confident going to the arbitration, certain the hearing would deliver a verdict in favor of DMI. Whether Dave asked Frank or not, his brother typically went along to provide support. "I'm going to court tomorrow. Want to come with me?"

"Not this round. I'll sit this one out," Frank said. "I'm too busy to run down to the courthouse with you this time. I'll catch up with you later. Good luck."

Dave didn't move after Frank left. He gave serious thought to what had just happened. He loved Frank. That was true, but he was determined not to let his brother and Madeline's discontent seep into his heart and create bitterness. He was forgiven and free from the guilt of his unrighteousness and poor decisions. Dave jotted a few more notes, refusing to be defeated. He felt victorious and still excited about DMI being the industry leader. When that revelation was placed in his soul fifteen years ago, it was there for good. Other decisions and priorities would have to line up, no exceptions.

Chapter 24

Madeline lingered in the kitchen, allowing the weight of DMI, Andre's challenges, and her responsibilities at home to fully manifest. She was exhausted. Being back at DMI, in the midst of the hoopla and action, was an adrenaline boost she couldn't get anywhere else. But being a mother to four rambunctious and very diverse children was an equal reward; actually it ranked slightly higher. Madeline leaned against the wall, wanting to float away, not forever, but just for the afternoon, until she felt recharged.

"Mommy, Mommy!" Tamara came tearing into the kitchen. "Andre called me a mean name."

She didn't realize the other children had gotten home already. It was too early. Her mini-retreat was over. Instead of four or five hours of refuge, Madeline had stolen about five minutes. More was not likely to come, with the children riled up and the East Coast meeting waiting to claw at her time too.

"What are you doing home?"

Tamara was too choked up. She struggled to get the words out. Madeline waited patiently. Finally her daughter said, "The lower grades only had a half day today. Don't you remember the note we brought home yesterday?"

Of course she didn't remember the note, or several other items. Thank goodness for Mrs. Jenkins. If not for her, the children would have been waiting outside the school, with Madeline totally unaware. For a split second, Madeline thought about Dave. He had the best of all worlds: a wife at home, staff at DMI, and a caregiver for his children, which would be her. She was constantly irked, realizing how free he was to live, while she carried the full burden of the life they'd created together. Something had to change.

"Where is Mrs. Jenkins?" Madeline asked.

"She's washing our clothes."

Don came charging into the kitchen, crying.

"What's wrong with you?" Madeline asked.

"Andre hit me," he said, crying as Tamara went to him and gave her brother a hug.

Before Madeline could figure out what was going on, she heard shouting in the family room. She ran in, with Don and Tamara on her trail. The shouting intensified as she entered the room. Shock overtook her when she saw Sam and Andre wrestling on the floor, with fists and profanities flying in equal rhythm. She drew in a deep breath unprepared to do battle.

"Andre and Sam, stop it!" she yelled, rushing to the boys.

Mrs. Jenkins must have heard the commotion and ran in too. She helped Madeline pull the boys apart. Tamara and Don were screaming and crying. The scene was a nightmare.

The boys were finally separated, with one on the couch and the other on a wingback chair off to the side. They were fuming, and so was Madeline. She stood there in disbelief. When had her home fallen apart? Had her going back to work fostered this much dysfunction?

"Mrs. Mitchell, would you like me to take one of the boys into the kitchen with me?" Mrs. Jenkins asked, standing close by.

Madeline, who typically had an answer for just about everything, was totally baffled. She didn't know what to do. The situation was too surreal and raw. "Give them a minute to sit there and think about their actions," Madeline told Mrs. Jenkins.

That would allow extra time for Madeline to figure out what to do. Nobody moved for several minutes. When the intensity of the moment had dwindled, Madeline was poised and ready for answers. "What happened?" she tossed out, not directing her question to anyone in particular. She wanted answers from everybody.

"Andre called me a spoiled brat," Tamara said.

"You *are* a spoiled brat," Andre barked.

Madeline walked over to him, knelt down, and said, "Shut up until your turn comes to speak."

His eyelids were squinted. He slapped his hands on his thighs but kept quiet. It was good enough for Madeline. "What else happened?" Madeline asked.

Tamara continued. "After he called me a brat, I told him that I wasn't. Then he said, Shut up, Daddy's girl, before I punch you in the mouth."

"Is that what happened?" Madeline asked Andre.

"Yeah, but she is a Daddy's girl, and we all know it. She's the only one he cares about."

"But the way you said it was mean," Tamara said.

"So what? Stop being a baby," Andre said.

"Young man, I'm not going to keep asking you to watch your tone."

"If she doesn't want me to bother her, then she should leave me alone and stay out of my way," Andre muttered.

Madeline wasn't going to argue with a child. She glanced at her watch. Barely an hour left to get back

to the office for her meeting, and nothing had been re-
solved yet. She wasn't close to leaving. This was a mess,
she thought. She had to hear the rest of the story. "How
did Don get involved?"

"He told Andre he'd better not hit me in the mouth.
So Andre said, 'Fine. Then I'll hit *you* in the mouth.'
And he hit Don," Tamara said.

Madeline prided herself on not taking sides, but in
this case, she was upset with Andre. "You hit a little
boy, as big as you are?" She knelt down to his level
again. "The next time you want to hit somebody, why
don't you come and hit me?" she said, fuming but determined to give as much discipline as her frustration
allowed.

Don was still whimpering. She figured his feelings
were hurt as much as his lip. He'd recover, but she
wasn't so sure about Andre.

"That's when I had to jump in, because I'm not letting somebody hit my little brother or sister. I don't
care how much they get on my nerves," Sam said, still
riled up a bit.

"I'm supposed to be your brother too," Andre said in
an antagonizing tone, which was hard for Madeline to
describe fully. There was definitely an underlying message that she couldn't easily decipher.

"Everybody, settle down. Fighting is not the way
that our family solves problems." Madeline turned to
the nanny. "Mrs. Jenkins, will you be able to stay a few
extra hours this evening?"

"Yes, of course, Mrs. Mitchell. Whatever you need,
just let me know."

If only she had an idea of what she needed. Madeline
needed to leave now in order to get to DMI in time for
her meeting. She also needed to stay at home to make

sure the children didn't kill each other. The tug was too much. She'd had enough. "I want the four of you to find a spot and sit down. Don't talk to each other, don't move, and don't say a word until I come back in this room. Do you understand?"

The fervor in their responses varied, but each child agreed, giving Madeline a small window of opportunity. She grabbed the phone and dialed Dave's office. His secretary answered.

"Sharon, I need to speak with Dave."

"He just went back into a meeting with clients from the Faith Coalition. Can I have him give you a call when the meeting ends?"

"No, get him on the phone now. This is urgent," she said boldly, refusing to be put on hold.

"Oh, okay, I'll get him."

Within a minute Dave was on the line. "Madeline, what's going on?"

"This place is falling apart here. The boys are outright fighting. Andre punched Don in the mouth. Sam took it upon himself to hit Andre for hitting Don. It's a nightmare here. I need your help."

"What should I do?"

"I don't know, but I certainly can't take care of this home, the children, and my business at DMI. It's too much. I have to get a break."

"I'll do whatever I can. I have to go now, but let's talk later."

"This *is* later. We need to talk now. Don't you hear what I'm saying, Dave? I'm drowning. I need help. The children need help. We need you."

"Since the Faith Coalition team is in my office, I'm standing out in the open, at Sharon's desk. This isn't the best place to talk," he whispered.

"Dave Mitchell, I'll see you in thirty minutes. You better make time to see me, and I mean it. These are your children, too, and I'm not letting you off so easily anymore. Before you worry about adding a fifth child, you'd better do right by mine," she said and slammed the receiver on its base. Enough was enough.

Chapter 25

Dave was trapped between the business waiting in his office and his obligation on the other end of the disconnected line. He pondered his predicament for a second. Then it dawned on him. He'd held down the job of running DMI, but his reliance on Madeline had become too great. Where was his faith? Had he abandoned his firm belief in God's ability to provide, direct, and sustain him in both his business and his personal life? Honestly, he couldn't answer the question, which caused him concern.

"Mr. Mitchell, is there anything I can do to help? Do you want me to tell the client that you'll be back in a few minutes?"

"Actually, that would be perfect. Give me ten minutes," he said. "I'll be in Madeline's office."

His secretary took action, and Dave retreated into a quiet space. He entered the office, closed the door tightly behind him, and locked it. His clarity had been blurred for weeks. Dave meditated, not letting any particular thought take precedence. He had to get back to the basics, and seek direction. He understood the source of his confusion. He'd gotten away from who he was. He'd allowed the influences of others to shape his perspective—Frank, Madeline, and his clients. He had to make a clean sweep if God was to return as head of his life. The chatter had to be eliminated.

He assumed his favorite position in the building, which was standing in front of the windows and peering out at the majestic sky, evidence of the Almighty's greatness. His resolve was rising, and clarity came with it. Suppressing the influences of outside pressures wasn't sufficient. If he was going to be free from the burden of confusion, sustain his peace, and fulfill his purpose, he had to force Frank's words, Madeline's anger, Sherry's concerns, and his clients' demands out of his head. An air of resolve swept over Dave as he reflected on how he'd achieved success in the past. He'd done it through reliance on a God that was bigger than his abilities. Dave grabbed ahold of that same faith today that had repeatedly worked for him in the past. It must have worked now, because he was suddenly ready to close out the meeting with Mr. Richardson and then tackle the discord with his kids.

He opened the door and stepped into the hall. He wasn't going to allow anyone to heap guilt upon him. They probably did think that he was being punished, with a dip in revenue and problems with his kids. He didn't see it that way. The God he served was loving and longed to shield him from wounds once he repented, and He didn't have to make Dave pay every day to reinforce his failure. Dave walked down the hallway as a renewed man. Fear and doubt were blown away as faith nudged ahead. Fifteen years of vision hadn't been lost. Nothing had changed. His dedication to the Lord hadn't, either.

He walked into his office, energized, eager to take on the world. "My apologies for the interruption," he said, resuming his seat at the head of the conference table. He glanced at his watch. "We've spent nearly two hours working the numbers and trying to restore your confidence. We're done with that," he said, raising a few eyebrows from his clients. "Either you want to do this deal or you don't. Let's face it. There will always be a headline in the media about me or someone on my team. I can't control that, but what I can do is offer you a solid service for a fair price." He closed his portfolio. "Now, either we have a deal or we don't, but this meeting is over." He was fully prepared to let the client walk out the door if necessary. Dave wasn't willing to let anyone pin him in a box that he had already climbed out of.

Mr. Richardson glanced at the file and back at Dave for several rounds before saying, "I'm satisfied that you and DMI are the right partners for us. We have a deal. I'll let the accountants and attorneys work out the details, but I honestly believe you're the one to give us the guidance we're seeking." Mr. Richardson said, extending his hand. Dave gave him a firm handshake.

"That's what I want to hear," Dave said, accepting no less.

"Our leaders need training, but they also need to understand the spirit of humility and redemption. Thank you for your time."

The general counsel shook Dave's hand too. The deal was sealed, and Dave was pleased. This was one more step in the right direction.

Chapter 26

By four, Dave was sitting in his office alone. Madeline burst in without warning. Before she spoke a single word, he could see the fury on her face. It was indiscernible to others, but having been with her for so long, he knew the sign. Her neck was stiff, her lips were pursed, and she had a piercing stare. Most noticeably, she came right up to him and stood there with her arms folded.

"I see you made it in," he said, not sure what was coming next. He'd braced for whatever.

"Yes, I finally made it back, with no help from you, thank you very much."

"Well, you're here now. How can I help?" he asked, gently reaching for her hand.

Madeline seemed to soften a bit; at least she took a seat as her neck relaxed. "We have big problems with Andre. I can't handle him alone."

"What about Mrs. Jenkins? Is she helping you?"

"Mrs. Jenkins is his nanny, not his parent," Madeline said, testy.

Dave detected the tone and immediately went into salvage mode. The only way for them to have a meaningful conversation was to keep Madeline from boiling over. He was committed to keeping her out of the red zone, but he was sure it wasn't going to be easy, based on the way she'd entered his office.

"I'm sorry. I didn't mean to imply that it's her job. I know we have to figure this out, and we will," he said.

She fingered the curls in her hair and said, "We better, because he's in a crisis and will continue getting kicked out of school until we do something."

"I didn't realize he'd been in trouble so many times until you told me earlier. I had no idea."

"Because I don't tell you everything."

"But you should."

"For what? It's not like you're going to leave DMI to pick him up when the headmaster calls or babysit him when he's suspended. Apparently, that's my job." He let her say as much as she wanted without interrupting. She deserved his attention.

"I'm sorry if I've missed opportunities to help with him and the other kids. I mean it, but sometimes I'm strapped to this place without many breaks. Maybe my other obligations end up suffering more than I realize."

"Dave, you're not the only one who's busy around here. I work my buns off here *and* at home. A lack of time is no excuse. I handle both jobs every day and on weekends. So you get no sympathy from me."

"I get your point," he said after determining there was no value in defending his weakened position when it came to spending time with the kids. Madeline was right in many ways. He was seeing that more and more.

"Anyway, Andre has a really bad attitude, and this fighting is going to get him into real trouble. It's just a matter of time before he gets expelled from Cedarbrook Academy, and then what will we do? I can't work with you here at DMI and take care of a troubled child." Her gaze slumped. "This isn't what I signed up for when we adopted him."

Dave sat up in his seat. "It sounds like you're regretting the decision."

"Definitely not." Her gaze continued panning the floor. "But this is challenging. I know this sounds cruel. I don't want you to take it the wrong way, but you were the one who decided to bring Andre into our family permanently. It was your idea. You were adamant about getting him. I told you then that it might be too much for me, didn't I?" He nodded in affirmation. "And you brought him, anyway. Okay, I could accept him as my son, and I have. But you have not done your part."

"I didn't know you felt that way."

"How else can I feel? You brought him to Detroit, dropped him in my lap, headed back to DMI, and started a new family with Sherry," she told him.

"Now that's not true."

"Really?" she fired at him. "What part?"

"Sherry isn't involved in this discussion."

"Ooh, yes, she is. You're expecting another child, and the ones you have are starving for a piece of you. And don't think I'm going to let you forget it. Sherry's illegitimate seed isn't the only child deserving of your attention."

"Madeline, we're doing well here talking. Let's not go there."

"Oh, we're going there. Sherry's child is not taking center stage when there are four Mitchell children waiting in line ahead of that baby, and don't you forget it. I don't care how many babies your woman has. The estate on Mayweather Lane belongs to my children. It has always been their home and always will be. No one else is going to shove them out. You're their father, the only one they have."

"You don't have to worry about that. My heart is big enough for all five of my kids."

"Good, because I can promise you that I'll fight for my children's rights until the day I die. It's a promise that I will keep, no matter what happens."

Dave knew they were headed down an awkward path, one that he'd prefer to avoid, but when she was like this, there was no stopping her. Madeline's words were crisp, and the burning gaze in her eyes said she was serious. He took note and kept silent.

"I might not be living with the children, but I'm here for them."

"Great, because I think Andre should move in with you."

"W-what?" Dave stammered.

"You heard me. Andre should move in with you. His problems are too much for me to handle. What he needs more than anything in this world right now is his father. He needs a man to speak to, to provide direction and discipline. I can nurture and mother him all day long, but only you can teach him to be a man. It's your turn now," Madeline said, rearing back and crossing her legs.

Dave was generally prepared for most things that happened within the confines of DMI, but he was genuinely caught off guard with this suggestion. He didn't know how to respond or if he should respond at all. What was there to say? Should he say yes and then have to deal with Sherry? Or no and then suffer Madeline's wrath? The answer wasn't coming easily. He wanted to meditate on the request, but Madeline didn't give him a chance.

"When do you want him to move in?" she asked.

"I don't know. I'll have to think about this."

"There is nothing to think about," she said, raising her voice slightly. "He's your son. He's in trouble. He needs you, and I'm bringing him to your house this week, period."

Madeline stood to leave. He knew this wasn't the time to argue the point. Madeline was too upset. He'd think it through and see what could be done. Maybe she was right. He just wasn't prepared to act as quickly as she wanted.

"Let me talk to Sherry and see what we can do."

"No problem." Madeline leaned on the table. "You can talk to Sherry, God, Bobo, the tooth fairy, or Batman if you'd like," she said in an eerily calm tone. "But Andre is coming to live with you for a while. I hope you've kept the children's rooms intact. It will make his move easier." She strutted to the door. "See you later," she said, exiting.

Dave remained in his seat. There was nothing left to say or do. Madeline had said it all.

Chapter 27

Madeline was gone, and tranquility was creeping back into the room, but not as quickly as Dave wanted. Dave closed his eyelids tightly and let his mind rest. He yearned for wisdom, because he really didn't know what to do. He was a father to Andre, which meant Madeline's request was reasonable. Yet Sherry was his wife, but she and Andre didn't get along. Having the two live together could be a disaster. There was no easy answer. Dave muddled through a prayer, grasping for direction.

Frank walked in.

"I'm stopping by to let you know I'll be out for a few days. It's my anniversary, and my wife wants to make the three-hour drive up to Mackinac Island for a four-day weekend. I'll be back on Monday."

"You don't need my permission," Dave responded.

"I know that, but consider it a courtesy."

Dave didn't look in Frank's direction. "All right," he said, with no more to add.

"What has you acting so uptight?"

Dave heard Frank say something but didn't catch it. "What did you say?"

"I asked what has you this uptight."

It was probably wiser to tell Frank nothing and move on, but he had just prayed for guidance and was open to any method God chose to answer. There were count-less times in the past when Frank had given Dave support, sown seeds of wisdom, and provided a listening ear. Dave missed those conversations.

"I have a tough decision to make. Actually, the decision has already been made for me," he said, twiddling a few paper clips on the table.

"What decision is that?"

"Andre has been constantly getting into trouble at school this year. He's been suspended twice this month alone, and Madeline's tired."

"I guess so," Frank commented.

"She's tired to the point of no longer feeling like he can stay with her."

Frank squinted. "Wow. Where's he going? Because I thought you said he doesn't have any other family?"

"He doesn't. We're it, which means if Madeline can't keep him, I have to."

Frank chuckled. "You and what army?"

"Come on, he's not that bad."

"No, I don't mean the boy is bad. I'm saying that you can't handle raising a kid."

"How do you know?" Dave asked, feeling slighted by the comment. He had the potential to be a great parent like everyone else, if given the chance.

"Face it. You're a businessman first and a father second or third."

"That's ridiculous. I'm a father with four kids."

"Okay, then when was the last time you missed two consecutive DMI meetings?"

"I haven't. I don't miss meetings."

"Exactly. Didn't you tell me Andre plays baseball?"

"He did last year."

"How many of his games did you miss?"

"Most," he grunted.

"Case closed," Frank said, grinning.

Dave hated acknowledging Frank's input when his brother was in the "I told you so" mode, but the truth was the truth. "I guess you're right. Apparently, Madeline feels the same way, because she wants Andre to move back to the estate with me."

"Since you took him on as a Mitchell, I guess you'll have to do what you have to do for him. If living with you is the answer, go for it."

"If only it was that simple."

"Isn't it?"

"I don't think Sherry will think so. She struggles with my kids. I think Madeline has taught them to dislike Sherry, and they do. Having Andre move in will be a problem for Sherry."

"Letting him stay at Madeline's would be a problem too," Frank said.

"That's right. Now you understand my dilemma."

"It will come down to choosing which problem is the biggest and tackling that one first."

"Andre getting into trouble is, hands down, my main concern."

"Then solving his problem should beat out Sherry."

"I wouldn't put it quite that way."

"Man, you know I call it the way I see it. Somebody is going to win and somebody will lose in this situation."

Dave didn't want his decision framed in such direct terms, but there was the truth again, bold and out front.

"You're right. Bringing Andre home to stay with me feels like the right thing to do. I just hope Sherry understands."

"So what if she doesn't."

"She's my wife." Dave was slightly disturbed by Frank's persistent disregard for his marriage.

"Correction, she's your second wife. She knew you had kids and an ex-wife when she married you. I hope she realized you weren't going to be hers alone."

"She expects me to respect her wishes."

"She better wish Madeline doesn't have other demands, because those will mostly move to the top of your list."

"It's not like that with Madeline and me."

"Yeah, right, whatever you say," Frank said in a dismissive tone. "You created this situation, all by yourself. You didn't want to listen to me when I said that Sherry was going to be trouble down the road. The affair was bad, but you didn't have to go and marry her. Huge mistake. You're what? Less than a year into the marriage? And there's already big trouble brewing." Frank laughed out loud. "I'll tell you this. When you mess up, you do it big. The great Dave Mitchell has two wives, four kids, and issues that I wouldn't wish on my worst enemy," he said, continuing with his streak of humor. "Let me get out of here. I have work to do." Frank finally stopped laughing but kept the smirk. "Tell your wife I said hello."

"I'll tell Sherry."

"No, I meant the other one," Frank said, patting Dave on the shoulder and cackling on the way out.

Dave closed his eyelids and let Frank have the last word. His fate was already sealed.

Chapter 28

Sherry lay across the bed after waking from her nap. She didn't feel refreshed, having tossed and turned for most of the past two hours. She actually felt worse. The afternoon had trudged by, and she had nothing to show for it. She wanted to be at the office, but Madeline had killed that job. Sherry acknowledged that although Madeline's interference had nudged her out of DMI, she was planning to leave soon, anyway. This pregnancy was much more difficult than the last one, and the sensation of being overwhelmed was constant. Seven months along and her nerves were shot.

She grabbed a magazine from the nightstand and flipped through the pages. A few minutes later, she nestled into the stack of pillows and balled up in the fetal position. Boredom was hounding her every second. She reached over to grab the phone. Hopefully, Dave was coming home soon. She yearned for his company. She dialed his number at the office.

Her husband answered.

"I'm so glad you answered. Thank goodness," she said, not hiding her relief.

"Why? Is everything all right?"

She could hear the concern in his voice, and it was soothing. That was what she needed, reassurance of her husband's love. After the run-in with Madeline this afternoon, her confidence had been bruised, but a few words from Dave and she was bursting with joy. She smiled within.

"Don't worry. I'm well. You don't have to dote on me," she said. "I was just a little tired."

"Take a nap."

"I tried, but it didn't work out too well." The picture of Madeline kicking her out of the office wanted to take hold again, but Sherry resisted. She wasn't going to let doubt creep in, not while Dave was near. "I'm not used to napping during the day. I'm used to being at DMI working with you."

"Hmm, how about that."

"But I'll have to find other activities to fill my day, at least until the baby comes."

"Sherry, I have something important to talk to you about."

Due to the change in his tone, she instantly began to worry. "What is it?"

"I'd prefer to tell you in person."

"Dave, you're scaring me," Sherry said, sitting up in the bed, drawing a pillow to her stomach, and clutching it tightly, as though it represented her grip on maintaining the joy she was finally feeling.

"There's no need to be scared. It's a family matter that we'll need to discuss when I get home. And then we have to make some decisions."

"When will you be home?"

"I'm planning to leave in a few hours. I should be walking in the door between seven thirty and eight."

She glanced at the clock. It was only five o'clock. A few hours was going to be like an eternity. She was already dreading each minute but didn't want him to feel pressured to get home sooner. Her greatest wish was that Dave could spend more time with her so they could be a true family, but that wasn't possible for now. She accepted his priorities but didn't like how it made her feel. Sherry put up a good front and acted as if she didn't have any doubts. This night was no different than last night or the one before that.

"Take your time. I'll be here waiting for you when you get home," she said, rubbing her belly. "Me and baby Mitchell will be happy to see you."

They exchanged loving good-byes and ended the call. Sherry wanted to relax and maybe take another nap, but Dave's tone wasn't easy to forget. She racked her brain about what Dave wanted to discuss. She figured it had something to do with Madeline. It always had something to do with Madeline. Sherry pulled the pillow to her chest and rocked back and forth, fighting with her emotions. She had to stay calm for the baby. The memory of losing her first baby was too raw and served as a constant reminder of why she had to avoid danger at all costs. She rubbed her belly gently, incessantly, yearning to connect with her baby, one who would love her unconditionally, the one she wouldn't have to share with another woman. She slid down under the covers and let the indescribable love for her baby wipe away the looming fear.

Chapter 29

Madeline was calm when she rolled into the garage. Her body said, *Wait in the car for as long as you can.* Her rational thinking said, *Go inside and give Mrs. Jenkins a break.* On a good day, her body might have responded to the load, but not today. Madeline was exhausted between Andre, the other children, Dave, and both the Midwest and East Coast expansion projects. She didn't have the energy to fight. Someone could walk by with a feather and be able to push her over. She let her neck relax and her head rest against the steering wheel. After a few minutes, she mustered the strength to go for round two. She hoped the children were settled and eating dinner with a dab of normalcy. She could only dream. She got out of the car and slowly made her way to the back door. Her key turned slowly in the lock, almost like she was going to sneak in, get past her brood, and escape upstairs undetected.

As she opened the door and took a few steps, Tamara and Don waged an attack, clinging to her relentlessly and talking at the same time.

"Stop. I can't understand a word you're saying," she said, attempting to set her bag down and collect her thoughts. Chaos was flying overhead. It felt like she couldn't breathe, and the children didn't seem to care. They wanted their needs met. "What is going on?" she asked Tamara and Don, letting whoever could speak the loudest get a shot at telling her what was happening.

"Andre keeps picking on us," Tamara said.

"Were you picking on him?"

"No. He keeps hitting us when Mrs. Jenkins isn't around," Tamara told her.

Madeline prided herself on trying to stay neutral, but in some cases the younger children did get extra consideration, and she didn't feel wrong about it. She rushed from the mudroom, through the kitchen, and into the family room. Don and Tamara were on her trail. "Andre," Madeline shouted, "what's going on? Don and Tamara told me you're picking on them again. Is that true?"

He was watching television and didn't answer Madeline.

Her fury boiled. She was ready to snatch him and shake some sense into his head but was able to catch herself. Instead, she snatched the remote from him. "Do you hear me talking to you?" she said, bending over and getting her face close to his. There was no way he could ignore her.

"Yesss,'" he said, making her madder, but not to the point of breaking, not yet.

She was teetering on the edge but was not there yet. She had to make a move, fast. "Get up and get your bags packed. You're going to your father's."

"When?" he asked, seeming to show the only spark of enthusiasm she'd seen all day.

"Right now, as soon as you can get packed. Don't worry about taking a bunch of clothes. Get enough for a few days. You can get more clothes on the weekend."

"For real? Cool." he said as his frown, which had appeared to have taken permanent residency, faded. "Later for you," he said to Tamara, leaping to his feet and bolting out of the room.

"Are we going to Daddy's too?" Tamara asked, showing a spark too.

"Not tonight."

"Oh, why not?" Tamara asked.

"Because Andre is the only one going tonight. He needs special time with your dad."

"Me too."

"No, you don't. You get time with him."

"Not that much," Tamara said, frowning.

Poor child, Madeline thought. No one was going to get too much of his time. "You get enough. It's Andre's turn, and that's the end of it."

"But—" Tamara began, but Madeline cut her off.

"That's the end of it, young lady. Now, go tell Mrs. Jenkins I'm home."

Madeline's head was throbbing, swirling, and ready to explode. She grabbed the phone and dialed while her decision was still firm. She hurried, frantic not to let her motherly instinct kick in and cause her to change the plan. Her fingers couldn't dial fast enough.

Dave answered, and she blurted out, "I'm bringing Andre tonight."

"What do you mean? You said sometime this week. We didn't talk about him coming tonight."

"I know, but it's not going to work here. Andre has to stay with you for a little while. I don't anticipate it being forever, but you have to give me this break. He needs it, and I do too." She was desperate. No wasn't an option. She had to push harder and get Dave to agree. "Dave, I'm begging you."

"I don't know, Madeline."

"What don't you know? That he's your son? That he's in a crisis? That I need help raising your children? Tell me, Dave, what exactly is it that you don't know?"

"I have to talk with Sherry before I agree to do this."

"You haven't told her yet? What are you waiting on?" Madeline said, getting frustrated. They'd spoken about Andre hours ago, and he hadn't taken a single step to put her request into action. Too bad for him, because she wasn't backing down. "You better tell her by eight o'clock, because that's when I plan to be at the estate with Andre and his suitcase. No way am I going to let you discount your family just to accommodate the wishes of your mistress turned wife."

"Don't do that, Madeline. Give me a chance to talk to Sherry about it tonight, and then we can discuss this tomorrow."

"Why does Sherry get a say in this? This is between you and your children, not her."

"Come on, Madeline. We've been over this. She's my wife, and I will respect her."

"Like the respect you gave me when you cheated with her?"

"I'll talk with you tomorrow. I have to review a few more documents before getting out of here tonight."

"I mean it, Dave. I'll see you by eight o'clock."

Madeline was off the phone but not out of his space. Her words were circling overhead. This was a bad situation, and he absolutely knew it. Madeline was forcing his hand. He had no choice but to run home and break the news to his wife. She wasn't going to be happy. She found it challenging when his kids came for a two- or three-day visit. He was certain Madeline had instigated their lack of interest in Sherry, although he couldn't prove it. Sherry was distraught after each visit and required about a week to regain her composure. He couldn't imagine her reaction to Andre staying indefinitely.

Dave gathered several files and shoved them into his briefcase. He had to get home before Madeline arrived. There was no telling what she'd say or do to Sherry. His wife was already frazzled with the pregnancy. News of this magnitude might easily send her over the edge.

He craved deliverance from this place of confusion and Madeline's load of bitterness. He truly believed that if she didn't find peace with their situation soon and move on, her anger and animosity were surely going to destroy the person that he knew her to be. He could not stand idly by and watch his children take the ride of despair with her.

Chapter 30

When Sherry heard Dave calling out to her from downstairs, she was startled. It wasn't quite 6:00 P.M. She dashed to the stairs.

"I wasn't expecting you for a few more hours," she said, wrapping her arms around his neck and hanging on tightly. "This is a wonderful surprise."

He grinned and gave her a peck on the cheek as she slowly released her grip.

"We can have an early dinner, and then maybe we can catch the midweek movie on the television. That will be a nice treat for a change," she said, bursting with excitement.

He took her hand. "We have to talk."

There was that serious tone again, the one that had caused her to worry before and was doing the same this time too. "I don't know if this is going to be something I want to hear."

"Let's sit down and talk," he said, leading her into the master bedroom.

"Dave, you're really scaring me. Please tell me and get it over with," she said, refusing to sit.

He took a seat and said, "There's no easy way to say this."

Her fear was mounting. She had no idea what was coming, but she knew it was bad. She could tell.

"I spoke with Madeline today, and she explained how much Andre is struggling at school and at home.

Apparently, the divorce has impacted him more than any of us realized. Apparently, he's been getting kicked out of school enough to raise concern. As a matter of fact, he's on suspension the rest of this week." Sherry couldn't figure out why this news had Dave acting weird. She remained silent as he continued. "She believes it will be best for Andre to stay here with us for a while."

"Here? Oh no, that's not a good idea. Your children hate me. It's absolutely miserable for me when they come over. They ignore me, talk over me, and show me no respect. They don't want anything to do with me." Since she was an adult, Sherry didn't think it appropriate to tell Dave the feeling was mutual. He'd have to figure that out on his own.

"I tried stopping her, but you know how Madeline can be."

"No, I can't survive with your son living here. I'm already under stress, and it's not good for the baby." She panicked. "Dave, I can't lose this baby. Your son can't stay here. I'm sorry, but no." She loved Dave and didn't take satisfaction in putting him in an awkward situation. Normally, she didn't, but this was a unique set of circumstances. She had to stand up to Madeline.

"I don't see how we can say no if my son needs help."

"But how can we save Madeline's child at the risk of hurting mine?"

"That won't happen."

"How can you be so sure?"

"Because I'm trusting in the Lord."

"You trusted Him with the birth of our son, and he died. Where was He then?" The words slipped out, and she felt badly, but it was too late. She quickly moved to diffuse the tension between them. "I have another idea."

"What is it? I'm open," he said, raising his hands in the air.

"Have you considered sending him to boarding school or boot camp?"

The color drained from his cheeks. "I can't do that."

"Why not? It's a great option. Many parents send their children to military school or boarding school to help them with disciplinary problems. It's a great option."

"Not for my son," Dave said firmly. "I can't bear the thought of throwing away Jonathan's son. No way, never. Jonathan was as much a brother to me as Frank is. He was my dearest friend. He wanted me to take care of his son, and I will honor his wish until the day I die."

Sherry could tell it didn't make sense to continue objecting. She couldn't argue the point any further.

"If Madeline can't take care of Andre right now, then it's my job to step up," he said and drew Sherry close to him. "It's done. The decision has been made. Andre is coming to stay with us tonight."

Sherry was disappointed more than words could convey, but she didn't protest any further.

Chapter 31

Sherry wasn't alone. Dave had forgotten an important file at the office and ran out to get it, but he left plenty of anxiety to keep her company. He planned to return before Madeline and Andre arrived. She hoped he would.

Around 7:50 P.M. the doorbell chimed. Sherry tensed and shut her eyelids tightly. Maybe she could blink into a different fairy tale, because this one was over. Frozen in place, she didn't move, not until the chimes sounded a second time throughout the first floor of her house. She shuffled to the door, slow to open it and have to deal with the hurricane on the other side. Left with no way out, Sherry grabbed the knob, turned it, and gradually pulled the door open until Madeline's face was front and center. She stood there with the children.

Before Sherry could invite them in, Madeline had pushed past her and was standing in the foyer.

"You're early," Sherry said softly while closing the door after everyone had entered.

"Where's Dave?" Madeline asked.

"He had to pick up a file from DMI. I expect him back any minute."

"Oh, you do, huh?" Madeline said, letting her eyes wander up and down Sherry, giving her an eerie feeling. Sherry couldn't wait for Dave to get home. He had to hurry.

"Hello, Sam," Sherry greeted.

The boy gave her a halfhearted wave and said, "Mom, can I watch TV until Dad gets here?"

"Sure," Sherry responded before realizing who he was speaking to.

"Can I, Mom?" Sam repeated.

"I guess so, but don't get too comfortable. We're not going to be here long," Madeline told him.

"As you know, the TV is in there," Sherry said, pointing toward the den. "Feel free to watch whatever you'd like."

Sam was already gone before she finished speaking. Andre plopped down on the bottom step of the staircase.

"Of course he knows where the TV is," Madeline said, giggling. "This was his home for many wonderful years, remember?"

It was already starting. Madeline was finding ways to steal what little peace Sherry had managed to preserve. *Please let Dave get home soon,* she thought. She couldn't handle an hour of Madeline, not alone. No one could.

"I don't want to fight," Sherry said, throwing her hands in the air.

"Then don't," Madeline snapped in front of the children. Sadly, they didn't seem fazed. "Where is Daddy?" Tamara asked.

"Do you want to wait in the den or the kitchen until he gets here?" Sherry asked, trying to be nice. "I'm tired. I have to sit down."

"I guess having Dave's baby doesn't agree with you."

"Madeline, wait wherever you'd like. I don't really care," Sherry said and went to the staircase and took a seat. Andre jumped up and went up four or five steps. Don was just standing around. He didn't seem to know where he wanted to go.

"When is Daddy getting here?" Tamara asked.

"I don't know," Madeline told her. "He better get here soon, because we have to get going."

Tamara pouted and went into the den to join Sam. Don followed her out of the foyer, leaving Sherry with Madeline and Andre. Sherry couldn't have asked for a worse scene.

As the tension thickened, Sherry decided she wanted to surrender and threw down the flag of defeat. "I'm going upstairs. Dave should be here soon. Do what you'd like. I'm gone," she said, slowly getting up.

She took five steps, reaching Andre on the stairs, and then heard her rescuer coming in. *Thank goodness,* she thought.

"I see you made it," Dave said, entering the foyer from the back hallway, which led from the garage.

"Daddy!" Tamara cried out, running from the den. She jumped into his arms. I'm glad you're home. I love you, Daddy," Tamara said, clinging to him. She wasn't letting go, and Dave didn't push her away.

Sherry understood. Besides, she was his only daughter. Sherry was touched by the rapport between the two. One day her child would have the same love and attention heaped upon him or her. That was what she hoped. The more she watched Dave and Tamara together, the more Sherry felt jealous. It was like no one else existed. But how could she be jealous? Tamara was his daughter.

In the midst of the commotion, Andre didn't move, but Sherry could hear him sighing and breathing hard while Dave showered Tamara with his attention.

"What were you doing at DMI?" Madeline asked.

"We have to finalize the Faith Coalition contract."

"That's a huge account if we can keep them," Madeline said as Sherry watched her entire disposition change from that of a raging bull to that of a calm and collected businesswoman. The transformation happened in a blink.

"Based on my meeting this afternoon, it's a go for us."

"That's wonderful," Madeline said. "The vote of confidence will certainly boost our expansion strategy with potential clients."

"I have to tweak the discount structure. It entails just a few minor details. There aren't any major changes for them."

"If you can make the numbers work, I'll definitely help with the training plan. It's not my strength, but you know I'll pitch in where I can."

"You always do," he responded, causing Sherry to quake.

"This will be a huge win for us this year. I'm excited," Madeline said, more cheerful than Sherry was accustomed to seeing her, but then, she had never really worked close enough with Madeline to see that side.

"Me too," Dave said.

Andre stormed off.

"Where are you going?" Madeline asked.

"I don't know," Andre said, almost growling.

"Well, you better not go too far. We'll want to see you before we leave." Andre kept walking toward the kitchen. "Do you hear me, young man?" Madeline said, having to speak louder.

"Andre, do you hear your mother talking to you?" Dave asked, cutting in.

"Yeah," Andre replied.

"Then answer her right now," Dave said. Sherry could tell he was serious.

Andre must have known it too. He responded immediately and in a better tone than he had used at first. Then Andre ducked into the kitchen.

"See what I'm dealing with?" Madeline told Dave.

"I see. Don't worry. I'll work with him on that attitude. I'll get him straightened out."

The two spoke as if Sherry wasn't in the room. She felt awkward standing on the stairs, slightly removed from the space he shared with his other family. She could have inserted herself next to Dave, but her body wasn't willing to move.

"I'm trusting you with my son, Dave. You'd better take good care of him."

"It goes without saying. He's in good hands, and you know he is," Dave said.

"Dave, I'm tired. I'm going to turn in for the night. What time will you be coming up to bed?" Sherry said, looking at Madeline.

"I'm not sure. I want to get Andre settled for the night—"

Madeline interrupted. "We're going to get out of here now, anyway, and let you get to work. The Faith Coalition plan isn't going to get done on its own."

"I guess you're right," Dave said, touching Madeline's shoulder.

Sherry stood there watching, not sure what to do. *Go away, silly thoughts.* Dave had told her many times that she didn't have to worry about him and Madeline. Sherry believed him, until instances like this when she saw them together. It was hard to overlook how well they clicked. How easily they slipped in and out of conversations related to DMI. Sherry was disgusted. Madeline's hooks in Dave were real. No matter how hard Sherry tried shifting Dave's focus to his new family, Madeline's grip didn't appear to be loosening.

"Sam, Tamara, and Don, let's go," Madeline called out several times, until the children came to her. Nobody was ready to go.

"Why are we going so soon?" Tamara asked. For a young child, she always had so many questions, Sherry noticed.

"Because you have to get ready for tomorrow, and I have to work," Madeline said.

"But can't we stay longer?" Tamara whined, clinging to her father.

"I said no," Madeline said firmly. "Don, go get Andre."

"Where is he?" Don asked.

"I don't know. You and Tamara go find him and tell him I said to come out here," Madeline demanded.

A few minutes later Andre surfaced with Don and Tamara.

"Give your brother a hug. Say your good-byes so we can go," Madeline told the children.

"Why does Andre get to stay and we don't?" Tamara asked.

"Yeah, why does he get to stay?" Don echoed.

Much to her surprise, Sherry caught a glimpse of Andre smiling. At least he was until his father began consoling Tamara. His frown reappeared, and he ran upstairs with his suitcase without saying bye to anyone.

"Andre, you get back down here," Madeline called.

"Let him go. He's probably upset about having to stay here for a while," Dave said.

Madeline seemed upset. Dave gave her a quick hug and then said, "It's going to be all right. You'll see. Go on home, and try not to worry. He's with me now. I will take care of him. I promise."

Sherry turned and walked up the stairs. She couldn't bear to watch Dave and Madeline any longer. The ache was too great, and her pregnancy was too important to stand there and ask for heartache. She'd leave, and hopefully, Madeline would too—permanently.

Chapter 32

One fifteen. Two thirty. Three twenty, and now five thirty. Sherry had stared at the clock next to her bed most of the night. The longest stretch of sleep she'd claimed was the past two hours. Dave's alarm clock startled her when it sounded off at five thirty. She was wide awake and would be unable to get back to sleep. Yet her body craved the rest.

"Dave, are you awake?" she said, nudging him slightly.

"I am, at least I better be. I have to get out of the house by six thirty," he said, tossing the covers off and sitting on the side of the bed. "How did you sleep?" he asked, leaning on the bed and giving her a peck on the cheek.

"Not well," she said, feeling compelled to be honest. He had to know that she wasn't in favor of Andre staying with them. She had nothing against Dave's son, but any child of Madeline's was bound to cause trouble for Sherry. She knew it and was prepared.

"Is it the baby?" he said, lying next to her.

"Yes and no."

"What does that mean?" he asked, placing his bent elbow on the bed and resting the side of his head on the palm of his hand.

"The baby is fine for now, but if Andre stays with us, that might change."

"Nonsense," Dave said, lying down again.

"If Andre's here, that means Madeline will be here. And she's more than I care to think about."

"Oh, she's not that bad."

Maybe he didn't think so, but his opinion was clouded when it came to his precious Madeline. She was tough, maybe even vicious, when it came to protecting her interests. Sherry was fully aware of how much power and fear Madeline could display.

Dave went on. "This is his home. He's sleeping in his old room, for goodness' sake. I'm pretty sure he's settled in."

Dave was probably right, which made Sherry's suggestion about him going to boarding or military school, less appealing. She didn't want the child to think he'd been kicked out, but Sherry wanted this baby. She didn't do a good job protecting the last baby from Madeline's constant tirades. This child wouldn't be left to the wolves. She was willing to protect it at any cost. No sacrifice was too great, not even Dave's validation. Sherry had a plan.

"Let's face it. Andre doesn't like me."

"That's not true."

"It is, and I can kind of understand. He's a child. I don't blame him, but the truth is that he doesn't like me. So I suggest you get a full-time nanny or companion to babysit him while you're at work. With the proper supervision he won't have to interact with me. It will be like he's not here," she said, not intending for her comment to sound quite the way it came out.

"You worry too much. Andre won't be a problem for you. Once his suspension is over, he'll be at school most of the day. Yes, I can get a nanny, or maybe he needs more of a mentor at his age. Either way, I can get a full-time person to sit with him until I get home at night."

Sherry was somewhat relieved, but nowhere near satisfied with her personal life. "The best option is for Andre to move back in with his mother, but I see that's not happening."

"Give it a few months. Let's see how this works out, and then we can talk about making changes, if necessary." He sat up and peered at her. "I'm hoping no changes are necessary. I really want this to work for Andre. He's been sacked with repeated losses in his life. It's not his fault. I'm his father, and he needs me. I have to be here for him. It's my obligation, and I gladly take on the challenge." He stroked her hair. "I'm going to need your help to make this work."

"I'll try," she said, acquiescing the second he touched her.

"I can't ask any more of you," he said and gave her a long kiss on the lips. The moment didn't linger. In a swoop he was out of the bed and heading to the bathroom.

"You think you might be able to come home for lunch today? Since he's out of school, this will be the first day that Andre and I will be stuck together."

"Don't say it like that."

"You know what I mean. We're going to be here together. It would be nice if you could have lunch with us, at least this once. It would help me a lot."

"I wish I could, but my calendar is booked with meetings most of the day. Madeline and I have to finalize the strategy for the Midwest expansion."

"Of course you do," she whispered.

"I'm sorry I won't be able to come home for lunch, but I promise to try tomorrow," he said and disappeared into the shadows. She wanted to join him, but there wasn't room for her. It wasn't 6:00 A.M. yet, and his day was already filled.

***

Andre woke up in his bed. He looked around the room, struggling to figure out where he was. *That's right,* he thought. He was in his old room on Mayweather Lane. He rolled over and stretched his arms across the queen-sized bed. He was home. He giggled like a school kid. He let his gaze roam around the room, side to side, up and down. He could hardly believe his move to the old house was true. Being with his dad was like a dream, and the other kids weren't with him. That made it the best. He jumped on the bed as if it were a trampoline. He hadn't had this much fun in a while.

He eventually stopped horsing around and went downstairs to get breakfast, skipping and humming with each step. His happiness was boiling over until he reached the kitchen and saw an unfamiliar face.

"Can I get something to eat?" he asked.

"Absolutely," the lady said.

"I haven't met you before," Andre said. "I never saw you on any of the weekends when I came to see my dad."

The lady poured him a glass of juice. "You're right. This is my first day here. Your father had the temporary agency send me over this morning to help out."

"But he already has a cook."

"I'm here specifically to help take care of you."

"I'm a teenager. I don't need a babysitter," he told the lady.

"I'm sure you don't, but your father wants me to be here for you. So here I am," the lady said, smiling. "Consider me your personal assistant."

Andre didn't have anything against her, except that she didn't need to be there. He could take care of himself. He wasn't a little baby. He wasn't going to let her help him. He figured after a few days, his dad would have to let her go. He'd prove she was a waste of money.

"What would you like to eat? Pancakes, waffles? You name it."

Whoa, nobody said anything about having fresh waffles for breakfast. *Not bad,* he thought. Maybe this lady wasn't going to be so bad. He'd get waffles and see how he felt about her afterward. "Sure. I'll take some waffles. Do you have warm syrup too?" he asked, taking a seat at the table.

"If we don't, I'm sure I can warm it for you."

Andre was in heaven. He was away from his annoying sister and brothers, was sleeping in his favorite room, and was eating waffles with warm syrup for breakfast. The best part was that he was living with his dad. His situation didn't get any cooler than it was at the moment.

Chapter 33

Sherry rolled out of bed and strolled down the hallway around eleven thirty. Breakfast had long passed. She just wasn't hungry, but the baby required food regardless of how she felt about eating. She meandered down the stairs in her robe, exhausted from tossing and turning most of the night. The hours of sleep she'd claimed after Dave left this morning were too few. Sherry eased into the kitchen, almost like she was sneaking in. She braced to see Andre. When she poked her head in and found no one there, she relaxed. She poured a glass of milk and decided to sit and enjoy the cold drink with a handful of crackers while looking out the back window.

For five minutes, every noise had her jittery. Finally, her nerves couldn't handle any more. She retreated to her room, afraid that staying in the kitchen, out in the open, could get her caught in the enemy's trap. She wanted to avoid Andre indefinitely. He was Madeline's son, which automatically meant he couldn't like Sherry. How could he? She was sure Madeline didn't allow traitors to exist in her world. If Andre showed the slightest kindness to Sherry, he might be tossed into the abyss or eaten alive by his mother. Madeline was vicious, and it was best that Sherry stay away from Madeline and her troops, at least until the baby was born. Sherry took a seat by the floor-to-ceiling drapes and grabbed a book. She wasn't taking any chances.

After intermittent naps, a chapter here and there, and a few game shows, Sherry was ready to pull her hair out. Being stuck at home without a job was dreadful. Being held hostage in her room in fear of what a teenager might say or do was the absolute pits. Sherry couldn't think straight, she was so annoyed. They were only one day into the arrangement with Andre, and she was ready to scream. This wasn't going to work. She called her husband.

"Is Dave in?" she asked his secretary.

"No, he's not. Who should I say is calling?"

"Mrs. Mitchell." There was a pause. "Did you hear me?" she asked, wondering why the secretary wasn't responding.

"Yes, Mrs. Mitchell. Is it Madeline or Sherry?"

"It's Sherry," she answered, totally deflated. "Sharon, don't you recognize my voice?" she said, letting her dissatisfaction speak loudly.

"I apologize, Mrs. Mitchell, but Sharon is out for the day. I'm a temporary assistant filling in."

"Okay, well, please give my husband the message," she uttered.

Sherry was wondering how much humiliation one person could take. Her torment was never-ending. Thoughts rushed in like a tidal wave, and her emotions overtook her. Marrying Dave had been the joy of her heart, but each day was proving that the price of this marriage was more than she wanted to pay.

The mood remained long after her book was finished. She watched the clock tick by. She attempted to call Dave several more times with no luck. Sherry sat in the room, alone, until the sun set. She couldn't wait for Dave to get home, whenever that was going to be. They had to figure out another way. Her sanity depended on it.

Giving up on the day, Sherry decided to go to bed without dinner. The sooner she got to sleep, the quicker morning would come. Dave was certain to be home by then. She'd catch him bright and early and have the discussion he didn't want to hear. Andre had to go. Just as she was putting on her gown, Dave walked in. "When did you get here?" she asked, surprised to see him. Sherry wasn't sure if she was happy or sad to see him. Nothing was clear.

"Just got here," he said, giving her a hug and the usual peck. She wanted him to take her into his arms and caress her, blocking out the distractions and the threats to their marriage. But he didn't. She had to accept a peck on the cheek and a quick embrace. "You aren't getting ready for bed this early, are you?" he asked, glancing at his watch.

"Actually I was."

"Have you eaten?" he asked.

"No . . ."

He took her hand. "Come on down and have dinner with Andre and me. This is our first night together. I rushed home before eight so we could sit down to the table together as a family."

She didn't want to. Who was he kidding? They weren't a family. She screamed within, feeling trapped. "I'm not hungry."

"But you have to eat for the baby. Come on. Do it for me," he said, words that would normally have swayed her instantly. Not this time. She was reluctant and was not in the mood to pretend otherwise. Sherry knew he had children when they married, and she thought she was okay with it. The more honest she allowed herself to be, the more Sherry realized she wasn't okay with him having an existing family. His children hated her, and the feeling was becoming mutual despite her best effort to form a relationship with them.

"I'll go down with you, but don't expect me to do much talking."

"Why not? You're not feeling well?"

Too bad he couldn't tell. "You can say that I'm tired, real tired," she said and left it there.

Chapter 34

Madeline and Dave sat at the conference table in his office, with a thin space separating them. She watched him flip pages as he peered over his reading glasses.

"How's it going with Andre?" she asked.

"Good, I guess."

"What does that mean?" she said, staring at him.

He pulled off his reading glasses. "Well, we haven't had any problems. So far so good."

"But it's only been two days."

"I know, but I believe it's working."

Madeline picked up her pen and pretended to be writing a note. "What about Sherry? Is she as happy about this arrangement as you are?" she asked.

Dave gave her a quick glance that provided the answer she anticipated. "It's an adjustment for her, but she realizes how important this is to me. She's totally on board."

"Sure she is," Madeline said.

"I'm grateful to her for supporting Andre and me. She could have said no and refused to bend."

"I would have," Madeline said.

"But she's not you."

Madeline dropped the pen down on the table. "You are right about that. She most certainly is not and never will be," she barked.

"I didn't intend to offend you. I'm sorry," he said. "There is no one like you. There is only one Madeline Mitchell in the world. You truly are one in a million."

His words were laced with enough sugar to make her gag. If he really felt that way, they'd be living together at the estate. Instead, he had his own family. She had hers and wasn't swayed by his charm. Those days had long passed.

Sherry sat at the kitchen table, miserable. Andre's babysitter had to take the day off leaving Sherry alone with the teen. She'd grown tired of being stuck in her room. Friday morning had escaped, but she had a grip on the afternoon. Nodding in and out of sleep, the beel rang at the front door. Sherry wasn't expecting anyone. She leapt to her feet, excited at the thought of having company. She rushed to the door and opened it. The anticipation drained from her veins.

"What do you want, Madeline?"

"What do you think I want? I'm here to see my son. Where is Andre?" Madeline asked, waltzing into the house as if she was still the owner.

"Upstairs, I guess," Sherry said, lingering at the doorway. Her spirit was too weak to duel with Madeline. Today wasn't the day for her to take on the lioness. Sherry was willing to surrender immediately if it would spur Madeline to get out quicker.

"Why are you guessing? Either you know where he is or you don't!"

"Like I said, I think your son is upstairs." She wasn't Andre's keeper. That was Madeline's job.

"Excuse me," Madeline said in a nasty way and headed upstairs.

"Who gave you permission to walk freely around my house?"

Madeline halted in her tracks. "You don't even want to go there with me."

The contempt in her gaze made Sherry pause. "Just go on up," Sherry said, flailing her arm, disgusted.

"That's what I thought," Madeline said and kept walking up the stairs.

Sherry felt a slight pain in her side. She sat at the foot of the staircase, determined not to get overly concerned.

A minute later Madeline came barreling down the stairs and stepped over Sherry. "He's not upstairs. Where is my son?"

Sherry wasn't able to pay attention. Making sure her baby was safe took priority over Madeline's ranting.

"Where is Andre?" Madeline asked again, her tone meaner.

Sherry pointed in the direction of the family room. "Maybe he's in there. I don't know," she said in a soft-spoken tone, trying not to put any pressure on her stomach. Sherry wasn't going to let Madeline's presence affect her pregnancy.

"Don't bother getting up. I know the way."

That was fine with Sherry; she hadn't intended on getting up, anyway. She rubbed her side, trying to soothe the pain away and the fear that followed.

Suddenly Sherry heard yelling as Madeline darted back into the foyer. Sherry was in the same spot, at the bottom of the staircase.

"This boy needs supervision, not a free pass to just sit around. Why are you letting him watch TV all day?"

"I didn't *let* him watch anything. He's watching what he wants." If he was in school like the other children, instead of being suspended for most of the week, there wouldn't be an issue, she thought. This wasn't Sherry's problem. It was Madeline's.

"Aren't you the adult in the house?"

"Madeline, this is ridiculous and childish. When are you going to accept me in Dave's life?"

"Probably never."

Sherry wanted to fight back, but Madeline was too much to handle. Avoiding a fight for the sake of her baby's health was easy. Madeline could yell and scream as much as she wanted. Sherry wasn't going to be dazed. Intimidated, maybe, but Madeline would never know how much.

Sherry got a series of sharp pains in her abdomen, causing her to double over. "Oh, my gosh," she moaned while clutching her abdomen and side.

Madeline stood there, appearing shocked.

"Help me, please," Sherry begged.

"Andre, get in here now!" Madeline called out. He came in right away. "Go dial the operator, and tell them to send an ambulance."

Madeline ran toward the kitchen.

"Don't leave me in here alone," Sherry cried out.

"It's okay. I'm getting you a glass of water. I'll be right back."

As the water ran, Madeline's thoughts swirled uncontrollably. What in the world was she doing? How cruel could fate be? There she stood, forced to nurse her husband's pregnant mistress in their family home. Madeline would have laughed if it could have alleviated her overwhelming sense of defeat. She would have cried, too, but it wouldn't make a difference. Her soul was crushed, but she stayed focused on helping Sherry. It had never been her intent to cause any problems for Sherry and the pregnancy. How could God and life be so cruel?

The ambulance arrived pretty quickly, and the paramedics rushed Sherry to the hospital. Madeline had to call Dave.

There wasn't an easy way to tell him, so she blurted it out. "I'm at the estate. Sherry just left in the ambulance, with some kind of pain in her side."

"What happened? Please tell me that you didn't get into a fight with her. Please tell me that," Dave said, sounding distressed.

"No, we didn't get into a fight. I'm shocked that you would ask such a question. You should concentrate on getting to the hospital. I'll find out where they're taking her and let you know as soon as I can."

"Thanks for letting me know," he said, and they ended the call.

"Let's go, Andre," she said, opening the front door.

"Where am I going?"

"Home with me."

"But I'm supposed to be staying here with Dad."

"For now, you're coming home with me. I'm not up for an argument. So, please, just come with me. You can come back after your dad checks on Sherry," she said, leaning against the door frame.

He walked out, expressing no resistance. Thank goodness for small miracles. She walked out behind him and closed the door to Sherry's home.

Chapter 35

The constant beeping sound of the heart monitors and other machines was contributing to Sherry's uneasiness. "Can you please call my husband again?" she uttered.

"Mrs. Mitchell, your blood pressure is elevated. You have to calm down. We don't want to get the baby in distress. Please lie back and take nice slow breaths."

"But you don't understand. I need my husband." Dave was the medicine she needed. He knew how to put her at ease. Just his presence was sufficient.

"I'll dial the number for you, if that will help," the emergency room nurse offered.

Sherry was desperate to say yes when she heard Dave.

"I'm here," he said, rushing through the doorway to her bedside.

She hugged him and wouldn't let go. Time stopped, and she felt safe in his arms. The baby was too. There was nowhere else she would rather be than in his strong arms, protecting her and their child. She felt him pulling away, but Sherry didn't want to let go. She couldn't. He was her lifeline, and she clung to him with all her might.

"You can let go now. I'm here, and I'll be here with you for a while," he said, loosening the grip she had around his neck. "Looks like you've had a rough day."

She asked for a tissue, and he gave it to her. "I can't tell you how frightening this has been," she said, rising up and feeling anxiety rushing in.

"Lay down, Sherry, and don't worry," he said. "I know God's mercy will be on this baby, and it's going to live."

Sherry wasn't much into religion or going to church but didn't have a problem with Dave's beliefs. At a time like this, she was willing to accept prayers and anything else that would lead to a healthy delivery. She let Dave finish his prayer, hoping it meant something. He seemed to think so, and it was good enough for her in this delicate situation. Hope from just about anywhere was going to be warmly received.

"Thank you for the prayer. This baby can use as many positive thoughts as it can get," she said, wiping the corners of her eyes with the tissue.

A nurse came in. "Let me check your blood pressure," she said, grabbing the arm band. After completing the test, she said, "One hundred sixty over ninety-five is higher than we like. Do you have a history of high blood pressure?"

"No, I don't," Sherry said, responding immediately. "Should I be worried?"

"We definitely don't want you worrying under any circumstances. That will keep your pressure up, and we want it to come down."

"Nurse, excuse me, but when Sherry was pregnant a few years ago, her blood pressure shot up too."

That was right. She'd forgotten. It was probably more like those days were blocked out. Thank goodness Dave was there with her to speak to the nurses and doctors; otherwise, she'd be alone.

"Is that common during pregnancy?" Sherry asked.

"For some women. The most important action you can take for the baby is to calm down and stay relaxed." The nurse rested her hand on Sherry's shoulder. "I know it's hard to do, but you have to take it easy. We want to give that little guy or gal the best shot we can at getting here on time and not a day early," she said, patting Sherry's hand.

"Thanks, Nurse," Dave said.

"Just ring the bell if you need me," the nurse said, sliding a pen into her pocket and leaving the room.

Sherry and Dave were finally alone.

"When I got the call from Madeline, I was concerned, but you seem to be doing better," Dave said. "Do you remember what happened?"

Sherry collected her thoughts and poured out her emotions to Dave. "It was Madeline and Andre. They were arguing, and I didn't want to be in the middle. They kept pushing me until I began feeling pain in my side." "Madeline and Andre pushed you?" he asked with utter seriousness in his voice. She wanted to melt over his concern.

"Not physically, but it might as well have been. I was going bonkers watching them go at it. Dave, I know you want your son there, but it's not working. Every day I have to stay in my room. It's dreadful."

"Why are you staying in your room?"

"Because I'm trying to avoid him. He seems to be doing the same."

"Is it really that bad?"

"Worse. That's why I can't stay in the house with Andre. I just can't. I'm sorry, but I have to look out for my child."

"Me too. I have to look out for all my kids, including Andre."

Sherry shifted her gaze away from Dave. She didn't want him to feel badly, but honesty was what he had to hear.

"We'll work this arrangement out."

"No, Dave, we won't," she said, so boldly that it shocked her. "I have to be serious. I won't come to the house unless Andre is gone."

"You don't mean it."

"I do."

The doctor entered the room and read Sherry's chart. "Mrs. Mitchell, I have good news and bad news. Which one do you want first?"

"I'll take the good. I could stand a bit of good news for a change," Sherry said, peering at Dave.

"The good news is that you won't have to wash dishes or clean the kitchen for several months." The doctor rested his arm on the bed rail. Dave sat near the bed, on the other side, seeming to be listening intensely. "The bad news is that you'll have to stay on bed rest for those months, and I'd like to start by keeping you here at least several days until we're sure that you're stable."

Sherry frowned. "That's not what I wanted to hear."

"I'm sure, but I know we'll work hard to get this baby born healthy and on time," the doctor said, looking at Dave.

"Yes, indeed," Dave chimed in. The doctor left after Dave thanked him for helping out.

"Did you hear what the doctor said? I can't be under pressure. Andre has to go back home," Sherry declared.

"Our house is his home. It's as much his as ours."

"You must know that I don't take any pleasure in having him leave. But I have to be. Home is my refuge. If I can't be comfortable there, I can't be anywhere."

"I don't want to kick my son out. It will crush him, not to mention what Madeline will say."

"Dave, forget about how Madeline feels. What about me? Don't my wishes count?" she said, getting loud.

The monitor began beeping. The nurse came in right away. She pushed a few buttons, and the beeping ended abruptly. She checked Sherry's pulse and asked a few questions. The nurse must have been satisfied with Sherry's condition, because she left the room.

Thank goodness, Sherry thought.

"Am I coming home or going to a hotel until the baby is born?"

"As of now, you're in the hospital and may be for several days. We can revisit this discussion when you're stronger."

"No, Dave, I'm not going to let you do that."

"Do what?"

"Brush off my question without giving me an answer. Am I coming home or going to the Westin?"

Reluctantly he said, "Coming home, of course."

"With or without Andre?" she said, sitting straight up, stiff.

"Without."

Sherry could see the grief etched on his face but didn't offer any consolation. Andre had to go. "Thank you," she said, reaching for him.

"Don't thank me yet. I have to tell Madeline and Andre the bad news. I already know it's not going to sit well." His eyes widened as he said, "We've taken care of Andre. Now, what about you?"

"I'm feeling better all ready," she said, lying back.

"Maybe your getting sick is for the best." She wasn't following him. "Now that the doctor has put you on bed rest, I'd like to see if we can talk them into letting you stay at the hospital."

"But I want to come home."

"I know, but there's no one at home to take care of you. The housekeeper is around, but she's not a nurse. I'd be much more comfortable at DMI every day knowing you're in capable hands here at the hospital with a team of doctors and nurses, instead of being alone at the estate. Once Andre leaves, you'll basically be on your own, and that bothers me."

"When you put it like that, I guess I can stay here a few weeks if the doctor thinks it's best."

"I'll talk to him. Maybe we can keep you here nice and safe for a month or two," Dave added.

"I can't promise that I can last for a month in here. A few weeks I can do, but that's about my limit."

"Okay, let's start with a few weeks and go from there," he said, rubbing her hand. "I'll talk to your doctor before I leave and take care of it. Extending your stay is the right decision for us."

Her heartbeat slowed to the same pace as Dave's. She lay in the bed as their hearts beat in unison. She was home. Wherever Dave was, that represented home.

Chapter 36

Madeline considered going into the office after leaving the estate but decided to go home instead. Andre was in his room. She was in hers. The other children would be home soon.

There was a knock on her bedroom door. Madeline slowly got up. It was Andre.

"Is Sherry going to be okay?" he asked.

"I honestly don't know, but I hope so," Madeline told him, and she meant it. "You want to sit in here with me for a while?" She could tell he was shaken up after watching the ambulance cart Sherry away.

"Nah, I'll go to my room. I just wanted to find out if she was going to be okay."

"Maybe you can say a prayer for her," Madeline said though she wasn't being sincere. Her children weren't big on prayer or church because she wasn't. That was Dave's thing. He had tried swaying her into his religious camp early in the marriage. As time passed, he didn't push his religion on her, and she didn't force it on the children. Against Dave's wishes, she preferred to let them make their own choices when they were older. Once in a while Don and Tamara would go to church with Dave, but it was rare.

After Andre schlepped to his room, Madeline leaned against the door, replaying the scene at the estate. She felt for Sherry. She didn't want to, but her heart wasn't biased. They were both mothers who loved their children. Sherry's wasn't born yet, but the love existed already. That was evident. Madeline understood.

Madeline closed the door softly and returned to her bed. Her emotions were dancing back and forth between compassion and reality. Rational thinking told her it wasn't the baby's fault that it had been conceived and was falling into a messed-up family predicament. Jagged fragments of her shattered love repeatedly convinced Madeline that she was justified in opposing every aspect of Sherry, including the new baby. Madeline sank down into the covers and pulled the sheet over her head. She knew it didn't make sense to dislike a child, which was why Madeline didn't want anyone to know how she really felt. Reality was harsh, and thank goodness she wasn't the only one who had to deal with it. Thanks to Dave, all of them had been dealt their share, but leaving him hadn't solved her problems.

Madeline dosed off and woke up an hour later from a bad dream. Sherry was chasing her down a dark road. She was everywhere. When Madeline was awake, Sherry was there. When she closed her eyes, she was there. She couldn't escape Sherry. Madeline finally gave in and called Dave. By now he had to be at the hospital. She'd try there first.

"Is Mr. Dave Mitchell there?" she asked someone at the nurses' station after being transferred by the hospital operator.

"He's in the room with Mrs. Mitchell. Would you like to speak with him?"

"Yes, please. Tell him it's Madeline," she said, intentionally not giving the Mitchell name. There was one too many already in the hospital.

The nurse was gone briefly, and then Dave was on the phone.

"Madeline, you're looking for me?"

"Yes, I'm checking on Sherry's condition." She was reluctant to ask about the baby, in case the prognosis wasn't favorable. Curiosity and compassion made a bold concoction. "Are Sherry and the baby out of danger?"

"We believe so, but she's going to need rest, and it's critical for her to stay calm. I want her to get comfortable in here, because it's the only place where I'm assured Sherry and the baby will get top-notch treatment. This baby means the world to her and to me too."

"At least Sherry is doing better. What time do you want me to bring Andre over tomorrow? Since it will be Saturday, perhaps the other children can come too and spend the day with you while Sherry's in the hospital."

There was a long pause on the phone before Dave said, "Why don't you keep Andre over the weekend? I would get him Monday, but I need the extra day, just in case. I'll promise to get him after school on Tuesday."

"Why wait? I thought you'd want the company while Sherry's gone."

"It will be best if he stays with you. Sherry needs me, and I can't let her down."

Madeline was hurt, hearing Dave sound so endearing. Her pride kicked in, like it had for the past couple of years, and she instantly converted the hurt to a more manageable emotion, filtered fury. But the fight just wasn't in her today. She was going to let him have this one.

"I can keep him over the weekend, but can you at least get him Monday? He's already going to be disappointed as it is."

"Madeline, I really need the extra day."

"All right, Dave. I'll keep Andre with me until Tuesday, but you'd better get him after school, or we're going to have a big problem. He needs you just as much as Sherry does. Remember that," she said before they ended the call.

The children were in the family room, and everything seemed to be a challenge. The TV, the games, and the snacks contributed to the mayhem. Madeline was exhausted watching the circus unfold among her children. She yearned for peace and quiet. If she could have only one, that was okay too.

"I don't want to watch that stupid show. Tamara always gets what she wants," Andre shouted.

"We watched your stupid show twice because you kept complaining. Now it's my turn," Tamara shouted back. She was five years younger but didn't let the age difference keep her from going at Andre.

Two more nights might as well be a month. Tuesday couldn't come too soon for Madeline.

"Stop, please! You guys are getting on my nerves. Please, be quiet. I've had enough of this bickering," Madeline told them.

"I'm going to my room," Sam said. She let him go. He wasn't the main one causing the ruckus, anyway. It was mostly Tamara and Andre going at it. Don was content with his Jiffy Pop popcorn and *Superman* comic book. He must have grown immune to the constant quarreling. Madeline wished she could too, but as the only parent in the house, the job of problem solving was exclusively hers.

After Sam left the room, there was calm for about ten minutes before Andre started up again. He got up from his seat on the couch and walked past Tamara, who was sitting on the floor. When he passed her, he gave her a slight kick, messing up the tower she was making with her cards.

"What did you do that for?" Tamara yelled, ready to cry.

"Andre, why did you do that?" Madeline said, jumping in.

"It was an accident. Jeez, what's the big deal? Everybody makes mistakes," he said and kept walking until Madeline leapt to her feet and grabbed him.

"That wasn't an accident, young man," she said, gripping him by the collar. "Now, apologize."

Don was staring at her with a disheartening expression of fear.

"Yeah, apologize," Tamara taunted.

"Stop that," Madeline said to Tamara, pointing her finger to indicate this was serious.

"It was an accident. Why should I have to apologize?"

"Because I said so," Madeline said emphatically. There was no room for additional questions, and she was sure he knew it. She pulled his collar. "Do it now."

"I apologize," he said under duress. Madeline let him go. "I hate this place. That's why I want to go back to Dad's, but you won't let me."

Madeline had told him he had to stay at her house until Tuesday, at his father's request. Once again, she had to be the villain, when it was Dave who didn't want his son with him. Madeline wanted to shield Andre from rejection, but maybe he was old enough to hear the truth.

"I'm not keeping you from your father. He's the one who wanted you to stay here so that he could spend time with Sherry while she's in the hospital."

"That's not true."

"You don't believe me? Then call your dad and ask him yourself." She grabbed his hand and led him to the phone. She handed him the phone. "Here, call him. Find out for yourself." She felt a hint of guilt about being so candid, but her frail human side prevailed.

Reluctantly, he took the phone, dialed the number, and then pushed the speakerphone button. When his father was on the phone, he spoke in a subdued way. It was surprising to Madeline given the energy he was pouring out only a few minutes ago.

"Dad, can I come home tonight?"

"Tonight isn't good, son. I'm heading to the hospital in an hour. There will be no one here to sit with you."

"I don't need a babysitter. I can stay home by myself."

"I wouldn't feel right leaving you here alone."

"I can go to the hospital with you."

"That's not such a good idea."

Madeline listened quietly.

"Please let me come home tonight. I won't get into trouble. I promise. Just please come and get me. I can't stay here."

"I'm sorry, son. I have to be with Sherry, but I'll pick you up by Tuesday."

Andre pushed the speakerphone button, disconnecting the call without saying bye. "I bet he would come to get Tamara if she asked."

Madeline didn't agree, but Andre wasn't going to hear her opinion. His mind was set. "I hate everybody in this whole house," he said and stormed out of the kitchen. As long as he didn't go back into the family room to torment Tamara and Don, Madeline was willing to let him find his own refuge. As much as he pressed her nerves, her heart wept for her son.

Chapter 37

Dave was ready for the 10:00 A.M. meeting with the Midwest Clergymen, but where was Madeline? The client would be arriving any minute. He went to the open doorway and called out, "Sharon, have you seen Madeline?" Just as the words crossed his lips, he saw her going down the hallway. "Madeline, are you coming to the meeting?" he asked, rushing to catch up with her.

"I'll be right there, Dave," she said, sounding uninterested. Given that the Midwest Clergymen was one of the largest clients currently in negotiation with DMI, he was concerned about her lack of enthusiasm.

"I'll be waiting in my office. Mr. Ingles should be here in less than an hour. You'll need to hurry."

"I'm going as fast as I can," she said. "Remember, I have young children at home." She stopped in her tracks. "You have none. So there will be days when I can't get here as early as you. Now, I'll be down to your office as quickly as I can. Proceed without me until then," she said, spewing nails of aggravation at him, and retreated into her office.

Dave turned around and went back to his office. He had suspected there would be a fallout from leaving Andre at Madeline's over the weekend. But he didn't have a gauge on how deep it would go with her. He was certain to find out before noon.

The hour whisked by.

"Mr. Ingles is in the lobby," Sharon announced over the intercom which connected her desk to Dave's office.

"Go down and bring them up please," he said. Madeline popped in. "Perfect timing. Mr. Ingles from the Midwest Clergymen has arrived."

Once everyone was in the office, their meeting got under way.

"Mr. Ingles, we've crafted a full-service plan for you," Dave told his client.

Madeline was normally engaged from the start, but today she repeatedly tapped her pen on the table, causing Dave to become distracted and lose his train of thought.

"Uh, what was I saying?" he said, fumbling through a few of his notes. "I'm sorry, Mr. Ingles."

"Call me Martin."

"Then Martin it is," Dave told the client. "Excuse me. I was distracted. It won't happen again."

"It's no problem. Your company's performance speaks for itself. I'm interested in hearing what the two of you have to say. Take your time," Martin said.

Dave was mortified. Professionalism was his calling card. He was disgusted by his lack of concentration. Madeline might have been the catalyst for his distraction, but ultimately it was his own doing. He wouldn't blame her.

The meeting moved forward, and Martin seemed pleased with the presentation. Madeline chimed in once or twice, but she said nothing meaningful. Her body was in the chair, but it was evident to Dave that the rest of her, the piece DMI needed, had stayed home.

"I'll review your figures with my team and get back to you," Martin said, standing and extending his hand to Madeline and then Dave. Dave walked the client to the door and handed him off to Sharon.

"Make sure he gets to the lobby," Dave instructed.

Everyone exchanged good-byes. Dave could hardly speak to Madeline, he was so frustrated. She had some explaining to do.

"Do you have a few minutes?" he asked Madeline.

"I guess," she said, repeatedly peering at her watch.

"Am I keeping you from being somewhere?" Dave asked.

"Maybe," she said.

"Madeline, what is going on with you? You didn't participate in the presentation."

"I was here. What are you talking about?"

"You were in the room, but your enthusiasm and professionalism must have stayed at home today." Typically a comment like his would have prompted a retort from Madeline, but she didn't respond. "Did you hear me?" he asked.

"Actually, no, I didn't, Dave," she said, tapping her pen on the desk rapidly. "I can't get Andre off my mind."

"Isn't he at school?"

"For the moment, but he was in such a bad way last night after speaking with you that I'm prepared for him to get into trouble at school today."

"Don't be so sure."

Madeline stopped tapping and said, "I know him as much as a parent can. I'm telling you, today is going to be rough for him. It will be a miracle if he gets through the day without expulsion. I'm going to call and check on him." She sprang up and grabbed the phone on Dave's desk. He stayed out of her way.

"This is Madeline Mitchell. Can I please speak with the headmaster?"

Dave waited patiently to get the update, hopeful for good news. She wasn't on the phone long before getting off. Her facial expression didn't give any indication of what she was thinking.

"What did he say?" Dave asked, eager to find out.

"Just as I suspected."

"What has he done?"

"Nothing yet, but the headmaster said Andre is despondent and has been unwilling to do his work. They're concerned, too, and think it might be best to let him take the rest of the day off."

"Really? The headmaster was that concerned?"

"Apparently," she said, sighing. "Andre should be picked up before he gets into trouble. It's not a matter of if, only when."

Dave had to acknowledge her suggestion. "Are you going to get him?"

"I can't," she blurted out. "I told you before. I can't keep balancing DMI and the children alone. You have to help more. I can't do it." She approached Dave. "No, I take that back. I'm not *going* to do it."

"But I can't pick him up early, either."

"Of course you can't. You *never* can," she retorted. "Dave, I mean it. You have got to get involved or be willing to watch this child implode. It's your choice."

She wasn't yelling, but her words were resonating more than Madeline realized. "I can't pick him up today, but I'm still planning to get him tomorrow." Dave didn't dare tell Madeline the full truth. He'd told Sherry that Andre wasn't going to live with them any longer. He was wise enough to know this wasn't the right moment to share his decision with Madeline. He also knew it wasn't the ideal moment to tell Sherry that Andre was going to stay at the house for a short period.

Truth was, Dave couldn't tell either woman the full story if he had any chance of helping Andre. He had to tread water until Sherry and Madeline were both in healthier states of mind. Since the doctor had extended Sherry's hospital stay four more weeks, Dave had extra time to concoct a way out, or at least he hoped so.

Chapter 38

It was Tuesday, and his mother had promised Andre that he was going to his father's house after school. She had to keep her promise. He'd kept his by staying out of trouble for the whole day. Andre actually couldn't remember the last time he'd gone an entire day without getting into trouble. It definitely wasn't recently. He'd done his work without sassing the teacher or getting really mad at other students for saying stupid things. He hadn't paid much attention to what the other kids said today. He was determined to do a good job and get to go home with his dad.

He kept checking the wall clock every few minutes. Two more minutes and class was out. He quietly tucked his notebook and pencils into his knapsack. He had one foot forward, ready to bolt out of the classroom, past his schoolmates. When the bell rang, he darted out, running down the hallway until a teacher told him to slow down. He did as he was told without arguing. The door was a few steps away, and Andre wasn't going to mess up this close to getting what he wanted.

Andre looked around, anxious to see his mother's car. There she was, parked behind the buses, just as promised. A warm feeling came over him, like hot fudge poured on ice cream. He couldn't hold back his smile. He jumped inside the car.

"How was your day?" Madeline asked.

"Good," he said, excited.

"Like what?"

"I did my work, and I didn't get into any trouble."

"Wow, that's fantastic," she said, giving him a big hug.

Even the praise felt good for a change. He didn't like being mean, but people bothered him too much. Being the oldest in his family put extra pressure on him. His kid sister and brothers got away with much more than he did. Sometimes he didn't know how to handle the pressure, but nobody seemed to listen to him. So he stopped talking. But today was special.

"We're going to Dad's, right?" he asked, hoping they hadn't tricked him.

"Yes, we are. As a matter of fact, he's leaving work early to meet us at the estate." Andre smiled wider. "You know he never leaves work early unless it's for a very important reason. Today would be you," she said, easing into traffic.

In twenty minutes they were parked in front of the family house. He hustled out of the car and ran to the door. Nobody answered. He knocked for ten minutes, until his knuckles were sore. His excitement ran away.

"I know your dad is going to be here. He'd better be here," his mother said, banging on the door too.

Andre plopped down on the stoop, feeling his anger coming up. He should have known everything was going too good for him.

When his mother had given up on knocking and had taken a seat on the stoop next to him, he heard his father's Cadillac roaring up the driveway. Andre jumped up, with his excitement oozing. He ran up to the car before it came to a full stop.

"I was beginning to wonder if you'd forgotten," his mother told his father.

"How long have you been waiting here?" Dave asked.

"Not long," Andre said. He didn't care how long he had to wait if his father was eventually going to get there.

His father grabbed him around the neck and gave him a hug, which Andre was glad to get. He was happy, because he was home.

"Looks like the two of you don't need me here. I can go to work," his mother said and left.

Andre went into the house with his father. He ran his knapsack upstairs to his room and jetted down to the family room, where his father was.

"It's just the two of us. What do you want to do?" his dad asked.

"I don't know. Maybe shoot a few hoops and then watch TV."

"That works for me."

The two ate pizza together a few hours later. Andre couldn't be happier. He was in a dream and didn't want it to ever end. When the phone rang, his father went to answer it. He followed him into the kitchen for no real reason.

"How are you feeling?" he heard his father ask. "As long as you're in the hospital, I need you to relax and not worry about what's going on here."

Andre knew it was Sherry. He was agitated about her interrupting their evening. A couple minutes later, when Dave ended the call, Andre was super glad that the call was short.

"That was Sherry," Dave told him.

"Oh . . ."

"She has to be in the hospital for at least another month."

"Oh, that's a long time," Andre said, beaming inside.

"Son, do you mind if I do some work for a few hours in my office?"

"Okay with me," he said. As long as his father was in the house with him, Andre was satisfied.

Chapter 39

Madeline sat in her office, feeling well rested for a change. Last night actually seemed odd. It was pretty quiet. The children weren't fighting. They weren't even arguing. She should have been relishing the calm, but Madeline wasn't euphoric. She missed Andre. He had more challenges than she could handle alone, but he was her son. She would never abandon him or any of her children.

"Mrs. Mitchell, I have a printout of your schedule for tomorrow," her assistant said around three thirty.

"Come on in," Madeline said, reaching for the sheet of paper. "I can't believe the week is half over." She glanced over the sheet. "Have I gotten any calls from Cedarbrook Academy today?"

"None that I'm aware of," her assistant replied. "Were you expecting a call?"

"Kind of," Madeline said. "Let me know right away if they call."

Her assistant nodded and walked out.

Madeline was tempted to call the school and relieve her concern. A few minutes later she caught a glimpse of Dave in the hallway. He had his briefcase, which was surprising. There were at least another four hours of daylight.

"Where are you going?" she asked.

"To meet Andre at the house."

"Oh, I see," she said.

"We had such an enjoyable evening yesterday that I wanted to spend more time with him tonight. Andre talked more last night than he has since being in Detroit. I actually saw a breakthrough."

Madeline was overcome with defeat as she listened to Dave rant on and on. He had won again. Even though he rarely spent more than a handful of hours at a time with his children, they loved him. Madeline didn't mind their adoration for him, but jealousy crept in when she heard about Dave's immediate impact on Andre. She felt like a failure.

"Apparently, Andre did pretty well at school today. I guess you can take the credit for his improvement," she remarked.

"You've asked me to do my part, and that's what I'm doing."

"Think you're father of the year now, huh?"

He chuckled. "I'll talk with you later."

Reason took hold of her. "Dave," she called out to him. "Don't pay any attention to me. I'm only feeling sorry for myself. Getting help for Andre is the most important priority for me. So thank you for making him a priority. Clearly, it's what he needed. Regardless of what I say, please know how grateful I am to you."

"No thanks needed. He's my son too and it's my job just as much as yours," he said. She felt his sincerity and returned a smile. They were of one accord regarding Andre, and she didn't take it for granted.

Thursday brought the same worries for Madeline. Ten A.M. had passed, and there was no call from the school. She'd picked her phone up twice in the past hour to make sure there was a dial tone. There was, which assured her the phone was working. It was odd

that they hadn't called yet. She should have been ec-
static, but that would require her to be in denial. She'd
grown accustomed to the school calling practically
every day.

Her assistant entered the office. "I have the file for
your upcoming meeting with the Evangelical Group at
four o'clock."

Madeline thanked her and took the file. "Uh, no
calls?"

"No calls from the school, Mrs. Mitchell," her assistant said, smiling. "I'll put it through right away if we
get one."

Madeline was slightly embarrassed, having to ask
constantly about the school. Thank goodness her assistant understood. If she weren't an employee, they
might have become friends. After the inappropriate
behavior between Sherry and Dave, Madeline kept employee relationships strictly professional.

Another hour passed, and Madeline couldn't stand
the suspense any longer. She jetted down to Dave's office and found him there.

"Have you heard from Andre or the school today?"

"No, I haven't," he said, taking off his reading glasses.
"Why? Were they supposed to call?"

"Yes and no. He's usually in trouble by noon, but I
haven't heard from anyone yet, not yesterday or today.
It kind of has me worried," she said, bracing her hand
on her hip.

"Based on what he told me at home last night, he had
a good day yesterday. No trouble."

"I find it hard to believe that suddenly he's a totally
new child, problem free. Come on, Dave. Surely, you
don't believe it."

"I do," he said, smug. "Maybe this is your day."

"How so?" she said, folding her arms.

"Maybe, just maybe, he's having another good day."

"That would be a miracle. Two in a row."

"Miracles do happen, you know," he said, grinning.

For an instant, it felt like old times. The radiance in his grin tapped into a sealed part of her feelings. He was still Dave Mitchell, the man she'd planned to build a company with and raise a family. His choices had crushed her dreams, but they didn't have to ruin those of her children.

"I meant to thank you again for keeping your word and picking up Andre on Tuesday," she told him.

"We're having a good time together. I enjoy having him with me."

"That's good to hear. Who knows? Living with you might be the solution we needed," she said. "Clearly, he's doing better with you. Having no calls coming in this week is shocking. To be on the safe side, maybe I should call the school and find out for sure."

"Don't worry so much. He'll be just fine. Besides, I'd like for you to sit in on the Southern Bible Institute meeting. I'm sure Mr. Cooper would love to have you join the discussion."

"When?"

"Two o'clock."

"Sure, I can join you."

Madeline spent the next hour and a half picking through her files. She glanced at the mahogany-encased clock resting on her desk. It was almost one o'clock and not a peep from the school. Maybe it was true. Maybe Andre was trying harder to stay out of trouble. By now surely she should be dancing in the hallway, but Madeline wasn't cheering, not yet. She just couldn't believe Andre could make such a drastic change after spending just two evenings alone with his father. The notion made her sad as she thought about how hard she'd worked over the past couple of years to get Andre stable. Out of nowhere Dave, Mr. Anointed, had swooped in and seemingly saved their son. Madeline moped in her office until Dave poked his head in.

"Do you have a few minutes to prep before the client gets here?" he asked.

"Sure," she said, gathering her file and notepad.

They went to Dave's office. Frank joined them.

"I didn't realize you were joining the meeting," Madeline asked.

"What meeting?" Frank said.

"Oh, I guess you're not," she answered, directing her attention to the file in front of her.

"We're meeting with the Southern Bible Institute in fifteen minutes. What can I do for you?" Dave asked Frank.

"We need to make a final decision on how to handle the latest civil case," Frank told him.

"Which one?" Dave said while looking over the client file, like Madeline was. There wasn't much time. The client would be arriving any second. They had to be prepared.

"You remember, the small church in Kentucky is suing us for breach of contract?" Madeline listened but not intently. Lawsuits weren't her specialty.

"Refresh my memory," Dave said, seeming to pay more attention.

"Last year, apparently, they fell into financial trouble."

"What does that have to do with DMI?" Madeline asked.

"Well," Frank said, chuckling, "they claim our financial training services didn't help them avoid bankruptcy. As a result, they're blaming their misfortune on our ineffective training."

"That's ridiculous," Madeline blurted.

"Tell me about it," Frank echoed. "It's a waste of energy, but this is what we repeatedly have to deal with. I'm used to it after fourteen years."

Sharon rapped on the door to get their attention. It was already open. "Excuse me, Mr. Mitchell, but someone from the hospital is on the line. It seems to be important."

Dave jumped up. "Please forward the call in here right now." He grabbed the phone on the first ring. Madeline heard some of what he was saying, but it was difficult to catch every word since Frank was talking too. Dave was off the phone abruptly. "I have to get to the hospital."

"Are Sherry and the baby all right?" Madeline asked without overthinking her reaction. She truly hoped both of them would come out of the hospital healthy.

Dave shrugged. "I don't know. I have to go and find out what's going on."

Sharon popped in again. "Mr. Cooper is here. Should I send him in?"

Dave grabbed his suit jacket. "I have to go. Frank, can you sit in on this one with Madeline for me?"

"No, I have a meeting with the legal department and a boatload of other priorities. I can't do this one for you."

Madeline was stunned. Back in the day, Frank never said no to Dave. He'd been inconvenienced repeatedly to help Dave without complaining. His younger brother had always been like an idol to Frank. Regardless of what Dave had done, Frank was still his brother and needed his help.

"Come on, Frank. You can cough up an hour, can't you?" Madeline asked.

Frank hesitated and then plopped into a seat. "For you, why not?"

"We can handle this, Dave. Go and see about Sherry and the baby. Don't give a second thought to this meeting. We got it," Madeline told Dave. "I hope everything works out," she added.

"Madeline, I appreciate that more than you know." Dave sighed. "Hopefully, I'll be here for the three o'clock meeting." He thanked them and bolted from the office.

Chapter 40

Sin was sin, which included knowingly breaking rules. That didn't prevent Dave from ramping up the speedometer to seventy seven in a seventy-mile-per-hour speed zone. Sherry had been frantic on the phone. He didn't want to believe the worst and opted not to.

Dave was about ten minutes away, but his thoughts were farther. He reflected on his kids, each of them, and felt a twinge of sorrow. He hadn't provided the spiritual leadership they deserved. Madeline believed in God but didn't see a reason to have Him present in the Mitchell home on a daily basis. So he had never pushed the kids into church or taught them how to genuinely pray. He couldn't help but feel that the lack of spiritual covering had left them vulnerable to many of the challenges they were confronting. His soul was weeping, but no tears were visible on the outside. Dave felt compelled to repent for not being the spiritual head of the family that he should have been.

He put on his signal light and eased toward the exit ramp. He'd blown his role with Madeline and their kids, but by the grace of God, he was getting another chance to do it right with Sherry and their family. She wasn't big on religion either, but their baby would be raised in the church. That was going to be a require-ment for him if this baby lived. It had to live. A fear of death tried to grip him. Dave resisted with all his might. He pulled into the hospital parking lot, leaned into the steering wheel and wept.

Dave drew in a few deep breaths, gathered his emotions, and stepped boldly into the hospital, comfortable that his prayers had been answered. He made his way to the fourth floor and to Sherry's room.

"Oh, Dave, I'm so glad you're here," Sherry said, crying and reaching out to him.

He sat on the edge of her bed and held Sherry. "You're very upset. What's going on?"

He caught most of what she was saying. It wasn't easy deciphering her words in the midst of loud sobs, but Dave was willing to do the best he could.

"I want to go home. I'm tired of being in the hospital."

He drew away in order to make eye contact. "But this is the best place for you until the baby is born."

"I can't stay here. I'm alone, and home is where I want to be."

"But I'm at work most of the time. You know that."

"It's okay. At least I'll see you in the morning and in the evening. We can have dinner together every night."

"What if I get in at ten o'clock?"

"Then that's when we'll eat," she said, not crying as dramatically.

He wanted to object further but couldn't give an adequate reason. She continued pressing him. What was he going to do? Before she could come home, Dave had to be honest and tell her about Andre being at their house. Dave didn't know how she was going to react, given that he'd already promised to send Andre back to Madeline's last week. As far as Sherry was concerned, Andre was already gone. The composure Dave had gathered in the parking lot was wilting. Yet the truth had to prevail, despite the consequences. He searched for the right words, not wanting to push Sherry farther into distress.

He took her hand, peered into her gaze, and said, "I have to tell you something important."

"What is it?" she said, flinching.

"Andre isn't at Madeline's."

"Where is he?" she asked. He could feel her tensing. His gaze dropped. "He's at the estate."

"Dave!" she yelled and jerked her hand from his. "Why? You told me he was going home."

"I know, but he sees the estate as home. I tried sending him to his mother's, but he just wouldn't go without putting up a fight. Madeline and I decided it was best to let him stay with me."

"Madeline doesn't get to decide what happens in our home."

"She meant no harm. She was purely looking out for Andre. We both were," he said, letting his gaze join hers again.

"This isn't fair, Dave," she said. "I'm not coming home until Andre is gone. We agreed."

Suddenly the heart monitor began beeping rapidly, until the sound was too piercing to sit idle. He was about to run out to the nurses' desk but didn't get past the doorway. The nurse was already on her way in. She immediately pressed a few buttons to shut off the noise. Dave was alarmed and on his feet.

"Nurse, is there a problem?" he asked.

The nurse checked Sherry's blood pressure and did a bit of poking. "Looks like Mrs. Mitchell's heart rate was elevated. Your vital signs seem to be fine for both you and the baby," the nurse said to Sherry. "But remember that we have to keep you relaxed. Every single day the baby can stay inside your womb is going to give it a better shot at a healthy birth."

"I'll make sure she stays calm," Dave said, staring at Sherry. "This time I truly promise." He knew what the promise entailed, and she did too. Madeline and Andre, on the other hand, weren't going to like his decision.

"I have a meeting that I have to attend. I'll see you later," he said, kissing her. Dave left the hospital room and braced for a long evening.

His thoughts didn't settle during the drive from the hospital to DMI. Any other day, twenty or thirty minutes would be plenty of time to concentrate on an issue, come to a resolution, and consider it closed. He didn't brood over matters, never had. He'd learned at an early age that worrying didn't get the problem solved. He'd pray first and leave fretting as a second option. Challenges and attack after attack on DMI had caused him to grow spiritually. Having faith worked for him to the point where he didn't have to go to the second option, at least not until recently.

He believed wholeheartedly that God was fair, which was why he couldn't blame Him for the current Mitchell family predicament. Dave had to bear the full weight of the family problems on his shoulders. He wondered who could have known that one moment of weakness would sow seeds of discord too great for him to manage well over three years later. Even when he was at peace, those around him weren't, which chipped away at him. He desperately needed the Lord to give him strength and guidance before his second option overpowered his prayers.

Chapter 41

Madeline was bringing the Southern Bible Institute meeting to a close. "We've covered the training plan and the timing, and we'll have to take your cost proposal under advisement."

"I hope we can work the numbers and close this deal," Mr. Cooper said.

"If you're willing to accept our original price, we can sign this today," Frank said, sliding his pen to Mr. Cooper.

The moment was frozen. No one responded. Then laughter erupted.

"I look forward to hearing from you . . . hopefully, with something I can work with," Mr. Cooper said. "I have to tell you," he said turning to Madeline, "the divorce between you and Dave threw us for a loop."

"Things happen," was the most Madeline could offer. Mr. Cooper didn't need to know more. Details weren't relevant to him. He cared only about the stability of the company that was taking his money. She understood his perspective and took no offense.

"I can't tell you how pleased we are to have you and Dave still working together." Madeline smiled but didn't interrupt.

"Your reputation as two powerful leaders is what prompted our decision to go with DMI initially."

"And we're grateful for your faith in us."

"Please give Dave my regards. Hate that I missed him."

"I'll be sure to let him know," Madeline said, seeing the client out.

For a brief while, she'd been able to successfully block out Dave and Sherry's medical ordeal. She was hoping for the best, but it didn't change her personal feelings about Sherry. Not wanting someone to live was very different than not wanting them to live in her house with her husband. A pill of such magnitude was still too bitter for her to swallow.

Frank remained in Dave's office after the client left. "Whew! Coop was a tough old bird."

"I know. He didn't want to budge on his price cap of two fifty. If Dave had been here, he would have pushed him closer to our original price of four hundred thousand," Madeline stated.

"Dave, Dave, Dave," Frank said, getting up to close the door.

"What did you do that for?" Madeline asked.

"I figured we could wrap up the meeting," he said, reclaiming his seat at the table and gesturing for her to sit too.

"There's not much to talk about. We presented the proposal. Mr. Cooper agreed to every component except the cost, which means Dave will have to follow up in order to close the deal." He kept gesturing. So, she decided to sit. "For two people filling in for Dave at the last minute, I think we did pretty well."

"Face it. The two of us are always covering for Dave," Frank said.

Madeline had given her support to Dave freely. She hadn't thought of the meeting as a burden. "I do my job, and it just so happens that I'm pretty good at this. If Dave benefits from my hard work, so be it."

"You're something else, Madeline Mitchell."

"If you say so," she said, flashing a partial grin at him, almost a smirk.

"I definitely do say so. My brother isn't smart enough to know what a gem he let get away. Look, don't get me wrong. I'm not bad mouthing his new wife. But the reality is that she's no Madeline. I tell Dave that every chance I get."

"I'm sure it's not something he wants to hear," Madeline said, a bit embarrassed by the flattery.

"Am I your type?"

"Excuse me?" she asked, shifting her body in the seat.

"If circumstances had been different and you hadn't married Dave, would I have been someone you would have been interested in?"

"No," she said, emphatically staring him down.

Madeline genuinely cared for Frank. He was Dave's only brother and, until recent years, his loyal friend and colleague. They were both grateful to Frank for his sizable investment in DMI from day one. There was a time when Frank would have done just about anything for his brother and DMI. Dave's inability to shield DMI from his personal mistakes had shattered the brothers' relationship, but there were bridges Madeline wasn't willing to cross, not for revenge, not out of contempt, and not in the pursuit of happiness. Even though she was no longer living with Dave, she had to live with her conscience. Her heart and emotions didn't get a vote. Common decency had to rule.

"Is it something I said?" he asked, his face stamped with a grin, which let her know he might not be serious. Who could be sure with him? Although, the Frank she knew was usually very direct. He made his words count, with few spoken that he didn't mean wholeheartedly.

"Frank, you will always be a special brother-in-law to me and an uncle to my children. Whether I'm married to Dave or not won't change our bond as far as I'm concerned. But the truth is my heart was built to love only one Mitchell man."

"Need I remind you that he's married to another woman?" Frank responded.

There was no need for a reminder. The sobering fact ate at her soul daily. "That doesn't affect how I feel."

"Are you telling me you're still in love with a man who's married to another woman?"

"I'm not telling you anything," she said, slightly agitated at the question. He made it sound like she was chasing after a married man. What irony. How could she be the wife, lose her husband to the mistress, and then become the other woman because her feelings hadn't died with the betrayal and the ultimate divorce? She wasn't having this conversation with Frank. Her feelings weren't for public scrutiny. "Dave was my husband, and now he isn't—end of story."

Instead of shutting the conversation down, Frank pulled himself closer to the table and leaned on his elbows. "Why did you let Sherry have him? You could easily have beaten her out for him. There's no competition in that race." He chuckled.

She didn't respond to Frank, but his words were resonating. Why hadn't she expressed her true feelings to Dave? Maybe it was only her pride that had won. Maybe it was her anger. Perhaps it was hurt that had kept her mouth shut when it came to telling Dave she still loved him before the divorce. Her feelings were irrelevant now. He was married, with a baby on the way. To express any inkling of love for him now would render her the other woman, a title she despised.

"Well, sis, good luck with waiting around for a man that's not coming back."

Dave opened the door unexpectedly, causing Madeline to cut off the conversation abruptly. She was certain Dave hadn't heard any of the discussion. *Thank goodness.* She hoped he wouldn't pick up on the awkwardness between her and Frank. Silence cleansed the room. She'd leave it at that and get back to work.

Chapter 42

When Dave walked into his office, he wasn't prepared to see Madeline and Frank. "What did I interrupt?" he asked, figuring the meeting with the Southern Bible Institute must have been a doozy if they were lingering this long afterward.

"Not much," Madeline said immediately.

Frank said nothing.

"How are Sherry and the baby?" Madeline asked which actually rejuvenated Dave. He understood how tough it was for Madeline to accept Sherry as the new Mrs. Mitchell, and appreciated her concern.

"She's not doing as well as I'd like."

"But is the baby okay?" Madeline asked with a strong hint of compassion.

"Yes, the baby is doing fine, so long as Sherry keeps her stress level down."

"Then I guess it's good for her to be on bed rest in the hospital," Madeline said.

Dave agreed, but Sherry didn't. She wanted to come home. He was pretty certain that once Madeline found out how his wife's trip home was going to cost Andre, she wasn't going to be as genuinely concerned about Sherry and the baby. Dave kicked the swirling conflicts from his mind and jumped into the one area that usually served as an effective distraction, DMI business.

"We have another meeting with the Evangelical Group in twenty minutes," Dave said.

"You cut it close," Frank said, perking up. Dave had noticed how unusually quiet his brother was but hadn't read anything specific into it.

"I got tied up at the hospital, but I'm here now and ready to go."

His secretary popped in. "Mr. Mitchell, the Evangelical Group just called. They had a flight delay and will have to reschedule."

Dave was glad. Normally, he wasn't excited about losing or deferring business opportunities, but today's events had forced him to deviate from his routine. "Let me know when you have a new date."

"Let my secretary know too so she can work it into my schedule," Madeline added.

Frank didn't chime in. He seemed overly disengaged. Dave had too much on his mind to guess what was irking his brother. Lately, there was always something.

"I didn't ask how the meeting went with the Southern Bible Institute. Cooper can be challenging," Dave observed.

Frank finally spoke up. "You can say that again."

"Actually, I thought the meeting went well. As a matter of fact, he told me to tell you hello," Madeline said.

"Your wife saved you on this one," Frank said, pointing to Madeline.

"Will you stop?" she told him.

"Well, I'm telling the truth. You *are* his wife, and you *did* save him. Coop told us that if you and Dave weren't working together, they would have pulled out. Am I telling the truth?" Frank asked, rearing back in his seat and grinning at Madeline.

She appeared to shake his comment off. Dave jumped in to rescue her from Frank's weird mood.

"Madeline, do you have a few minutes? I need to speak with you."

"Sure," she said without opposition.

"I guess that's my cue to get out. Good. I'm out of here. I have to go and put out a few fires," Frank said, chuckling. "See you later, Madeline."

She waved as he left.

"Excuse me, Mr. Mitchell, but your wife is on the line again," his secretary said over the intercom, her voice dropping on the word *wife*.

"Please, transfer the call in here," Dave said as Madeline fidgeted in her seat. He imagined she was thinking something like *not again*. Their conversation had ended abruptly when the hospital called earlier in the afternoon. Dave answered the phone as soon as it rang.

"Dave, are you busy?" Sherry asked.

He was always busy at DMI. Today wasn't an exception. "Yes, I am."

"Oh," she said, sounding sad. "Okay."

He was busy, but her well-being was a priority. He hadn't left her in the best shape. "Is this an emergency?"

"No, not really."

He glanced at Madeline, who was pretending not to be listening. No way was he going to tell her Madeline was in his office. Sherry would insist on talking this very minute, and the anxiety wasn't good for her, for the baby, or for him. He kept the small detail out of the conversation. "Then let me call you in about an hour."

"Okay, but don't forget."

"I won't."

"I love you," she told him.

Dave gave another quick glance at Madeline, who had her back to him. "Relax, and I'll call you soon." He was pleased to end the call smoothly. Good for him, because he suspected a storm was on its way.

"Everything okay with Sherry?" Madeline asked.

"She's fine, just lonely. She's not doing well with the bed rest."

Madeline didn't seem interested once he told her that Sherry and the baby were well. The concern she'd shown thus far was more than he could have asked for. Madeline was tough, no doubt. But to those who knew her as well as he did, she was a good-hearted person who on occasion let her passion overtake her logic. In the end her compassion and loyalty were going to show up. Those were a few of the many qualities he loved about her when they got engaged, and it hadn't changed. She wasn't his wife, but Madeline would always be more than a friend. He was banking on their bond getting them through what was sure to be an uncomfortable discussion. He delayed the inevitable as long as possible. Madeline had to be told.

"Sherry has to stay away from stress."

"Good for her," Madeline said, crossing her legs and stroking her nails. "The hospital should do the trick."

"Not exactly. She wants to spend the remaining pregnancy at home."

"And?"

"And I can't turn her down."

Madeline stopped messing with her nails and stared daggers at him.

"Which we both know means Andre can't stay with me when Sherry comes home."

"What!" she yelled so loudly that he was sure Sharon heard her out in the hallway. Dave rushed to the door and closed it. This was just the beginning. "You can't kick him out," she said, leaping to her feet and charging toward him. "Not now, not when he's showing real signs of progress. You can't be serious."

Dave took a few steps away from Madeline. "It's not what I want, but there's no other option. If Sherry wasn't pregnant, this would be a different conversation."

"Don't give me your lame excuse, Dave. You're a grown man. You always have another option," she said, folding her arms and maintaining direct eye contact with him. "Sherry can keep her behind in the hospital, with a team of doctors at her beck and call. Why does she have to go home?" Madeline wasn't giving him a chance to answer that question. Her venting wasn't close to being finished. "There's nobody at the estate to hold her hand during the day. We all know you live most of your life here. If she needs a babysitter, let her stay at the h-o-s-p-i-t-a-l," she said, stretching her neck toward him.

It wasn't that he couldn't argue with her. He chose not to. The frustration was justified. "If I had another option, I would gladly exercise it. But I have to take care of my wife."

"And who's going to take care of your children?" she said, poking her finger in his chest. "Tell me that, Dave. They were here before Miss Sherry came on the scene." Madeline placed both hands at her side. "Oh, I get what's happening here. Sherry whined and cried, probably threw a temper tantrum and begged for your attention. Why did she think you were going to change your world and spend time with her? Silly little woman," Madeline said, cackling. "I was with you a lot of years. I know you. Sherry's not going to get what she wants, because it doesn't exist."

"What doesn't exist?"

"Your ability to love anyone more than you love religion and this place."

"Come on, Madeline. That's not fair."

"Oh, it's more than fair. It's true, but I get it. I understand how Sherry feels. She is in love with you and is hoping to live out some fairy tale."

"She's not naive when it comes to our marriage."

"Sure she is," Madeline said, letting her gaze fall for the first time since she'd begun whaling on him. "Just like I was. We're both guilty of the same naive dream, that loving you is enough to overlook your true priorities."

"Madeline," he said, reaching for her hand, "what can I say to make this better?"

"You can say that Andre matters, that for once, the needs of our children will take priority. You can tell me that he's going to stay with you."

He pursed his lips, and the words weren't necessary. She jerked her hand from his.

"What was I thinking, Dave? You haven't changed a bit," she said, snatching her portfolio from the table and heading to the door. "What about Andre?"

"He decided to try out a chess class at the school. I think it will be best if you pick him up after school and take him home with you. I'll bring his belongings over later," Dave said.

"Absolutely not," she hurled at him. "I will not do your dirty work, you coward. There is no way on earth I'm going to crush his feelings. That's your job, and you're good at it," she said, turning away from the door and taking a few steps in his direction. "You know, I honestly feel sorry for Sherry. No, even better, I pity her. She sure didn't win the grand prize, did she?"

"What happened to you? All this anger, it's not you," Dave said.

"What do you think happened to me?"

"Don't you have any compassion for my unborn child, regardless of who its mother is? Where is the loving mother that I knew?"

"You left her behind, remember? And, yes, I do have concern for the baby."

"I can't tell."

"Well, I said I did. That will have to do. Look, I don't want to argue with you, and I do understand that you're worried about your baby and its mother. Honestly, I'm worried about the innocent baby too, and I want it to be healthy. But that doesn't mean my children can be shoved aside to make Sherry and her family happy. Why do my children always have to come second, third, fourth, and fifth?" she said, counting off fingers in the air. It's not fair to me or to them, Dave, and you know it."

No words were going to appease Madeline. He accepted her tongue-lashing and was grateful that she hadn't dished more at him. As far as Dave was concerned, the meeting went pretty well, considering. Telling Andre would be a different story. He braced for wave number two of the Mitchell family tsunami.

Chapter 43

Dave's soul was unaccustomed to worrying. Walking in peace and purpose had consistently been his calling card. Standing alone in his office, peace was nowhere to be found. Dave didn't know what to do. He yearned for guidance and direction like never before. He understood that regardless of which path he took, somebody was going to be disappointed. That was one of the by-products of his transgression. God had forgiven him without question, but he hadn't escaped the consequences. Watching each one of the Mitchell family members fall apart and be in constant turmoil was nearly unbearable, but fate was inescapable. He tried praying but still couldn't set the matter aside. Madeline, Sherry, and Andre weren't going away, none of them. Each wanted their due share of his attention.

He was twiddling with a key on his desk when Frank knocked. The door was open.

"You busy?" Frank asked.

"No. Come on in," Dave answered, beckoning him with a nod, sort of relieved to see a friendly face, even if it was that of someone who had issues with him. "What's up?"

"I came to check on you," Frank said, sitting.

"What made you do that?"

"Look, we might not be on the same page these days about the business," Frank said, leaning forward. "But you are my brother."

Dave nodded, glad to be engaged in a calm discussion for a change. It was a welcomed surprise.

Frank continued. "You were distracted earlier, more than I've ever seen you. That's not you. So I figured something big is going on. I came to see if you needed my help getting out of some jam you've most likely created," he said, chuckling.

Dave wasn't in a funny mood, but seeing Frank loosen up gave him cause to release the pressure too. He laughed a little. "Thanks, man. I could use a friend."

"So what did you get yourself into?"

Dave clasped his hands behind his head. "Man, I have a catastrophe on my hands. Sherry is in the hospital, on bed rest, but she wants to come home."

"And what's the problem?"

"Andre is staying with me."

"I remember you were thinking about that after Madeline put some pressure on you," Frank noted.

"Right. Initially, I was reluctant, but you know how Madeline can be. She wasn't taking no for an answer."

Frank was humored. "That's a fight you don't want."

"Actually, I'm glad she made the suggestion. Andre has made a miraculous change. Living with me is working for him, but the problem is that Andre and Sherry don't get along. They can't live in the same house."

Frank leaned back, and his eyes widened. "I see," he said, letting his head bob a bit. "You are in a jam."

"Tell me about it. Sherry won't back down, and Madeline won't, either. I have to figure this out and quick. Otherwise, this mess is going to get out of hand."

"I know you're Superman, but handling two families is not easy for any man, not even you," Frank said. "Have you thought about military school? One of my old army buddies runs a school in Colorado. It's also known for having strong academics."

"I wouldn't want to send him away."

"You may not have a choice. Send him to a school where he's going to get a good education and a swift kick if he needs it."

"I don't know, Frank."

"Well, you better come up with another solution quickly if you don't want two angry women storming this place and beating you to a pulp," Frank said, rising from his seat and tapping on the corner of the desk a couple of times. "If you change your mind, the school is called Gateway Preparatory Institute. It's right outside of Denver." He walked out, chuckling.

Dave remembered he had to call Sherry. He didn't want to break his promise to call back and have her become more upset. He dialed the number to the hospital and got her on the phone.

"I hope you're feeling stronger and more relaxed," he told her.

"I was just about to call you. I have great news. The doctor is willing to release me as early as tomorrow," she said, bubbling over. He was thrilled to hear the excitement in her voice but was disheartened at the notion of her coming home too soon. "Isn't that great news?"

What should he say? Should he agree that the news was good? That would be a lie. Should he remind her about the situation with Andre? That would be stressful for her. Yet another dilemma he couldn't readily resolve. Those were mounting. He decided to concentrate on the positive.

"Sherry, I can't tell you how pleased I am to hear you so happy. It does my heart good."

"I know. The thought of coming home and sleeping next to you every night always makes me happy. I can't wait for tomorrow. I wish he'd said I could come home today, but tomorrow will have to do."

She sounded giddy, and he didn't want to crush her spirit. He'd tread lightly but speak honestly.

"I'm glad you're coming home too," he said and paused. The next line was going to hurt her, but like a shot in the doctor's office, the pain would be brief. "It just can't be tomorrow. It's too soon."

"Dave, don't do this. I'm coming home regardless of what you say. That's my home too."

"Yes, it is, but I have to make arrangements for Andre."

"Why is he still there?"

Dave was at a complete loss for words. He fumbled with the next line. "Don't get worked up. I will take care of Andre."

"What about taking care of me? Who's going to make arrangements for me? I'm carrying your child, for goodness' sake. Doesn't that earn me any special consideration from you?"

He hated being put in a compromising position. "I will take care of this, just not by tomorrow."

"Then when can I come home? What's going to be convenient for you?" she snapped at him. Sherry didn't usually talk to him like she was now, but he understood her frustration.

"Next week is the earliest for me."

"You want me to stay in the hospital until next week? That's awful."

"Sherry, you have to give me time to make arrangements for my son. This isn't easy for me, either, you know. I can't kick him out on the street. If he can't stay with me, and he can't stay with his mother, then I'm going to have to look long and hard to find a place for him. It will take a few weeks." This time his tone was firm and unyielding.

He heard sniffles coming from Sherry. "I'm sorry," she sighed. "I didn't think about how this was affecting you too. I love you, and I'm sorry this is happening." He heard more sniffles. "I might not like it, but I'm willing to stay here until next week so you can find a place for Andre."

Her support calmed him. It was what Dave needed to hear. He ended the call, feeling hopeful. Frank's suggestion had lingered in his mind. He called in his secretary.

"Frank mentioned a prep school in Colorado. Can you do me a favor and get the contact information from him right away?"

"Absolutely, sir," she said, rushing out.

Dave was relieved that progress was under way. He hadn't solved the problem completely, but at least there was a plan in place. He'd work quickly to help his son and his wife through this quagmire. Admittedly, neither was making it easy for him, but it didn't lessen his obligation to both. He didn't take either lightly and hoped for the best.

Chapter 44

Dave paced in his office, wondering, planning, and worrying. He was tired of fighting with Frank, Madeline, and Sherry. They'd worn him out. *Forget about the adults for a second,* he thought. He had to decide on what was best for Andre.

His secretary came in and found Dave standing idle, a rare condition for him.

"Did you get the information?" he asked, relatively chipper.

"Yes, I did," she said, handing him a sheet of paper, which he immediately began to read.

"Do you need anything else?"

"No, not now. Thanks," he said, too engrossed in the details on the paper to look her way. He scanned the page for the phone number. He collected his thoughts en route to his desk, and that was the only preparation needed. He dialed the phone rapidly and heard ringing.

"Good afternoon. This is Gateway Preparatory Institute," a pleasant voice on the other end announced.

Dave was going to cut past the intros and get to the top guy, Frank's old military buddy. "My name is Dave Mitchell. Can I speak with the school's founder please?"

"He fell ill several years ago and officially retired last year. Can I help you?"

Help was exactly what Dave needed from somebody at the school. He was hopeful but was not certain this was the answer. Constant fighting and strong opposition had ripped his stash of faith to shreds. Desperation wanted to creep in, but he managed to hang on to a sliver of faith that this would work out.

"Yes, I'm hoping you can help. My son is having a few disciplinary challenges at school, and I heard that Gateway Prep might be the ideal place for him to attend school."

"How old is your son?"

"Thirteen with a birthday coming up very soon." "What grade is he in?"

"Eighth. Why? Is that too young?" Dave asked.

"No, we start as early as age five and keep students until eighteen."

That was a long stretch, Dave thought. Several weeks ago, he couldn't have understood a parent handing their kid off to boarding school for a single year, let alone from the age of five to the age of eighteen. The notion sounded excessive. That was how Dave felt last week, before his personal circumstances forced him to revise his judgmental perspective and look with understanding upon parents in the same predicament as he was. He had to repent.

"In some extreme cases, we can keep the child until age twenty-one with court intervention."

"Seems like a long time to be away at school."

"Sometimes it's warranted. We find that after students gets acclimated, they become very attached to the school. Believe it or not, there are cases where they don't want to leave."

Dave didn't think Andre would be in such a group. It was going to be difficult enough convincing him to go. Having him stay longer than required was not likely for his son.

"If I'm interested, what are the next steps?"

"We'd mail you an application form. We'd ask for school records and have you sign a release so we can speak directly with his current school."

Dave tensed. "What if he's had problems at his school? Would he most likely be disqualified?"

"Mr. Mitchell, we have many students here who came in with challenges. Our goal is to address those issues in a safe and structured environment. Each student is given personal care, and the program is tailored to their specific needs. So, we're prepared for him to come in with problems. When he leaves, your son should be a different person."

"Sounds like a wonderful program." Dave loved what he was hearing. Thank goodness for Frank's suggestion. He was reminded that an answer to a prayer could come from the least likely source. God was creative, and Dave had to be flexible. As he continued the conversation, his fretting dissipated as his sense of hope increased.

"I can mail a packet to you this week. You'll have plenty of time before the next school year begins."

"Oh, I was hoping to get him in much sooner, like in the next week or two."

"Wow. That soon? You do know that we're in the middle of our second semester, which goes from January to June."

"Yes, but unfortunately, we have a situation in the family that is forcing us to find a school for Andre right away. Time is of the essence. Is it possible to expedite the application process?"

"I don't see why not. I can fax the forms to you. If you can complete those in the next couple of days, we can get you out here as early as next week to do the parent walk-through."

"No problem. When we finish the call, I'll transfer you to my secretary. She'll give you the fax number and any other general information you need."

"One other request . . ."

"Name it," Dave responded eagerly.

"Please sign the release form for us to speak with your son's current school and get it to me by early tomorrow morning."

"You'll have it in your office tomorrow morning." Dave spoke with confidence, but it was wishful thinking to a large degree. His signature was only one of the two required. Getting Madeline to sign was going to be a chore. A miracle was his only hope.

Chapter 45

Delaying the inevitable wasn't his style. Dave was ready to attack the issue head-on. He proceeded to Madeline's office, mentally preparing for the backlash she was certain to provide.

Her door was open. She was at her desk, writing.

"Excuse me, Madeline. Do you have a few minutes?"

"Yes," she answered without lifting her gaze from the paper.

He closed the door, which caused her to look up.

"What's going on?" she asked.

"We have to talk."

"About what?" she asked, showing signs of distress or curiosity. He couldn't tell which.

"About Andre."

"What about Andre?" she asked in a stronger tone.

"Andre can't stay with me, and he can't stay with you."

"Dave, I don't want to talk about this anymore. We've beaten this topic to death. Let's move on."

"Wait. Please hear me out. I have an idea. Well, actually it's Frank's idea, but I think it could work for us."

"Frank?" she said, grimacing. "I have to hear this one." She pushed the palms of her hands against the desk.

"He told me about a preparatory school in Colorado. I called them up, and the program sounds like one we might be interested in exploring."

"Are you talking about sending Andre away to a boarding school?"

Dave's head bobbed. "Yeah, sort of. From what I understand, the school places a strong emphasis on education and discipline. It's exactly what Andre needs."

"Are you kidding me? Andre doesn't need a parole officer. He needs good old-fashioned love and support. You know, the basics, which should come from his parents."

"Madeline, we don't have any other ideas."

"You're pathetic. You know that? You're ready to ship him off to the first school that will take him off your hands." She shifted her gaze up to the ceiling. "I'm sure this isn't what Jonathan had in mind for his son."

"That's not fair."

Madeline was a lioness. She was a master at grabbing her foes by the neck and strangling the hope out of them if she felt threatened. "Might not be fair, but it's the truth," she said, leaning forward with a riveting glare. "Since you love the truth so much, chew on those words."

"I'm not here to fight with you."

"You never are. Quit with the crap and the 'I'm the victim' attitude. You created this mess, and now the rest of us have to deal with the fallout. I'm tired of cleaning up your mess, Dave. You know this boy needs to be with you. Look how well he's doing with you."

"I don't deny his progress."

"But you want to send him away because your woman threw a temper tantrum. So our son has to pay the price for Sherry's happiness."

He could tell Madeline that she wasn't being fair, but why bother?

"How long will my children pay for your shenanigans and Sherry's whims? Hmm?" she uttered. "How long?"

"I can only keep praying for a peaceful resolution."

"Stop," Madeline cried out. "Just stop. I don't want to hear your canned religious speech. The only one in this family who's benefiting from your so-called faith is Dave Mitchell, plain and simple. I'm thirty-eight years old. I'm a long ways from the silly, young twenty-three-year- old you married. You can't fill my head with your religious mumbo jumbo anymore. That's Sherry's role now, not mine." She lowered her voice. "Whatever relationship I could have had with God, your actions ruined. Why should I, or anyone else, for that matter, commit every breath I have to faith when it hasn't helped you a bit? Look around, Dave. Your life is a mess. You've failed me, your children, and probably God too."

Arguing wasn't going to change Madeline's mind. Plus, she was right in some ways. Dave didn't feel guilt about the past, but he did regret being a poor example. His actions could easily discourage someone's interest in marriage. He'd failed but thank goodness for redemption. It was his lifeline and saving grace. Madeline might not agree, but God was still God, not just with the good outcomes, but in all things.

Dave couldn't explain why Andre's life had taken such a troubled path, but there was a purpose for his son. Dave would never give up on him, but selfishly keeping him in Detroit when there was a better place for him wasn't the answer. He had to convince Madeline.

"You can't keep Andre, and I can't, either. He's too much for the nannies to handle, and there is no one else we trust to take care of him. I believe we have to consider this program. We have to do this."

Madeline let her gaze roll around. Finally she said, "Give me the name of the place and a number. I want to do my own investigation."

Dave perked up, seeing a sign of Madeline acquiescing. "If you'd like, we can visit the campus next week."

"Okay," she said reluctantly. He'd take it.

"Good. I'll have Sharon make the arrangements. Oh, I almost forgot. We have to sign a release form today. The school wants to call Cedarbrook Academy to get feedback on Andre."

"Oh, boy, that's not going to be good," she said.

"No, it's okay. They assured me there are plenty of students who come in with challenges and leave as new people."

Madeline snickered. "Sounds too good to be true. And you said Frank suggested this place?"

Dave nodded.

"Heaven help us," Madeline sighed.

Chapter 46

Sherry wasn't thrilled about spending another weekend in the hospital. It was already Thursday, and there weren't any plans for her to go home yet. With any luck, Andre would soon be away at the school Dave had told her about, and she'd be home. She pressed the TV remote, searching for a show to watch until Dave arrived. He was on his way earlier, when they'd spoken. He should be arriving any minute. She stopped on one of the game-show channels and fell asleep.

"Are you asleep?" she heard someone say faintly. Her eyelids opened when she felt her hand being gently caressed. "Sherry, did I wake you?"

"I'm glad to see you," she said, groggy. She gripped Dave's hand in return.

"I intended to get here earlier but got tied up with Madeline and the school."

Sherry was eager to find out what progress Dave had made with Andre. The sooner the process was over, the faster she could get home. "How's the application for Andre coming along?"

"Almost finished." He nodded, caressing her hand some more. "As a matter of fact, that's why I'm here."

Sherry sat up, excited to hear the good news but careful not to make Dave feel badly, especially when her joy was at his son's expense. She had to be sensitive and support her husband. "Was he accepted?"

"Not yet, but it's looking good. Madeline and I have completed the application and our individual interviews. With a little favor, Andre is in."

"How soon would he start?" she said, concentrating hard on concealing her joy.

"Maybe by the end of this week, but definitely by next week."

"That soon?"

Containing her excitement was becoming more difficult. How could she not be excited at the idea of Andre getting out of her house? Deep inside, she wished her relationship was better with him as well as with her husband's other children. There wasn't much she could do if Madeline was coaching the kids to hate her. She decided to concentrate on pleasant thoughts. Soon she and the baby would be at home with Dave.

"The school understands how important this is to our family. They've done an excellent job of expediting the process. There's one step left. A site visit," he said. "I have a late flight booked for this evening. I'm going to stay overnight and be at the school bright and early tomorrow. If all goes well, Andre could be approved for admission tomorrow." He patted her hand. "Madeline is going too. They want both parents to attend the site visit. We figured it was easier and faster to go together."

"You and Madeline are constantly making plans together."

Dave pulled his hand back. "You don't have to worry about me and Madeline."

Sherry wasn't absolutely certain that was true. She was quite aware of what could happen when two people were alone together and felt alarmed. "Do you have to stay overnight? Can't you fly in the morning?"

"We have a nine o'clock appointment. We have to fly out tonight," he said, tracing his index finger down the side of her face. "But I don't want you to worry about a thing. We'll fly in, take care of business, and be back for dinner tomorrow. How's that sound?"

She mustered a smile, although it was a lie. She felt awful but was not sure if it was from worrying about the baby or about Madeline being with Dave. She didn't want to lose her husband or the baby. Worry and jealousy felt identical.

The flight was uneventful. Madeline took it as a positive sign that maybe their family chaos was turning around. As they were being driven from the airport to the school, Dave sat close to one door and Madeline was on the other side, with a considerable amount of space between them.

"I guess we're almost there," Madeline said.

Dave nodded, peering out the window. The car slowly maneuvered down a long road lined with trees.

"We're actually going to do this to Andre."

Dave turned toward her. "Not to him, for him," he said, patting her hand and then clutching it. "We're not bad parents. This is best for our son."

She looked away, not feeling like a model parent. As far as she was concerned, Andre was being tossed to the wolves. "I just don't want him to feel abandoned. He's a good boy with a few challenges that arose through no fault of his own."

"You know it and I know it, but unless we help him get a grip on his anger, one day he's going to be a grown man and society might not be as lenient with him."

She couldn't refute what Dave was saying. That was what she'd do: concentrate on Andre's future and not his present state. She gripped Dave's hand in return. No words were spoken. There was no need. Their history together wasn't easily erased. Having Dave there with her was the only way this trip could work. She couldn't bear making this decision alone.

Thank goodness her children had a father. He didn't always act right toward them, but his limitations had to be tolerated. Had Madeline known two years ago what she knew now, she might not have decided in favor of divorce so easily. She gave Dave one last glance and then shifted her gaze while letting his hand go. Regrets were few in her life, and it was becoming clearer that letting Dave go couldn't be on the list. It just couldn't be; otherwise, working with him on a daily basis and watching him rush home to another family would be debilitating. Madeline didn't dare take a sip from that bitter cup. She'd rather stay indifferent. It was easier to get through the days that way, as she'd proven for the past year.

The ride wasn't long. Madeline took in the view as the limousine passed under an archway labeled GATE-WAY PREPARATORY INSTITUTE. "This is a pretty nice-looking campus."

"It reminds you of a college campus."

"It does, and I didn't think the school would be this nice." Her hope was stirred. "At least there isn't any barbed wire."

"Madeline, Gateway Prep is not a detention center."

"Humph. Good luck convincing Andre."

"Once he gets here, settles in, and makes a few friends, I'm sure Andre will do well. Who knows? Maybe he'll be glad to be away from us."

"I highly doubt it," Madeline said. Their family was high-strung, but Andre was a member of the family. She didn't foolishly believe this was a move he would endorse. He was going to protest. That much she already knew. Dave should too.

The limousine finally reached the front of the administration building.

"Are you ready?" he asked her.

"As ready as I'll ever be."

Chapter 47

Andre didn't mind staying at his mother's house one night while his parents were out of town. He could deal with the rug rats for a day, but that was about it. He was older now, an official teenager. It was lame hanging around his kid brothers and sister. They were always in his stuff. Nobody wanted to respect his room. He didn't understand why his parents didn't make the other kids leave him alone. *Ugh.* Sometimes he wanted to scream at the top of his lungs to make them get away.

For now, he sat on his bed, reading a comic book and glancing at his watch every five minutes. His father was supposed to pick him up at 5:30 P.M. He couldn't wait. It was already 5:20. He had read the same page over three times, unable to concentrate. Now it was 5:22, then 5:25. He put the comic book down and stared at his watch as each second ticked by. Five twenty nine came, and his heart was pounding. Then it was 5:30, 5:32, and 5:35. He hurled his comic book across the room and fell back on the bed.

"Mommy's home," Don said, running past Andre's room.

Andre leaped off the bed and shot out of his room. He caught up with Don on the way down the stairs and bypassed him. He jumped from the third stair from the bottom to the floor below. There stood his father. Andre gave him a bear hug.

"Are you okay after jumping down from those stairs?" Madeline asked, rubbing his shoulder.

"Ah, it's nothing." He gave her a hug too. He was so excited. He was willing to hug everybody in the house, including his bothersome sister and brothers. "I'll grab my bag and be right down, Dad. You won't have to wait long for me," he said.

Andre was ready to charge up the stairs when his dad said, "We're coming up with you. We need to talk."

"Okay," he said, leading the way. They seemed very serious, which caused Andre to think about the past couple of days. He had worked hard not to get in trouble at school. He'd done his work and gotten good grades. He'd even avoided arguing and fighting with his pesky, annoying sister and whiny brothers. He'd been good. He couldn't imagine what his parents were going to say. It had better be good, was his only thought.

"Don and Sam, you stay down here," his mother said.

"Tamara too," his father added.

"But you just got here," Tamara told their father.

"I'll be back. Just give us some time to talk with your brother privately, missy."

"Okay."

Watching her whine and coo over their dad made Andre uncomfortable. He took two steps at a time to get up the stairs faster and to get his father away from Tamara. This was his chance to be with his parents, not hers. She got plenty of chances with them both, more than anybody.

He entered his room, and his parents followed. His father shut the door, and his mother sat on the bed, waving for him to sit next to her. She put her arms around him.

"Why are the two of you acting so weird? Did the school say that I did something wrong? Because that's not true," he said, getting loud.

His father sat next to him on the bed too. "We didn't get a bad report from the school."

Then they must have gotten bad news about him from home. "I didn't get into a fight with Sam, Don, or Tamara. You can ask them. Seriously, I didn't," he said, feeling nervous.

"No one said you did," his mother assured him.

"Then what is it?" He had to know now.

"We went to Colorado," his mother said.

"I already know that. You told me before you left where you were going."

"What you don't know is that we went to check on a college preparatory school for you," his father told him.

"College, for me? I'm only in the eighth grade. I have four years of high school before I have to think about college." His parents wouldn't look at him, which made Andre antsy. They were hiding something, and he couldn't stand it. "What's going on? Please tell me."

"We've decided that you should finish school in Colorado," his father blurted out.

"Colorado? How am I going to go to school there when we live in Michigan? Are we moving?"

His mother gave him a hug, but he pulled away from her.

"We're not moving. You are," his father told him.

"Why? I've been doing good. My grades are good. I haven't been in trouble in almost two weeks. I know how to stay out of trouble. I do."

His mother rubbed her hands on her thighs and sounded like she was sniffling.

"Son, you're doing well, and we want to keep it going," his father said.

"Then why send me away?"

"Because there's no other way to give you the help you need," his father told him.

"Tell him the truth, Dave."

"I am."

"The *whole* truth. He deserves to know."

"Know what?" Andre asked.

"You have to go to Colorado because you can't stay at your father's house any longer," his mom said.

"Why not, Dad?"

His father hesitated and then said, "Because Sherry is pregnant. She has to be very careful over the next couple of months. It's extremely important for Sherry to stay calm."

"So what? I won't bother her. I can stay in my room."

"Son, I wouldn't want you to stay in your room. That wouldn't be fair to you."

It would be better than going to Colorado, Andre thought.

"Having you and Sherry staying there together won't work. As much as I hate it, the two of you just don't get along."

"So you're picking her over me?" Andre said, feeling so mad, he could rip somebody's eyes out.

"No, I'm not, son. I'm picking your well-being over my desire to keep you here."

"Yeah, right. You're kicking me out for her," Andre said, jumping up. He wanted to break something, anything special that they'd given him. Why not? They were breaking him and didn't seem to care. They had never cared.

"Andre, you need to calm down," his father said, coming near him.

"Leave me alone, Dad. I mean it. Don't touch me."

"I won't touch you if you settle down."

"Don't tell me what to do. You're not my father."

"Yes, I am. I know you're hurt, and I understand."

"No, you don't," Andre said as tears and snot began flowing. He swiped the back of his hand across his nose. "I did what you told me to do. I did every single thing when I was at your house. I didn't say or do anything to Sherry. Why do I have to get kicked out?" he wailed. When his mother reached out to comfort him, he pushed her away.

"This isn't about Sherry." his father lied.

"Yes, it is!" Andre shouted, swiping his nose again. "I'm not going to Colorado. I'll just come back to my room here."

"You can't stay here, Andre," his mother said. "I'm at work most of the time. You and the other children are constantly fighting when I'm gone. This is not an ideal environment for you. I don't want you to go, but I have no choice. I have to agree with your father. Prep school is going to be the best place for you."

Andre stared at each parent, slowly and separately. As the anger swelled up in the pit of his stomach, he let the words fly. "I hate you. I hate you both, and one day you'll be sorry for sending me away."

"Andre, you don't mean what you're saying," his mother said, covering her mouth with her hand as tears streamed down her cheeks. "We love you."

He didn't care about her tears. She didn't care about his. From now on, he had to take care of himself. Every adult in his life had proven they couldn't. He was done with them.

"Can we leave tonight?" Andre asked.

"Why do you want to go so soon? You don't have to be there until next week," his mother said.

"I want to get out of here and away from all of you as soon as I can."

His burning anger began smoldering. He drew in a deep breath, vowing not to love again. Anybody or anything in his way was in trouble, and that was a promise.

Chapter 48

Saturday morning arrived with a fury. Madeline stood in the foyer, numb to her surroundings. Minutes were like hours. Andre descended the stairs with his duffel bag and backpack.

"Where's your trunk?" Madeline asked intent on not shedding tears.

"It's outside. I brought the trunk down early this morning, before anyone else got up."

"I guess you're eager to get going."

"I guess so," he murmured.

"You know it's not too late for me to throw on some clothes and fly out to Colorado with you."

"I don't want you to come."

He didn't want Dave to go, either, but his father had insisted. Against every motherly urge in her body, she'd agreed. It wasn't easy letting him go without being by his side when he walked into his new world, but Madeline didn't want to upset him further by tagging along. She was dying inside but didn't let her sorrow show. Madeline had to display strength in front of the children. They couldn't know about the crippling pain in her soul as her son prepared to walk out. Don came down the stairs, then Tamara.

"Did you come to see your brother off?" Madeline asked.

"Uh-huh," Don responded.

Tamara didn't give an answer, although she appeared to be upset. Madeline aimed to keep the farewell as lively as possible to avoid slipping into a total meltdown.

"Where's Sam?" she asked Don.

"Right here," her son said, coming from the family room.

"I didn't realize you were in there," she said, beckoning for him to come on in. "Anyway, your dad and the car service will be here any minute. This is your chance to say bye before Andre goes to school."

"Bye," Sam said, tucking his hands in his pockets and turning to leave.

"Stop right there!" Madeline shouted. "You can do better than that."

"What else do you want me to do?" Sam asked, as if he was irritated at the request.

Madeline was fully aware that the two oldest Mitchell boys didn't get along very well, but she was confident that maturity would erase their dislike. "I want you to wait in here with the rest of us, like a family should."

"What for?" Sam said snidely.

"Who cares if he doesn't want to say bye?" Andre said, slinging his backpack over his shoulder and grabbing the duffel bag by the handle. He dragged the bag past the family to the front door. "I'd rather wait outside by myself."

"Andre, come on. Sam didn't mean to hurt your feelings. Did you?" Madeline asked, staring at Sam.

Andre shrugged. "That's okay. I don't care. I just want to get out of here. Good riddance."

Don ran to Andre and gave him a hug. "Bye, Andre. I'm going to miss you."

Andre peered down at Don, who was almost a foot shorter. "See you later, squirt," Andre said in a kind voice, one that he hadn't used often in their house.

Tamara went to him, but Andre bolted out the door, closing it behind him. Sam left the room. Don was the only one who had had a successful good-bye. The rest of the family didn't seem to exist for Andre.

Shaving her flesh with a knife couldn't hurt any worse than the pain Madeline was wrestling with at this moment. She leaned against the door, the object separating a mother from her wounded son. They were close in proximity but miles apart in spirit. Don leaned against her, Tamara too, as defeat swooped in and claimed Madeline's waning motherly strength.

Chapter 49

Sherry lay across the bed. She couldn't find a comfortable position. She drew the pillow to her back for support and finally dozed off, taking a short nap. Dave was fast asleep. He had stayed up with her for a while earlier but finally fell asleep.

The coolness of the sheets startled Sherry into consciousness. She felt around her side of the bed, and it was wet.

"Dave, wake up," she said, shaking him. She didn't want to startle him, but he had to get up. "Dave, wake up."

He rustled a bit and then said, "I'm awake. What do you need?"

"My water broke. We have to get to the hospital right away." Sherry's bag was packed and waiting near the staircase.

"Oh, I'm up," Dave said, hopping from the bed. He wandered around aimlessly until she reminded him of what he had to do.

"I'm throwing on a pair of sweatpants. You're getting dressed and grabbing the suitcase by the stairs," she told him.

"It's June, won't sweatpants be hot?"

"Dave, it doesn't matter what I wear. I'm taking the sweatpants off soon as we get to the hospital. We just have to get out of here."

"Right," he said, moving in the direction of his closet.

Sherry was eager to get to the hospital and deliver a healthy baby. Memories of the death of her first one darted in and out of her mind. She was afraid of what could happen, but Sherry was going to think positively. Her baby was full term, which gave it four and a half months longer than the last baby had. By this hour tomorrow, she'd be a mother. She was overwhelmed by pain as the cramping sensation increased.

Dave rushed from the closet. "Are you ready to go?"

"Almost. Let me grab my sweatpants, and then we can go have this baby—our baby," she said with pride.

Madeline stood in the break room, repeatedly reading the announcement posted on the wall.

Dave and Sherry Mitchell announce the birth of their son, Joel. . . .

She glossed over the date, time, and weight to zoom in on the parents. Sherry had finally laid the golden egg. Madeline was relieved that the baby boy was healthy and alive. In truth, that was as far as her well wishes would go. To pretend to care beyond the basic level of common courtesy would be a farce. Since she didn't play games, there would be no pretending.

Several employees walked in and tiptoed past her. Awkward moments were bound to occur for the next couple of months, as the staff figured out how to celebrate their boss's new baby without teeing Madeline off. Perhaps she should put forth a statement to ease the tension among the workers. She considered the idea briefly and decided against it. The baby's birth wasn't her news to share or explain. She placed her hand on the announcement and lingered there until reality hit. Dave was officially the father of two sets of children and hadn't done well with the first one.

Madeline meandered from the room, sensing stares. She bumped into Frank, who was coming around the corner with a cup of coffee.

"Oops," she said, not sure if the run-in was her fault. She hadn't been paying attention.

He flicked drops of coffee from his shirt. "I'm glad it wasn't hot," he said, chuckling.

"I'm so sorry," she said, embarrassed.

"Don't worry about it. I have an extra shirt in my office."

"You keep extra clothes in your office?"

"Why not? You never know when somebody might plow into you in front of the break room."

Madeline smirked, although she wasn't in much of a jovial mood after reflecting on Dave's oldest son being tossed away in order for his youngest son to have the spotlight. Well, Sherry had won that round. Madeline was sure there were going to be plenty more rounds when it came to the children.

"Can I help?" Madeline asked.

"No problem. I got it," he said. "By the way, I've been meaning to ask you about Andre. It's been what, a couple of months since he went to the military school?" Frank said balancing the cup as coffee dripped down the side. He went into the break room. She did too.

"They call it a preparatory school." *Military* sounded too harsh for her.

"Preparatory, military . . . What's the difference?"

The difference was her ability to sleep without guilt. Believing he was in a casual college preparatory program versus being stuck in a rigid military camp was much easier. She remained silent.

"How's he doing in the preparatory school?" Frank said, dumping his remaining coffee into the sink.

"Let's grab a table in the corner." Madeline didn't want others in the company to hear about personal Mitchell business. She took a seat close to Frank and whispered, "Andre is adjusting, according to his counselor, but we haven't spoken to him directly. He hasn't taken our calls." She wanted to crumble.

"He'll come around. Give him time."

"I hope so," she said, sighing. Frank was more hopeful than she was. There were factors too huge to discount. "Andre was pretty upset when he left. The relationship between Dave and Andre was strained before the boy was shipped off. The two of them were reconnecting at the estate until Dave chose Sherry over him. At least that's the way Andre sees it. He blames Sherry for getting him kicked out."

"Not a good situation," Frank said rubbing the back of his neck.

"I'm just afraid Dave will lose Andre forever if he doesn't work hard at reaching him now, while Andre is young."

"The reality is that the separation will either force your son to change his mind-set and get right, or it will provide a lot of time for his anger to stew and turn into a full pot of well-seasoned contempt."

The words resonated with Madeline. "This is challenging."

"I'm not going to lie. Dave has a jacked-up situation going on between his two families."

"Tell me about it," Madeline said. "Did you read the announcement about Dave's new baby boy, named Joel?"

"I didn't see the announcement, but Dave called me around six this morning to tell me the news."

"I guess you would be on his list of people to call with his big news," she said, masking her feelings about Dave having another child.

"Must be a short list," Frank said. "I'm getting a fresh cup of coffee and heading to my office."

Madeline walked out with him, intent on rushing to her office, bolting the door shut, and hibernating until the mystique of baby Joel passed. She hoped it would be soon.

Chapter 50

Time was supposed to heal wounds, Madeline thought. Then why was her heart as wounded today as it had been four years ago, when Andre went away to school? She wasn't able to get him off her mind. The three-hour flight from Detroit to Denver had provided no relief. The nearly hour-long ride from the airport had added no clarity. As the driver pulled onto the campus, it felt like just yesterday they'd entered the gates for the first time. Each year they'd visited for family day, two parent-counselor conferences, and Andre's birthday. Madeline and Dave had made sure they attended every meeting. Nothing had taken priority over that. It was the only act of love they could show him while he was at Gateway Prep. This impromptu meeting requested by Andre's counselor was no exception.

"What do you think this meeting is about?" she asked Dave.

"I have no idea. I'm almost afraid to speculate," he said, staring out the window.

"His attitude toward us has gotten worse these past couple of years."

"I agree. He can't even visit on the holidays without there being problems. Look at what happened this past Thanksgiving." Dave winced. "He fractured Sam's nose."

"Don't remind me," she said as the sadness within her mounted. "Child protective services got involved." Madeline let her gaze plummet. "That was bad."

"We were fortunate to get him off with pure probation."

"I don't want to go through that again," Madeline said.

"Me, either, but what can we do? Andre is graduating and coming home in a few weeks."

Madeline's eyebrows arched. She didn't have the answer, but it didn't eliminate the issue.

The car reached the administration building and stopped. Before the driver could assist, Dave was out of the car, with the door open for Madeline. "After you," he said.

Madeline got out. She took in the moment, drawing on her inner strength. She drew in a long breath of air and released it slowly. Through those doors was the son she'd practically lost. "You think he'll be glad to see us?"

"I'm not sure," Dave responded.

They went to the office of Andre's counselor, who was waiting for them inside. Greetings were exchanged.

"I'm glad to see you again. It's always a pleasure to have you here, Mr. and Mrs. Mitchell," his counselor said.

Madeline didn't bother to correct him on the name. She was Mrs. Mitchell, but not the one attached to Dave legally. That one was at home with their boy, Joel. Madeline didn't want to think about them. Andre was the center of attention for a change.

"When can we see Andre?" she asked.

"He'll be ready in about a half hour. I wanted to speak with you first."

"Is there a problem?" Dave asked.

Madeline tensed. Andre was too close to finishing for there to be a setback.

"As you know, Andre has completed the high school curriculum."

"Yes, we're thrilled and looking forward to his graduation in a few weeks," Madeline said.

"This has been a long journey, but we're glad Andre has made it," Dave added.

"I certainly understand your enthusiasm."

Madeline didn't like the sound of the counselor's tone. "Are you trying to tell us something?"

"Actually I am."

"Then just say it," she said, getting annoyed, mostly out of fear of what might be coming next. She hoped Andre wasn't getting kicked out before graduation. That would be a nightmare.

"Ideally, this would be the moment for Andre to leave the school, but honestly, I don't believe he's ready," the counselor explained.

"He's not going to graduate?" Madeline asked, scooting to the edge of her seat.

"Oh no, he's definitely graduating."

"Whew," Madeline uttered.

"Then what are you saying?" Dave asked.

"Andre has made considerable progress academically since he's been with us here at Gateway Prep." Madeline stayed on the edge of her seat, her anxiety building. "Andre hasn't thrived socially, but he's been able to make a few friends. Overall, he's done well with us."

"So, what's the problem?" Madeline said, staring at the counselor. She wasn't interested in deciphering riddles about her son's welfare. She wanted direct answers. "Please tell us what's going on. Otherwise, I might explode."

"Then let me be direct."

"Please do," Dave added.

"In my professional assessment, Andre is not so-cially ready to leave the program. He—"

Madeline cut him off. "You just said he was mak-ing friends and doing okay socially. In the next breath you're saying he has a problem. Well, which is it?" Madeline asked, being very curt with him.

"Andre's anger is not under control yet. He battles with abandonment issues, and unfortunately, it mani-fests as anger. We feel it will be best for him to stay a bit longer to strengthen his anger management skills."

When the counselor said the word *anger,* he didn't have to convince Madeline any further. Andre had been mad at them for four years. Who carried a grudge for four solid years? There was much going on in her son's head, and she felt afraid as she thought about how disruptive he was going to be in the future unless his anger was controlled.

"How can we make an eighteen-year-old stay here if he doesn't want to?"

"Normally, we can't, but remember, Andre is on probation for the next three years. Since the court in Michigan approved his return to school here, I'm pretty sure we could get his stay with us extended if we all agree that it's best for him."

"What would he do for three more years here? Sit around and watch TV?" Madeline asked.

"Oh no, we have both a skilled trades and college curriculum. He would take classes toward a bachelor's degree," the counselor explained.

Madeline wasn't aware they offered programs be-yond high school. Her curiosity was at least piqued. "I'd like to hear more."

"Has he spoken to either of you about coming home?" the counselor asked.

"In one of our rare calls recently, he definitely talked about coming home," Madeline said.

"Not because he wants to be with our family. He just wants out of here," Dave commented. "But he might not have a choice with his problems."

"Rest assured; he's not the only Gateway Prep student with special circumstances. We have made exceptions in several cases and extended a student's enrollment. I believe Andre is an ideal candidate for the extension program."

"You have my permission," Dave said.

"I'm not sure," Madeline added, reluctant to keep Andre locked away. She was mad at Dave for committing to it so quickly. What did he care? He had a problem-free baby boy at home. She was certain Dave preferred him over his other children. Her disgust increased. Dave had managed to trade one son for another. She wanted to hate him for what they'd done to Andre, but she didn't have it in her to go that far. He'd get a tongue-lashing on the way to the airport, though. He deserved that much. They both did.

Chapter 51

Andre was drawing in his composition book when his roommate popped into the two-room unit. "Dre, your parents are here." Andre didn't move. "Did you hear me? Your folks are here."

"I hear you," he said, more cautious than excited. He'd stay put and let them come to him.

"I'll come back later. So you can hang out with your folks."

"You don't have to go."

"Really, it's cool," his roommate said on the way out.

Madeline came around the corner, leading the way. Dave was a few steps behind.

"Andre!" his mother cried out when he answered the door, rushing to him with her arms open wide. She hugged him, and Dave shook his hand.

"Graduation isn't for another two weeks. What are you doing here?" Andre mumbled.

His parents looked at each other, and nobody spoke. Andre shook his head, prepared for the usual.

"We came to talk with your counselor," his mother told him.

"About what?"

"We wanted to find out how you're doing," Dave answered.

"Why couldn't you ask me?"

"Because you don't take our calls, remember?" Madeline eagerly reminded him.

Andre didn't have a legitimate response. He wished there was one to shut them up. "So what did he say? Did he tell you how well I'm doing? I'm graduating with honors."

"That's wonderful news," Madeline said.

"He didn't tell us about the honors, but we're proud of you, son," Dave said, patting him on the back. "He told us you're progressing nicely. But—"

"But nothing," Andre interjected. "I'm doing great, and that's all there is to it."

"What are your plans, son?" Dave asked.

"Graduate, come home, and get a job, I guess."

"What about college?" his mother asked.

"Yeah, college is a possibility too."

"College is a requirement, son," Dave said.

"Maybe for some people, but it's too early for me to be sure what I want to do. Who knows? I might decide to go to art school. I just don't know right now and don't want to be pressured into doing what you want me to do."

Madeline rubbed his back briefly and said, "We're not here to pressure you."

"Then what do you want from me? I didn't ask you to come."

Who were they fooling? He wasn't stupid. He was becoming agitated speaking with them. He'd had this conversation during every visit, and Andre was sick of it.

"Son, we're here because the school asked us to come," Dave revealed.

"Who?" Andre asked very loudly.

Madeline shook her head. "It doesn't matter who."

"It does to me!" Andre shouted.

"Calm down," Dave told him.

"Calm down for what?" Andre snapped back. "I'm not upset." Not really, not compared to how mad he could get. That was the main reason why he didn't talk to them. It always ended in an argument, and he got blamed.

"Andre, the school believes you would be better off staying here longer," Madeline said softly.

"They don't know what they're talking about."

"We happen to agree with them," Dave said.

"Huh! Of course you would," Andre said in a snide way, and he knew it. "Agree as much as you want, but I'm not staying here. I'm leaving right after graduation."

"And where are you going, son?" Dave asked.

"I've already told you. I'm coming home. You've had me locked up in here for four years. I'm not staying one day longer," Andre declared.

"Actually, you don't get a choice, son. You have to stay," Dave told him.

"What are you talking about?" Andre asked, spewing anger and not trying remotely to conceal his feelings. He didn't have to. This was his place. They were the ones who had invaded his space unannounced. They deserved whatever treatment they got.

"Remember that you're on probation for assaulting Sam. The court can force you to stay here, and that's what we're going to ask them to do," Dave informed him.

Andre was fuming. Fracturing Sam's nose was an accident, but his parents didn't want to hear that. They cared only about their precious Sam. Thanks to all of them, he wasn't getting out. Reality sank in. "How long?"

"Another year or two, possibly until you turn twenty-one," Dave said.

"What? No way. You can't do that. Why do you hate me so much?" He fought off tears of rejection, vowing never to let them see him crushed. They'd never get the satisfaction.

"We love you, Andre," his mother said, attempting to console him. He shook her off. He didn't want her pretending to care when the truth was obvious.

"If you love me, then let me come home. I don't want to stay here anymore. I want to come home."

Dave shook his head. "We can't, son. It's not the right time for you to leave."

Andre thought about the other kids, about Don, Sam, and Tamara. He bet they wouldn't have to beg. He didn't know much about his dad's other son, Joel. But he was pretty sure the four-year-old boy didn't have to beg for a spot in their father's house, either. Andre couldn't stand being the only one who was treated this way. He plopped down on the beanbag chair and put a pillow over his face. If he wasn't going home, there wasn't anything left to discuss.

His parents tried talking to him, but they were ignored. They probably weren't thrilled about getting some of their same crap back that he'd lived with at home. Andre grinned slightly. Eventually, they gave up and left.

Andre's roommate came into the tiny living room area shared by the two upperclassmen. "Where did your folks go?"

"Who?"

"Your parents are gone already?"

Andre grunted. "What parents? I'm an orphan. My parents died a long time ago."

"But I thought . . ." his roommate said with a puzzled expression.

"You thought wrong, my friend," Andre said, getting up from his resting place on the beanbag chair. "Don't worry. I was wrong about them too."

Chapter 52

Four years later . . .

Sherry packed the gym bag, tossing in an extra pair of socks. "Which sneakers do you want to take?" she asked her son, who was now an eight-year-old.

"The blue and the red," he said, scarfing down a cookie.

"You don't need two pairs, Joel. Why don't you take one?"

"Because I don't know which one we're supposed to have. I better take both pairs just in case," he said, plucking two more cookies from the jar.

"How many cookies are you going to eat?" she asked.

He hunched his shoulders and kept eating.

"I'm surprised you have any left. I baked those for you when? Last week?"

He nodded and kept eating.

Sherry was beaming with satisfaction. She couldn't have dreamt of giving birth to such an amazing son. She watched his every move, ready to jump in and help Joel with whatever he needed.

Dave entered the kitchen.

"What are you doing home this early?" she asked, startled to have him home before nine. It was only five thirty. "What's wrong?"

"Nothing," he answered right away. "Does there have to be something wrong for me to come home and be with my family?" He kissed her on the cheek and raised his hand in the air for a high five with Joel.

"Ah, yes," she said, unable to relax. There was some reason he was home early, and she wanted to know it. "You don't normally come home this early. Go on. Tell me. What is it?" She braced for his answer.

"Okay, you got me. I left a file here. I've pretty much needed the file all day, but I didn't have a chance to come home earlier and get it."

"Great. You can come to my practice," Joel told his father.

"Not tonight, young man. Dad has to work this evening, but I'll catch your next one," Dave replied.

"You promise?" Joel said.

"I'll do my very best, son. That much I can promise."

Sherry cringed, listening to Dave. He had made only two of Joel's seven soccer games, the first one and the all-star game a few weeks ago. Sherry was 100 percent sure Dave attended those because she'd nagged him relentlessly until he finally agreed. She sighed, hearing Dave falsely boost her son's hopes, only to disappoint him later. He could disappoint her. That expectation had been established at the beginning of their relationship, but her son was off-limits. Sherry was well aware of Dave's professional obligations, having worked closely with him for a year. She had accepted the demands of DMI on Dave's terms, but he was also Joel's father. She wasn't going to let him forget, either.

"You know his championship game is this Saturday," she reminded.

"That's right, champ," Dave said, scratching his son's head with his fingers.

Joel laughed. He loved every second with his father. Sherry wanted more for him.

"You can't miss the game," she said firmly.

"I'll be there."

"You'd better be," she told him. "You've missed most of the season, but this is important, Dave."

"Yeah, Dad, this is our biggest game ever. If we win this, we each get a real tall trophy."

"Great," Dave said.

Sherry wasn't sure if Dave understood how special the game was for Joel, and how important it was for him to show up. She had four days to remind him, and she would every single day. Joel's happiness was worth the inconvenience.

"I'm not kidding, Dave. You have to come."

"I said I would," he said, embracing her.

"Yeah, Dad, you have to come. Will my sister and brothers be there?"

Sherry and Dave both looked at one another, a pause hovering over the conversation.

Finally Sherry broke the silence. "I don't know, Joel."

"Maybe I should call and invite them. The other players on my team said they're bringing their whole family. They're bringing their grandparents. I don't have any of those, so forget that. I might have some cousins, but I'm not sure. So the only other family I have for sure is Don, Tamara, and Sam," he recited, seemingly proud.

She didn't understand why.

"And Andre too," his father added. Dave went to his office, leaving Joel and Sherry in the kitchen, talking.

"Oh yeah, I almost forgot about my other brother. How could I forget a whole brother?" Joel laughed. "I don't think I'll ask him to come, since he's too far away. I can't ask Sam to come, either, since he's in college, right, Mommy?"

"Right. It would take him at least five hours to drive home from Indiana. I'm sure he won't be able to come," she said, intentionally sounding very upbeat. Her son didn't have to know Sam wouldn't come to his game even if it was across the street. Sherry knew it but hoped he would never have to endure the alienation that she had experienced from the other Mitchells.

"But the other ones are right here. I wish I could have my sister and brothers at my game. Everybody else is going to be there. You think I should call them, Mommy?"

"If you want," she told him, not wanting to douse his heated enthusiasm with negativity. But Sherry knew Madeline's children weren't going to give Joel a chance to share his excitement. They treated her baby like an infectious disease, wanting to be nowhere near him. She hated the rejection he had to endure, but there wasn't much she could do about it. Unless she had more children, living with few meaningful family ties was going to be his fate. It had been hers and was destined to be his too.

Chapter 53

Andre fidgeted in the seat as his counselor jotted some notes. For eight years he'd sat in this seat, and most of the time, it was an easy visit. He'd sit and talk about what was on his mind. The counselor would listen and give him advice. He'd go back to his room until the next session. When he came to Gateway Prep, he hated the sessions. He hated having a stranger nosing into his past, asking a bunch of questions, and making him feel embarrassed. But he grew to look forward to the sessions. Mr. Greene understood him. He listened. Nobody else did. It was hard to walk away.

"You just turned twenty-two. There are no more extensions for you. The program is over."

"But there are more classes I can take. Maybe I can get a job here."

"Doing what?" Mr. Greene asked.

"Maybe a counselor."

Mr. Greene scratched between his eyebrows. "You don't need a job here. What you need is an opportunity to go home and deal with the unresolved feelings you have toward your family."

"They're not my family, and it doesn't feel like my home!" he shouted, digging his fingernails into his jeans. "I'm not related to those people."

"See how much emotion they evoke in you?"

"That's what I keep telling you. If I go, there will be problems for me." Andre was frustrated. He didn't want to waste his hour talking about people who didn't spend two minutes a day thinking about him. *Forget them. They may as well be dead.*

"If you don't go home, I fear you will have problems."

"Why? I don't have problems here."

"Andre," Mr. Greene said, taking off the glasses that were sitting on the edge of his nose, "Gateway Prep is not the real world. You're not going to have counseling sessions three to four times a week once you leave here. You won't have the same dedicated support you have here."

"And so what?"

"You'll have to be able to control your temper."

Andre scooted around in the seat. "My temper is a whole lot better than it was before I came here."

"Agreed, but you have a ways to go."

"Okay, so why can't I stay here, get a job, and keep up my counseling sessions?"

"Because you've aged out of the program."

"I can't help my age."

"You're right. Certain events we can't control. However, regardless of how we feel about you being here, the fact remains that you're twenty-two." Mr. Greene stared at him. "Your time has come, Andre. You completed your probation a year ago. We let you stay on so you could finish our introductory college curriculum. Now that you have, it's time to leave Gateway Prep."

"But I'm not ready. I don't know what to do next."

"Have you considered joining the military? Many of our students do."

"Nah, it's not for me." Andre tucked his hands under the bottom of his shirt and stretched his legs out in the chair.

"Then go home, son. You can't stay here."

Andre closed his eyes and lifted his chin toward the ceiling. He wanted to float away. "When do I have to go?" he asked, trying to swallow Mr. Greene's words.

"Right away. We have to get your room ready for a new student."

"Oh, another kid whose parents are tired of him and want him out of the house," he said, snickering.

The counselor pressed his lips together and stared at Andre for a few seconds, making him uncomfortable. "I've already contacted your parents."

"Really?" Andre said, rearing back in the chair. "What did Dave and Madeline have to say?"

Mr. Greene gave Andre another one of those stares, the one that spoke disappointment. "Mr. and Mrs. Mitchell to me, Mom and Dad to you."

"Yeah, right, if you say so."

"You mother is planning to come out this weekend."

"She's wasting her time, because I'm not going with her I'm legal now, and my probation is over too. So I don't have to do anything I don't want to do anymore."

"You're right, but I'm hoping you're optimistic about reconciling with your parents. Most new and recurring challenges we face are the result of unresolved old ones that haven't been adequately addressed."

"You're talking about my abandonment issues, as you call them."

"Precisely. If you want to truly gain control, face your fears. Andre, I don't see you as a quitter."

"I'm not," Andre answered instantly.

"Good. Then don't quit on your family until you're absolutely certain there are no redeeming qualities in any of them."

"Why is my family so important to you?"

"Because I was an only child too. My parents didn't die as young as yours, but they were gone before I graduated from high school. I didn't have a family to take me in. I lived in foster care, and fortunately for me, I made it. But you don't have to take my route. You have a family who wants to be in your life."

"If you say so," he said, although it didn't feel that way.

"Andre, you need to see this as an opportunity to address your issue with them. Work out common ground, and then move on. If you're still interested in working with us after being home for six months, then give me a call." The counselor reached into his desk, pulled out a business card, and handed it to Andre. "I'm honestly hoping you have so much success with your family that you forget about Gateway Prep."

"I doubt that's going to happen."

"The future is what you make of it, young man."

Andre listened respectfully, but the future he saw wasn't as cheery as Mr. Greene's picture. "I guess I can give it a try."

"Great. Besides, how bad can it be?" Mr. Greene said.

Andre smirked. For him to ask the question showed just how little Mr. Greene knew about the Mitchell family and their boatload of issues. Andre was just one of many Mitchells needing a full-time counselor.

Chapter 54

Frank and Madeline convened in Dave's office. He hadn't arrived yet. The three were going to review the midyear numbers and determine if they were on track with the annual sales projections.

"Where is he?" Frank asked Madeline.

She peered at her watch. Four fifteen. "I don't know, but Sharon didn't say he'd canceled. You know Dave. He's pulled in five directions. He'll be here," Madeline said, flattening her hair around the sides of her head. "Why? What's your big hurry?"

"I'm trying to keep more balance between work and home these days," Frank said, plopping his pad on the table.

"Oh, really?" Madeline said, intrigued. "What prompted that change?"

"Your husband—"

"You mean ex-husband."

"Okay if you say so."

They laughed in unison.

"Is that why you stepped down as chief of operations last year?" Madeline asked him.

"Not really. I stepped down because it was time to let go. Dave doesn't need me over both finances and operations."

"I think he'd disagree. He trusts you. You've always had his back."

"Trust is overrated."

Madeline never did quite understand Frank's excessive reaction to her divorce from Dave initially. Back then it seemed like Frank was the one who was divorced by the way he handled the breakup. "I'm glad you and Dave have been able to get on good terms again. I know how much he adores you."

"Don't get me wrong."

Sharon interrupted. "Excuse me. Mr. Mitchell will be up in ten minutes. He's running way behind with a meeting in legal."

Madeline and Frank thanked her for the update.

"What were you saying?" Madeline asked.

"I love my brother. I couldn't stay irritated with him forever, although I don't have to agree with what he does. You know he made some jacked up choices that we won't rehash."

"Haven't we all," she said contemplating her decision to leave Dave when there had been the chance to work through their problem. To say she'd made the right choice wasn't clear yet.

"Perhaps, but every time I used to think about how righteous Dave was, it made me want to change my life in certain ways. I'm telling you, he almost had me wanting to get some religion based on his whole God routine."

"That's what you think it is?" Madeline asked, not offering her opinion to him. For the longest time she was not in agreement with the amount of dedication Dave showed to his God, because it seemed to come at the expense of her and the children. It was true that he'd told her before they got married about his love for the Lord and how He came first. Unfortunately, she married him without realizing just how honest he'd been. "You know I'm very familiar with him and God. I didn't like how much he put into religion, but that's who Dave is. Is it fair for you to expect him to change? He has a right to his beliefs." Madeline hadn't always felt that way, but the years had broadened her perspective when it came to Dave. He was definitely not perfect. Andre wasn't perfect, and admittedly, she wasn't, either.

"I just expected more from such a religious person."

Madeline squinted. "Why?"

"Because he should have been better."

"He's human, Frank," Madeline said, shaking her head.

"No, he had something special that other people just don't have. I saw him come out on top case after case. There were so many times we should have lost, but he won. There was definitely a special hand on him. If it was God, so be it. So I was upset watching him throw away his respect and the reputation of DMI for a woman," Frank said.

"Sounds like you put Dave on a pedestal."

"Maybe—"

"Then that was *your* mistake. You really couldn't blame him. That was your choice." Dave had his flaws, as she was well aware, but he'd always done right by Frank.

"You're right, which is why I let the tension go. Let's face it, I'm not going to abandon my brother, but he did lose some of my respect. That's why I stepped down as chief of operations. I'm not as motivated anymore to give Dave or DMI everything I have. It's not worth the grind for me any longer. One job is plenty for me."

"I see you kept the chief of finance role."

"You better believe it. I'm not giving up the money. I might be slowing down, but this Mitchell is not crazy," he said, and they laughed again. "I have to watch the bottom line myself, just in case Dave slips again." They both laughed.

Dave walked in. "What's so funny?"

The laughter subsided.

"Ah, we were just shooting the breeze while waiting on you," Frank said.

Madeline didn't elaborate. Dave wouldn't want to know more.

Chapter 55

Dave was feeling a bit tired, having run from one meeting to the next. He would take a break after this meeting, around five thirty. Frank slid the financial report to him. Dave flipped through the twenty-page document, checking for any red highlighted numbers. He found several.

"Tell me what's going on with the Southern region," he said, fumbling in his pocket for his reading glasses.

"Not much to tell," Frank said, glancing quickly at Madeline. "There were a few start-up issues that impacted the bottom line."

"You mean with getting Daniel up to speed as chief of operations?" Dave asked. He recalled several delays near the end of last year but didn't realize it had impacted sales three quarters later.

"His transition into my old role wasn't as smooth as I'd hoped, but it will work out."

Dave rolled his eyes at Frank. "I'm sure Daniel will be fine once he gets the rest of his team in place." No matter how good Daniel was in the role, he was never going to be as good as Frank was.

Having his brother step down from the operation's position had been a personal low for Dave. For a second he longed for the old days when he, Madeline, and Frank were a solid team, impenetrable. Those days were long gone. Operating with less support was one of the many consequences of Dave's transgression that lingered. Repentance, forgiveness, and even redemption had been immediate, but it had become brutally clear that God hadn't let Dave's sinful nature go unpunished. It felt as if the consequences of his actions were going to be spread across several lifetimes—his, Madeline's, his children's, and Frank's. God help his family to learn to live with this inevitable wrath.

Dave turned his attention to the report. Dwelling on the rest would bear no fruit.

"The numbers for the Southern region aren't great, and so you may also want to consider bringing in a regional director for the South," Madeline suggested.

"That's not a bad idea," Dave said.

"I basically cover the Eastern region now. I could focus exclusively on the East and keep my marketing role," Madeline said.

"With the extra help, maybe I can get freed up to finally build my leadership library. It has been a dream of mine for ten years," Dave remarked.

"Where's the oversight and finances coming from?" Frank asked. "Madeline just told us that numbers for the Southern region are down. Do we really have money to fund a pet project at this time?"

Dave knew Frank was more apt to question his decisions. He wasn't alone. Several clients did too, but the lack of trust in him didn't diminish his role as CEO. He was still in charge, with a vision to fulfill. "I'll expand the management structure. I'll also pull together a board of directors to provide objective oversight," Dave said, rearing back in his seat, grinning.

"So you have this figured out?" Frank asked.

Dave nodded. "Who knows? Maybe we can finally begin to build up the international sector too."

"Slow down, little brother. We want to lock down the United States first and then venture out."

"My dream is for us to expand beyond Detroit and the United States. I want to take our teachings to the masses," Dave revealed.

"Maybe you do, but I'm getting older, and I don't intend to work crazy hours like I used to," Frank remarked. "That's why I gave up the operations role. You'll be on your own with the international expansion, and the West Coast, for that matter."

Dave sighed.

"Speaking of hours, it's going on five o'clock. I have a few things to do before getting out of here for dinner with my wife. I have to go," Frank said, slapping the table lightly.

He left Dave with Madeline.

"That brother of mine is something else."

"He is, but Frank loves you."

"He does, but the past has changed him."

"I can relate," she said, cutting her glance at him briefly.

He let the comment drop, figuring it would lead to another discussion that wasn't going to bear fruit. He and Madeline had a functioning relationship, and he preferred to keep it working.

"Oh no," he blurted out. "I was supposed to meet Sherry and Joel at his soccer practice."

"What time?"

"At five."

Madeline snickered. "Some things change, and some things don't."

"I've missed most of the games this year. I have to make the one on Saturday. It's his championship match. The little slugger is so excited."

"Saturday!" Madeline shouted. "We have to pick up Andre. I told you on Monday to block off your calendar."

"Oh no, I forgot about Andre."

"You always forget about Andre."

"That's not fair, Madeline. Besides, he is twenty-two years old. He's not a kid who needs a chaperone. He didn't let us come to visit for his birthday. What makes you think he wants us there this weekend? He'd probably prefer to fly home alone."

"Dave Mitchell, we have to fly out to Colorado and pick up Andre. We haven't been able to do much for our son. So I'm not letting you get out of this. Come on, you have to go. Please," she pleaded. "We can't let him down."

"Wow. This is awful, but I guess you're right."

"I know I'm right," she said as she seemed to relax. "The boy could have come home last year or earlier in this school term, but he was so fed up with us being inadequate parents that he chose to stay away. It doesn't get much worse when your child would rather sleep in a cramped dorm room instead of coming home. We've let him down repeatedly. I know it, and you know it too," she said, her voice cracking. "The counselor said Andre is willing to give us a chance. We're the ones who dropped him off in Colorado, and I want us to be the ones who pick him up. His counselor agrees."

"All right, I'm going with you to Colorado. I'll have Sharon make the arrangements."

"Great," she said. "I'm heading home. Maybe I can catch dinner with Don and Tamara. Since they're teenagers, it's almost impossible for the three of us to be home together in the evening. I catch them when I can, and Thursday seems to be the best night. I'm out of here. I'll talk with you tomorrow."

"Have a good night," he said as Madeline left.

Dave clasped his hands together and meditated. He needed the extra reinforcement before calling Sherry. He already anticipated her reaction, and it wasn't going to be positive. *No more delay,* he thought. He dialed home. She answered sooner than he expected.

"Sherry, I've made a huge mistake, and I'm going to need your forgiveness."

"What is it?"

"I totally forgot that Madeline and I have to pick Andre up from school on Saturday."

"No, you don't. You have to come to Joel's game. He wants you to be there, and so do I."

"I know, but it's one of those situations I can't change."

"What are you talking about? There are plenty of other options."

"Like what?"

"Madeline can go alone. Plus, Andre is over twenty-one years old. He's an adult. He can fly home on his own. He doesn't need two parents picking him up, especially when one has another obligation."

Dave appreciated Sherry's frustration. He'd just used the same ineffective argument. He was frustrated by the scheduling conflict too, but a commitment had been made to Madeline. "Andre is an adult, but the counselor apparently wants us to come out there as a show of support."

"What about Joel's support? He doesn't have any other family members to attend the match. You're it."

"Sherry, my hands are tied here."

"Then untie them, and find a way to make Joel's game."

"I can't."

"No, you mean you won't choose Joel over Andre."

"I'm not choosing sides."

"Oh, you are, whether you admit it or not. You're definitely choosing Madeline over me. Will there ever be a day when Joel and I come first?"

He'd heard that question repeatedly from both women. He hadn't answered Madeline earlier. He wasn't going to answer Sherry now. No answer would be satisfying to her. There would be no benefit derived from an extended discussion about this, but there was hope. Eight years ago, Madeline was barely speaking to him. She was so mad. Day by day they'd managed to build a solid partnership again within DMI. There remained several sensitive topics between them, but overall they got along. He knew healing was possible.

Chapter 56

Madeline and Dave entered the counselor's office for what would be the last visit. Madeline's emotions were mixed. She was thrilled that Andre was coming home, but she simultaneously wondered what they could expect from a son who'd basically chosen to be estranged from them.

"Have a seat," Mr. Greene offered.

"Andre's joining us, right?" Madeline asked, feeling slightly anxious.

"He should be here in about thirty minutes. In the meantime, I wanted to speak frankly with the two of you before he arrives."

Madeline's anxiety spiked. "Why? What's wrong?" The counselor opened his notebook and peered at her in a way that didn't look like good news was coming. Her heart was pounding as she anticipated the words that might come out of his mouth. She desperately wanted to hear a positive report about her son; otherwise, their decision to send him to Gateway Prep had been a mistake from the beginning. It was Dave's idea, and she could resort to blaming him if the program hadn't worked. The notion drifted into her mind and right back out. He was no more to blame than she was. They'd chosen the best option from the short list available to them.

Frank's insight from eight years ago popped into her head. He'd basically told her that Andre's time away would either allow his mind-set to change for the good or his anger would get worse. Fearing the worst scenario had come true, she wanted to cry in anticipation of Mr. Greene's assessment. But she willed herself to hold off at least until he finished his speech. Then she could let the tears of motherhood flow.

"Andre has been a delightful student here at Gateway," Mr. Greene began, and Madeline's tension eased. "He is a very bright young man. He has strong interests in the sciences."

"I'm not surprised. His father, Jonathan, was a chemist, and his mother a pharmacist," Dave said.

"So it's a natural discipline for him to pursue," Mr. Greene noted.

Madeline was pleased. *So far so good.* She was eager to hear more praise, having completely dumped the anxiety. This was the report she came to hear.

"He's gotten certifications in a couple of our trade programs. Andre has also completed a series of college electives. Most accredited schools will accept the transferred credits, should he elect to continue his college course work."

"We sure hope so," said Dave, who was pretty quiet today. Madeline wasn't sure if it was because he had to miss Joel's game or if his silence had to do more with Andre. She couldn't always figure out Dave. As long as he was in the seat next to her as they picked up their son, then she was fine.

"Sounds like Andre has made major progress," she said, beaming. "We're very pleased."

Mr. Greene nodded. "He has made significant progress, but I do have a concern."

Oh no, Madeline thought. *Here comes the tidal wave of despair.* She should have known the report was too good to be true. She braced for the bad news.

"Since Andre is twenty-two, normally I couldn't share his information with you."

Madeline moved to the edge of her seat. There was no way Mr. Greene was going to rouse her interest and not finish the story. She had to know what was going on with her son.

"But he signed a waiver permitting me to speak with you directly."

"So he knows we're meeting with you?" Dave asked.

"Absolutely. He is willing to make amends with the two of you and the rest of his family. He at least wants to try."

"That's a relief to hear," Dave said with enthusiasm.

"But as you can imagine, his success will be contingent, to some degree, on how well the family embraces him—"

Madeline interrupted. "We love Andre, and we're looking forward to having him home. Whatever it takes, we're willing to do it for him."

"I'm glad he'll have the support." Mr. Greene's gaze moved to the notebook in front of him. "With his progress, there have also been setbacks."

"Like what?" Dave asked, apparently as eager to know as Madeline was.

"He struggles with controlling his rage. When Andre feels emotionally threatened, he puts up a defense that's nearly impossible to penetrate."

Madeline wasn't a psychological therapist. She needed the counselor to lay out what he was saying in basic terms. "What does that mean, emotionally threatened?"

"If he feels rejected, disrespected, or ignored, Andre tends to tap into a place of unaddressed rage," Mr. Greene explained.

"Does he get violent?" Dave asked.

It was a question Madeline didn't want to consider after eight years of treatment.

"There have been a few instances where he was not able to control the rage and resorted to a physical reaction."

"How long ago was the last episode?" Dave asked.

"Several months ago."

"We didn't know," Dave said.

"How would we?" Madeline added. "He doesn't talk to us." It was a harsh reminder that this wasn't a fairytale ending. They were living in the real world, and it wasn't pretty for Andre.

"Are you able to tell us what happened, since we know very little about his interactions here other than what you've told us over the years?" Dave said.

"I believe there was a young lady he was interested in. It took several months before he got the courage to tell her how he felt. She didn't reciprocate the interest, and he didn't take the rejection well," Mr. Greene revealed.

"What did he do?" Dave asked.

"He punched holes in the wall and broke a couple of chairs."

"My goodness. I'm surprised we didn't hear about this before now," Madeline said.

"Due to his age, we weren't obligated to tell you."

Madeline was surprised at Andre's actions this far into the program. "It doesn't sound like he's made progress to me. Actually, it sounds pretty much like it did four years ago." Madeline sat there without answers. Her son was like a spicy bowl of jambalaya, with plenty of pleasant bites and a few unexpected fiery hot ones.

"Is there anything we can do to help him?" Dave asked.

"I'm glad you asked," Mr. Greene said. "I highly recommend he continue with therapy. I'm hoping he'll ramp the frequency up to several appointments a week. I know it can be costly, but the counseling will be very important for him."

"Cost is not a factor," Madeline interjected.

"I'm also wondering if Andre was ever diagnosed with paranoia or schizophrenia," Mr. Greene asked. "I couldn't find anything in his file."

"No, he's a smart boy," Madeline answered.

"Yes, but I believe Andre could benefit from more extensive psychological testing if he wants the most appropriate help."

"It might be difficult convincing him to take those kinds of tests," Madeline said.

"Is there a history of mental disorder in his family?" Mr. Greene asked.

"None that we know of," Dave told the counselor.

"There's nothing wrong with him," Madeline insisted, willing to defend her son against ludicrous accusations.

"There may be a disability of some sort there that's gone untreated."

Nonsense, Madeline thought.

There was a knock on the door.

"Excuse me," Mr. Greene said, getting up and going to the door. He opened it, and there was Andre.

Madeline stood to give him a hug. Dave did too.

"Hello, son," Dave said.

Andre didn't make eye contact with either of them, but he extended his hand to Dave. Instead of shaking it, his father pulled Andre in and hugged him tightly, concluding with a big pat on the back and a firm grip on his shoulders.

"I'm happy to see you, son."

It was Madeline's turn. She reached out to hug him, not nearly as forcefully as Dave. He barely reciprocated the hug. She understood and didn't let her feelings get hurt too badly. There was time to restore what they once had, she hoped.

"Everyone, please sit," Mr. Greene said, taking his seat too. "Andre, we were just discussing your therapy sessions."

"Oh," he said.

"I was just explaining to your parents how important it is to continue your sessions, especially for anger management skills."

"I don't mind going," Andre said.

"Then we'll find someone you like as soon as we get home," Madeline offered, like it was the only thing she had to worry about.

"Speaking of home, where am I going to stay?"

Madeline and Dave glanced at one another. It was a great question. She was embarrassed to say they hadn't thought about where he was going to live.

"Where do you want to live?" she asked.

"Doesn't matter to me."

"Well, you have my home, your mother's, and I guess we could talk about an apartment too," Dave said.

Mr. Greene jumped in. "If Andre is going to restore his relationship with the family, I would suggest that he return to one of your homes, instead of the apartment, initially. More interaction will be helpful with his transition."

"Do you want to stay with us?" Madeline asked her son.

"Doesn't matter to me," Andre repeated. "Wherever I go, it won't be for long. I plan to get my own place as soon as I get a job."

"Let's figure out what you're interested in doing. I'm sure we can find something for you at DMI," Dave said.

"Oh no, I'm not working there. Too many Mitchells. I'll find a job on my own, but I still need a place to crash for a few months."

"Then it's settled. You'll come home with me," Madeline announced. She wasn't sure how Tamara and Don would react to the news. They had limited contact with Andre. One of the few times they'd seen him was when they came to Colorado for his graduation ceremony several years ago. With Sam away in college and the other children so busy, she figured Andre would mostly have the house to himself. She didn't expect any problems.

"Thanks, but I think I want to stay with Dad."

"With me?" Dave responded, seeming stunned.

"Yeah. I have some good memories from when I stayed with you."

"I enjoyed our time together too, but you know my situation is different than what it was eight years ago. I have Joel and Sherry staying there with me."

"I know, but it's a place I'd like to try."

Dave didn't respond immediately. Madeline was ready to leap out of her seat and urge Dave to wake up. Andre didn't have many requests, and the only one he did have needed to be fulfilled. She kept cool. Two anger management candidates in the same room was one too many. She took the rational approach and carefully controlled each word that was squeezed out. "Dave, don't you think we should honor Andre's simple request? We did ask him to choose a house, and he has," she said, plastering on a smile.

"I guess you're right. Andre, you are welcome to come home so long as you don't mind having an energetic little boy following you around."

"I don't mind. It might be fun to have another little brother since Don is all grown up now." Andre laughed, which converted Madeline's fake grin into a real one.

There was hope for Andre. There had to be. Otherwise, what was the alternative for their family?

Chapter 57

Dave meditated in the backseat as he rode from the airport alone.

"Sir, what would you like for me to do with the luggage?" Dave's driver asked.

"You can set the bags on the steps." Dave didn't want to take Andre's three suitcases and trunk inside until he could speak with Sherry.

Dave entered the house, prepared to come straight out and tell Sherry about Andre staying with them. He'd dismissed several opportunities to tell her over the phone somewhere between Colorado and Detroit. He chose not to tell her that way. She deserved to be told in person. He didn't look for excuses. He went in, determined to find his wife and talk to her.

"Daddy, we won," Joel said, catching him walking through the door.

"All right," he said, giving his son a high five. "I knew you could do it."

"Do you want to see my trophy?" his son said, bursting with energy.

"Yes, I'd love to see your trophy. But I have to talk with your mother. Afterward, I will see your trophy, and you can tell me about the whole game. I want to hear every detail."

"Cool," Joel said, seeming to accept the offer without resistance.

"Where is your mom?"

"In her bedroom, I think."

Dave climbed the stairs hurriedly and went straight to the master suite, where he found Sherry.

"You're home," she said, sprawled across the bed, reading a magazine. She got up to give him a hug. "I've missed you."

He didn't respond. He was too focused on Andre.

"When did you get in?"

"We landed about an hour ago."

"How did you make out with Andre?"

He sat on the bed. Sherry resumed her spot on the bed.

"I have to tell you something," he said.

Sherry popped up. "Oh no, Dave. That doesn't sound like anything I want to hear. What is it?" she blurted out.

"It's Andre," Dave said, wringing his hands.

"What about him?" she said as her eyes widened.

"He needs a place to stay."

"He's going to Madeline's house, right? Please tell me he's going to Madeline's." Dave's gaze sank. "Dave, answer me!" she screamed at him.

"He's not going to Madeline's."

"Then where *is* he going?" she said, almost getting hysterical.

"Here, to live with us."

"Dave, how could you bring him here without asking me? How could you? I thought we'd gotten past those days of you and Madeline making decisions about my home and my life without consulting me. You've totally disrespected me, and I'm not in agreement. So there. Now what are you and Madeline going to do?"

Dave didn't want to fight with Sherry or Madeline. Years of fussing and fighting had relegated him to the sidelines. Dave was doing the best he could to appease both mothers, but their reactions suggested he was failing. Most importantly, he had to put Andre's needs in the forefront. "Sherry, come on. It's been eight years since Andre stayed here."

"And it isn't a pleasant memory."

"But don't you think he deserves another chance, a fresh start? For goodness' sake, please give him a chance," Dave said, not holding back his raw emotions.

He prayed Sherry would come to terms with his decision and understand why he needed to do this for Andre. He could only pray for acceptance and get his son's luggage off the doorstep. He couldn't leave Andre outside his new family forever. His time to come inside and be a viable member of the Mitchells had arrived. Dave had realized it, and Sherry would have to also.

As their limousine approached the gate to his mother's house, Andre got scared. He wasn't afraid of any particular person. He was worried about not being in control.

"We're here," Madeline said as the car pulled up. His father had taken another car home alone. His mother had insisted on having Andre come home with her to see his sister and brother. He'd agreed, willing to make an effort at getting along with them.

"Are Don and Tamara at home?" he asked.

His mother peered at her watch. "It's after five. They should be home," she said.

"Do they know I'm coming?"

"I told them you were, but you never know about teenagers on the weekend. Enough about them. Are you glad to be home?"

Andre had to think about the question and then took even longer to formulate a truthful answer. "A little," he said, not willing to lie. Years of therapy had taught him to be honest about his feelings and deal with the rest afterward.

"I guess a little is better than none," his mother said.

Andre could tell her feelings were hurt, but that wasn't his intent. "The place hasn't changed," he said, getting out of the car.

"Home shouldn't change. It should always be the place you can rely on to remain as you left it," Madeline told him, wrapping her arm around his neck. "Regardless of where you go, this will always be your home, Andre. Always." She kissed him on the cheek and then let him go.

Madeline fumbled with the door key as the car drove off. She didn't have any luggage, and Andre's had been sent home with his dad. When the door opened, Andre stood in the entryway, unable to cross the threshold. The warmth of being home escaped him. The last time he was there, he'd busted Sam's nose and ended up in juvie until they let him out on probation. In hindsight, he was sorry about what happened, but the fight was four years ago. There wasn't much he could do about it. When everybody came to his graduation several years ago, nobody seemed to hate him. Maybe they were cool with him after so much time had gone by. He'd just have to see.

"Don't just stand there, Andre. Come on in. You're at home," his mother said.

He stalled for a few seconds longer. Finally, he took a few steps into the house and stood in the foyer. His thoughts swirled, and his gaze traveled around the room. Same room, same furniture, but a totally different sensation than what he remembered after they'd moved into the house. A cold sweat covered him, but he wasn't going to tell his mother. He'd let her enjoy the excitement she seemed to be experiencing.

"When do you think Don and Tamara will get here?" he asked, half expecting them to be standing in the foyer with a WELCOME HOME sign, like they had in the beginning, when he arrived from Arizona at age ten to live with them. They had made a sign, gave him gifts and a party. That was many years ago. Today there was no sign, no cake, and no eager kids ready and willing to make him their brother. Nobody was waiting for him today, nobody except his mother. The truth surrounded him, just as he knew it would.

Chapter 58

There wasn't much to do. Andre decided to hibernate in the family room and catch a bit of the tennis match. He loved watching Agassi play. There was guaranteed to be a fight or a screaming match with the line judge when he was playing. A lot of people didn't understand the tennis player. They thought Agassi was a hothead who got mad when he didn't get his way. Andre saw him differently. He saw Agassi as someone who was passionate about tennis, loved it, breathed it, and didn't like getting cheated after putting in so much hard work. Andre turned up the volume on the TV. He could relate. People didn't understand him, his mother and father especially. But he was going to try hard to get to know them again and be a family. He was willing to try.

Around seven Andre heard voices outside the family room. As he turned down the volume on the television, Don came through the door.

"Hey, Andre. It's good to see you," Don said, giving Andre a high five. Andre stayed seated.

"What's up, Don?"

"Sorry I wasn't here when you got home. I was working on a project with a few friends, and we ran late." Don plopped onto a seat at arm's length from Andre. "What are you watching?"

"The French Open."

"I didn't know you were into tennis," Don said, kind of hyper.

"Might as well be."

Andre wasn't surprised by Don's comment. The family didn't know much about him. They hadn't cared enough in the past to find out what his interests were. Andre wanted to shut down the chitchat with Don and get back to his match, but he was committed to making an effort. It wasn't easy.

"So now that you're home, what are you going to do with yourself? Work? Go to school?"

"I'm not sure."

"You know, Sam is a freshman at Purdue." Andre wasn't really interested in hearing about Sam. He was Andre's least favorite sibling. "He's doing a double major in business and political science." Andre's ears were burning, and his nerves sizzling. He wanted Don to shut up. Instead his brother kept going. "He wants to go to business school and law school after undergrad."

"Whoopee for him," Andre said, pushed to the point of wanting to scream at Don to shut up. "Don't you have anything else you want to talk about besides Sam being in school?"

"Jeez, I didn't think it would bother you. I was just talking," Don said.

"I know, but my tennis match is on."

"No problem," Don said with an attitude. "I guess I'll see you later."

"You're leaving?" Andre asked, not caring if he did or didn't, but feeling guilty for running the guy off.

"Yep. I only stopped in to say hello. I'm meeting friends at the pizza shop."

Their mother walked in. "Andre, what did you want for dinner?"

"Nothing. I'm ready to go to Dad's."

"Aren't you hungry?" she asked.

Even if he was, Andre wasn't planning on telling her. He was ready to go. "No, I'm not. I figure we should go before it gets too late and then I'll have to wait until tomorrow."

"You're not going to sleep here?" Don asked with a perplexed look.

"He's staying with your dad and Sherry."

"Why are you making him stay there?" Don asked.

"We didn't make him."

"Nobody is making me do anything. I asked to stay with Dad," Andre said, jumping in.

"Why?" Don asked.

Andre didn't want to tell the full truth, not while he was working hard at getting along with everyone. "Why not? I lived with Mom for a long time. Thought I'd go to Dad's and then get my own place in a few months."

Don seemed satisfied with the explanation. Andre didn't have to tell his brother he wanted to stay as far away from him and Tamara as he could. Not so much Don, but definitely Tamara.

"Have you seen Tamara yet?" Don asked.

"Nope," Andre said, not wanting her to come home on his account. They hadn't gotten along too well before Andre left for school. He hadn't missed her and assumed the feeling was mutual.

"If you want me to drop you off, let's go," Madeline said.

She didn't have to tell him twice. Andre turned off the television and jumped up.

"I could drive him to Dad's if you want," Don said.

"No, I'll take him," Madeline responded.

"Don, you have a car?" Andre asked.

"It's an old clunker, but it gets me from point A to point B."

Andre should have known Don would get a car as soon as he turned sixteen. "What kind does Tamara have?"

"She's a lucky duck," Don said cheerfully. "Dad got her a brand-new Toyota Celica."

"Sweet, and I bet she didn't have to do anything special to earn it, did she?" Andre said.

Don chuckled. "You know how Dad is when it comes to Tamara. You could say she milks the fact that she's his only daughter, but he certainly doesn't mind." Don chuckled again. He was the only one laughing.

"I guess she is the lucky one," Andre said, feeling resentment churning, but he was able to maintain control.

Andre was smart enough to know the family had kept going while he was away, but it was tough hearing how much they were able to function and thrive without him. It was like he hadn't existed, although admittedly, he'd refused to come home since graduating from the high school program several years ago. Being home for a few hours had reminded Andre why he didn't like coming home. He couldn't wait to get out of his mother's house. He had to hear repeated stories about the spoiled Mitchell children and their perfect lives, each one of them.

"Mom, can we go?" he said, practically running down the long hallway to the garage. She was right behind him, thank goodness.

Throughout the entire ride to his dad's, Andre wanted to press the gas pedal while his mother was driving. No matter how fast she went, it was too slow. Before Madeline could come to a complete stop in his Dad's driveway, Andre had the car door open.

"Andre, what are you doing? That's dangerous," his mother said, stomping on the brakes. "Are you that eager to get out?"

"I'm sorry," he said. The apology was not for being eager. It was for the disappointment she seemed to be showing.

"Go on in."

"You're not coming in?" he asked.

"No. I don't want to get in the way. Tell your dad I'll see him at DMI tomorrow."

Andre said his good-bye and knocked on the door. His soaring enthusiasm slumped to the ground when Tamara opened the door and leaned against it.

"Well, well, well, if it isn't the lost Mitchell son. Come on in," she said, attempting to give him a hug. He pulled away. "What is this? You're not going to give your sister a hug?" she said, scrunching up her face. He didn't want to make a scene, so as much as he hated pretending, Andre played along and let her hug him. He had to kick off his stay in the right way. "Now, that's more like it," she said. Her bubbly attitude was driving him crazy.

"I didn't realize you were going to be here," he said, standing in the foyer.

"I usually stop by to see Dad on the weekend," she said, smug.

He repeated her words in his mind.

"Come on into the kitchen. That's where everyone is," she said, leading the way. She had already ruined his evening just by being there. The last thing he wanted was her telling him what to do, no matter how big or small.

She was right. There they were, his father, Sherry, and Joel.

Joel came running to him and said hello with a gigantic smile. Even if Andre wanted to dislike the kid, it was hard, seeing that the little boy was so glad to see him. Andre had to acknowledge that he hadn't gotten such a warm welcome from anyone else.

"Wow. You've grown, little man," he said.

"I know. I'm probably going to be tall like Dad. That's what Mommy tells me."

Sherry grinned at Andre and said hello. Andre returned the fake grin and kept talking to Joel. Tamara was sitting at the kitchen table and leaning back against their dad. Sherry was doting on Joel. Andre felt invisible. He was unnerved. He was the odd man out. This wasn't the greeting he'd hoped to have.

In his dreams of reuniting, he'd come to his father's house. They would sit and talk, maybe watch TV, but mostly the two of them would have a chance to spend some time alone together and reconnect. Why not? Don, Tamara, Sam, and Joel had had him for the past eight years. He'd had a few visits here and there with him, but never alone. It was his turn to get some of his time back. They had to get out of the way. His emotions were bubbling over. Andre clenched his fists tightly. He was sure no one saw what he was doing. He had to maintain control, regardless of how painful it was, as his nails dug into the palms of his hands. He was determined not to get kicked out again.

Chapter 59

Dave sipped on a cup of coffee while glossing over a report Frank had dropped off earlier in the day. Madeline found him there.

"Well, how did it go last night with Andre?" she asked.

He glanced at her and then laid the report on his desk. "So far so good."

"Interesting," she commented, seeming awfully surprised.

"What were you expecting?"

"I didn't know exactly what to expect. Andre hasn't been home for years. His life and our lives have changed. This isn't the same family he left, not really."

Dave agreed. There was Joel now. Sam was gone. Tamara and Don were teenagers engaged in their own activities most evenings. The Mitchell family was in a different phase than they'd been in when Andre was with them. "I think he's adjusting."

"I sure hope so. Lord knows, I hope so," she said

"You worry too much, Madeline. Our son will make the necessary adjustments. I'm helping him, and you are too—"

"And he'll have to help himself," Madeline interrupted.

"True . . ."

***

Dave was bent on getting home for dinner. As the clock struck six thirty, he was overcome with contentment. He had to thank God for blanketing his family with a bit of peace. They desperately needed the breath of fresh air circulating in the Mitchell household. Lord knows, their days of distress had been many. It was time for a breakthrough, especially for Andre.

The house was quiet as Dave entered from the garage. "Hello, hello," he called out, sure Andre had to be around, and Joel too. By the time he reached the foyer, he heard noises coming from the kitchen. That was where he found Sherry and Joel. Dave greeted his family. "Where's Andre?"

"Watching TV," Joel said.

"Have you eaten dinner?"

"Not yet. We were waiting on you," Sherry said.

"Then let's eat. Joel, can you please go get Andre for me? Tell him we're ready to eat," Dave said.

Both sons came into the kitchen within a few minutes.

"We might as well eat in here. There's no reason to sit in the dining room," Sherry said.

The family sat down. Sherry passed the potatoes and vegetables as Dave sliced the turkey breast.

"Andre, how does it feel being back in Detroit?" Dave asked, reaching for his son's plate to put meat on it.

"Okay, I guess," Andre said, pushing the turkey into the middle of his plate and setting it down.

"Don't you worry. Each day is going to get easier," Dave said, putting meat on Joel's plate. "I'm just happy you're home. It doesn't get much better than this, a man having his family sitting at the dinner table, breaking bread together. I'm a blessed man."

"How long are you going to stay with us?" Sherry asked.

"Don't know," Andre said, taking a bite of his food.

"Hey, son, I'd like to pray over the dinner before we eat," Dave said, handing Sherry her plate.

"Oh, I didn't know," Andre said.

"It's no problem. Let us bow our heads," Dave said, determined to be the spiritual foundation in his household.

In the past, somehow he'd let DMI consume his life to the extent of neglecting his family. Thank goodness he had been given a second chance with Andre, and Dave wasn't going to blow it. Prayer was going to be at the forefront of the Mitchell household going forward and church too. He'd lost too much already. No more. He was reclaiming his household, his family, their God-given authority and favor. Dave spoke the promise in his mind, then let it marinate in his soul. *Peace*, he kept replaying in his thoughts. He yearned to find refuge in the Mitchell family. Dave was spiritually, but not necessarily emotionally, prepared to accept the fact that the promise might not be fulfilled in his lifetime and other challenges would arise along the way.

"Can I eat now?" Andre said, hyped up.

"Sure, son. Go ahead," Dave told Andre.

"How long did you say you were staying with us?" Sherry asked.

"Hopefully, for a long time," Joel said. "I've never had a big brother live with us. I think it's cool having you here. All my friends have brothers, except for me." They couldn't get Joel to stop talking. He was beaming. Dave was pleased for him. "You missed my soccer championship, but maybe next year you can come."

"Maybe I will, little guy," Andre said, forking a mouthful of food.

"The games will start in September. Will you still be here then?"

"Joel, give Andre a chance to eat. You have many days to ask him every question your heart desires," Sherry said.

"Oh, come on, Mommy."

"Andre doesn't seem to mind, do you?" Dave asked.

"Nah, he's okay." Andre peered at Joel. "I'm not sure if I'll be around for your games. I'm thinking about joining the air force."

"I didn't know you were interested in the military," Dave said. "What about more college?"

"I haven't made definite plans. I'm keeping my options open."

"Son, I'd love for you to finish college and then take a leadership role at DMI."

"Doing what?" Andre appeared interested.

"I have several positions in mind."

"I'll have to think about it. Hey, Dad, think you could help me get a car? That way I won't have to beg for rides."

"What kind of car are you thinking about, and how much are we talking?"

The phone rang. "Excuse me. I'll get the phone," Sherry said, getting up from the table. She returned a short while later. "It's Tamara. She wants your help with her math," Sherry told Dave.

"Tell her I'll call back after dinner."

"You tell her," Sherry said.

"I'm sorry, Andre. Can you excuse me for a few minutes? I have to speak with Tamara. I'd like it if we could continue our conversation when I return."

Andre didn't immediately give him the okay to table their conversation. Dave figured Tamara's questions would be quick. They usually were. He'd return to dinner in a jiffy and pick up where they left off.

"How are you going to leave when we're in the middle of a conversation? Can't Tamara wait an hour or two? Shoot," Andre snapped, causing Sherry to set her fork down.

Dave scrambled to quickly diffuse the tension. "I apologize. You're right. Sherry, please tell Tamara I'll call her right after dinner. Please tell her for me," he said, widening his eyebrows as she stared at him.

Dave hoped she was picking up his signal that he wanted her help in easing the awkwardness in the room. She got up, and Dave took a gulp of water. He calmed down. Andre calmed down, and the house was in a state of peace again. No problem. There were going to be bumps. What family didn't have them? This was Andre's third day at home. It would take space and patience for his son to get acclimated, and Dave had plenty of both. Not so for Sherry.

Chapter 60

Andre had to step away from the bonding session with his father at the dinner table. He lay on his bed as music from his Walkman blared through his earphones. Too many thoughts were attacking his mind: the car, Tamara, a job, school, Tamara, Joel, the military, and Tamara. He turned the music louder. His eardrums should have been hurting; the music was cranked so loud. Maybe if it was loud enough, he could drown out the negative emotions that were percolating. He struggled to settle down. He closed his eyes tightly and tried to rest. That might be his only hope.

A few minutes later Andre heard a noise. His eyelids popped open, and Joel was standing next to the bed. Andre could see his brother's lips moving, but the music blocked out all sounds in the room, thank goodness. Andre shut his eyes and ignored the little boy. He didn't feel up to socializing, not right now. Joel didn't go away. He began tapping Andre's leg.

Failing at the ignoring game, Andre finally snatched the earphones out and shouted, "What do you want?"

Joel jumped back and an expression of fear washed over his face. Andre didn't intend to scare him, but if that was required to get Joel out of the room, then so be it.

"I came to see if you wanted to play Battleship with me."

"No, not tonight, little man." Andre put one earphone back into his ear.

"What about Monopoly or Trouble or Sorry?"

"No," Andre said more firmly as he attempted to put in the second earphone.

"You can pick any color you want. I don't mind," Joel said, tapping Andre's leg again.

The irritation was unmanageable. "I said no!" Andre yelled, and before logic could catch up with his actions, he shoved Joel away.

"Why did you do that?" Joel screamed back. "I just wanted to play with you!"

Sherry must have been walking by the door or spying, one of the two, because she burst into the room like Wonder Woman and grabbed Joel. "What did you do to him?" she asked as the little guy started crying.

It wasn't that serious, Andre thought. He chose to let the two stand there while he ignored them. Maybe next time the little boy would listen when somebody told him to leave them alone. Not everybody found him cute and was interested in jumping to fulfill his every wish. Clearly, that was what Sherry did, and probably his father too. It definitely wasn't what Andre was going to do.

"Can you close my door when you leave?" he said, securing both earphones and turning the music up to the max.

Sherry snatched the Walkman, ripping the earphones out of Andre's ears.

"What's wrong with you, woman?" Andre said, hopping from the bed to the floor, ready to confront this psycho. Sherry was nutso if she thought he was going to let her grab his belongings. He wasn't a child anymore, and she'd better recognize that. "Don't touch my stuff."

Dave must have heard the ruckus. He came running into the room. "What's going on?" he said, immediately standing between Andre and Sherry. There wasn't much space separating the two. Dave literally had to push both him and Sherry back a foot to get in there. Andre didn't move willingly. Dave had to put some force behind the shove.

"Don't you ever touch my son!" Sherry shouted.

"Nobody hurt the little man," Andre retorted.

"Who do you think you are, picking on a little boy?" Sherry said, with Joel clinging to her.

"Look, I'm in my room. *I* wasn't bothering him. He kept bothering *me*. I told him to leave me alone, and he wouldn't. Didn't I?" Andre asked Joel. The boy was too whiny to answer, so Andre asked again. "Didn't I?" Joel cried harder and buried his face in Sherry's chest.

"I'm not going to have my son bullied. I want you out of our house," Sherry stormed.

"Wait a minute. Everybody, let's take a deep breath and settle down," Dave said.

"You have to be kidding!" Andre roared. "You want me to leave because your spoiled kid doesn't know how to take no for an answer? Puleassse."

"I mean it, Dave. I want Andre out of here. He goes, or Joel and I go."

"See you later," Andre said, plopping on the bed and giving a slow wave.

Dave placed his hands on Sherry's shoulders. "Let's not say anything we'll regret later. Why don't we all take a break, get our thoughts clear, and then sit down as a family and figure this out? We can't fall apart whenever there's a disagreement. Guys, we might not always get along, but we can make this arrangement work. That's all I'm asking us to do here. Let's step back. Then we can talk."

Sherry shook her head. "There is nothing to talk about. I am very serious. He goes or we go."

"Sherry, you don't mean what you're saying."

"If you think I don't, then try me."

"I don't know why you're riled up at me," Andre interjected. "Your son started this, but you're not mad at him. You want to kick *me* out. Tough, lady! This was my house long before you and little man came here. This isn't even your house. It belongs to me, my mother, my sister, and my brothers, not you. I might have been a kid when it went down between you and my dad, but trust me; we know how you got this house and my father." Andre laid back and shut his eyes. There was nothing else to say. He was done. His father had better handle Sherry before there really was a problem.

"How dare you?" Sherry blurted out.

"Can I speak with you in the hallway?" Andre heard his father ask Sherry.

"Why? I've already told you what I want."

"But, Sherry, for goodness' sake, he's my son."

"And I'm your wife. How many times will I have to remind you of your obligation to me and Joel? You can't just look out for Madeline and her children. We have to mean something to you too." she said, boohoo-ing. Andre wanted to gag. "I'm sorry, Dave, but I'm going to keep Joel safe, even if it means leaving you."

"Lord, help us," Dave cried out, sounding like a wounded animal. It gave Andre an eerie feeling.

Chapter 61

Dave appealed to Sherry once again in the confines of their bedroom. She wasn't willing to listen. Her mind was set. Dave's heart was crushed. Nobody was going to win. As the realization of his failure took root, he meandered down the stairs and traipsed to his home office. He closed the door as the window in his soul shut on his allegiance to Jonathan. There was no denying his overwhelming disappointment. It hurt to fail Andre repeatedly. Knowing he was letting his dear friend Jonathan down made the pain indescribable.

As he dialed Madeline at home, his heart bled tears. After several unsuccessful attempts to reach her at home, he tried the office and found her. "What are you still doing there?" he asked.

"Remember I have a big presentation tomorrow?"

"That's right. On the East Coast expansion."

"You got it. So what's going on?"

"Why do you ask?" Dave said, stalling for time. He just wasn't ready to share the news.

"Because you wouldn't be calling me at eight o'clock at night unless there was a serious reason. I know this is about Andre. So what is it?"

Dave couldn't stall any longer. He had to tell Madeline what she didn't want to hear. "I need Andre to stay with you for a few days, until we can get him an apartment."

"What are you talking about, Dave? The boy hasn't been in your house a full week and you're kicking him out already. You can't be serious. I thought we'd come farther than this?"

"Me too," he said.

Madeline would never know how badly he felt at this precise moment. Even when his baby died, it hadn't cut as deeply as this. Perhaps sending Andre away to school was the original dagger in his heart. Sending him away again was like twisting the dagger deeper. His sorrow filled the room, strangling him relentlessly. He could barely eke out his words.

"Listen to me, Dave Mitchell. You cannot do this to Andre. If you do, I'm afraid he will hate you forever. Based on what his counselor said, I'm honestly not sure if he can survive the rejection."

"What are you saying?"

"He could have a mental breakdown," she said.

"Oh, come on, Madeline. Don't you think that might be a bit extreme?"

"No, *you* come on. This is not a game. It isn't some dress rehearsal that we run through and fix the mistakes the next time around. We're talking about the life of a wounded young man. And, Dave, face it. We've contributed to his wounds. So I'm asking you to please let Andre stay in the house with you," she said, pleading with him.

Dave was in a familiar miserable place, sandwiched between Madeline and Sherry. He knew grace was sufficient in tumultuous situations. He just couldn't feel it.

"Madeline, I have to get him out of here. It's not safe for Sherry and Andre to be in the same room together. There's no way I can leave the two of them in the house together. It's just not going to work. We have to accept this and come up with a solution."

"No, Dave, you can't do this to me. When the situation gets out of hand, the two of you want to drop this in my lap. I can't fix this. You and I have to do right by Andre. Please, Dave, you can't kick him out," she said as her voice resonated.

"I understand why you're upset."

"Being upset is the least of my concerns. Dave, don't you get it? It's not about me or how I feel. Andre is not a piece of patio furniture we can move around as it suits us. Our children matter to me."

"To me too, Madeline."

"Then prove it. Who's it going to be? Sherry and Joel or Andre?"

"Don't reduce my commitment to a no-win choice between them. I love all of them equally."

"Uh-huh," she uttered. Madeline wasn't going to let up. Actually, Dave probably wouldn't have, either, if he'd been in her position.

"I have no choice."

"You've always had a choice."

"Not this time," he said, giving in. Her pummeling was too much.

"You are wrong for kicking him out, and you know it." She paused and then continued. "When are you planning to drop him off?"

"Tonight."

"I don't know if anyone is at home yet. The rest of the staff is gone for the evening at my house, and I can't get home until nine," she told Dave.

"I spoke with Tamara earlier," Dave said. "She was doing her homework at home."

"I guess she can let him in," Madeline said, sounding sullen.

"I can always take him to the Westin for a few nights until we can regroup," Dave told her.

"Is the Westin your answer for every tiff? Jeez, Dave, how many times are you going to bring him to your place and then ship him off somewhere else? You've dumped him for Sherry three times, and to make it worse, you want to abandon him at a hotel," Madeline said, sighing. "Dave, you've gotten so much better with the children, but right now I think you're being a lousy father. Drop him off, and I'll deal with this when I get home. You and I aren't finished with this subject. You can believe that."

Dave ended the call and laid his head on the desk. He yearned for a touch of encouragement, the only comfort that could help at this dire stage.

Chapter 62

Andre didn't react well to the decision. His father drove through the security gate at Madeline's house after Tamara buzzed them in.

"Son, please let me explain to you why I'm doing this."

"Don't bother." Andre had heard enough lies. He wasn't interested in hearing any more. He was done with the whole bunch of them.

Dave continued pleading with him to understand as they got out of the car, but Andre wasn't hearing it. He just wanted Dave to shut up. He turned his back completely to his father, hoping to give a clear message: "Leave me the heck alone." Dave must have figured it out, because he finally stopped talking.

Andre pounded on the front door.

"Son, Tamara is coming to the door if you give her a chance."

"You didn't give me one," he said while staring at Dave, the man who claimed to be his father, but it wasn't true. Dave had suckered him into believing crap about family for the last time. Andre had desperately believed him in Mr. Greene's office. *Lies, all lies.* His anger was warming. He wanted to hit something, anything, to release the pressure mounting in his head. The pounding sensation was driving him crazy.

He pounded on the front door again, and Tamara eventually opened it.

"What's your problem, banging on the door like that?" she barked.

"Get out of my way," Andre said, pushing past her with his backpack hitting her side.

"Excuse me!" she snapped.

"What did you say to me?" Andre growled.

Dave jumped in, of course, to protect his precious Tamara. "Settle down everybody."

First Joel, now her. Andre's anger continued to escalate.

"What are you doing here, anyway?" she asked, as if he needed her permission to come home.

"None of your business."

"It *is* my business if you're in our house," she snapped again.

He'd had plenty of her mouth. If she kept it up, he'd have to shut it for her. By now his anger was simmering steadily.

Andre stepped toward her, but Dave put the brakes on him. That was okay, Andre figured. Her father wasn't always going to be there to protect her and her big mouth. "This is supposedly my house too."

"Stop it, both of you. You're too old to be fighting like you did when you were kids. I've had about enough out of you both. Now, cut out the foolishness. Your mom will be here around nine. I'm going home. Call if you need anything."

"I'm sorry, Dad," Tamara said, giving Dave a kiss on the cheek.

"It's okay, dear. I know you mean well." They hugged, which made Andre want to gag again. "Are you going to be all right here? Because you can come home with me if you want."

"I'm fine, Dad. I have way too much homework to come over tonight. Go on. I'll be fine."

Was he invisible? Andre's anger boiled as they spoke
with each other as if he weren't in the room. He didn't
need a college degree to see who Dave loved. Andre
thought about how hard he'd worked to earn Dave's
approval and love. This moment summed up his lack
of success.

When Dave told him good-bye, Andre served him a
taste of the same invisible dish he'd been eating from.
He ascended the stairs in complete silence. Andre
couldn't care less whether Dave stayed or went. He was
sure the feeling was mutual.

Andre found refuge in his room, slamming the door
behind him. He didn't want to be disturbed by anybody. There was no one on earth he cared about or
wanted to see. Sadly, there was no one who cared about
him, either, except for maybe Madeline. She wasn't the
best mother, but he appreciated that she'd tried to help
him.

An hour passed, and Andre was being bombarded
with negative thoughts, painful images, and a constant
pounding in his head. He wanted to take a break and
step out of his body for a while. If it had been possible
to do, he would have. The pain and confusion were just
that bad. He was desperate for relief, but none came.

There was a knock on his door.

"Go away. Leave me alone." The knocking persisted.
"I said to leave me alone."

Tamara opened the door. "I'm just checking on you."

"I don't need you to check on me. Close my freaking
door, and get out of here."

"Don't you know when somebody's trying to be nice
to you?" she said.

"I don't want you to be nice to me. Just get out of
here," he shouted as loudly as his voice would go. He
grabbed the football lying on the desk next to his bed
and hurled it at her.

The ball barely missed her. Hopefully, she'd get out now, he figured.

"See, that's why nobody wants to be around you. You're mean and nasty."

"Shut your stinking mouth," he said, leaping to his feet. He'd warned her, but she kept mouthing off.

"You're crazy," she said.

The word *crazy* ran in his head and acted like a switch. He struggled to get free from his thoughts, but he wasn't able to control the anger. His emotions churned together, creating a weird vibe. It was as if his mind and his body were disconnected. He was a car flying down a hill without brakes. His anger boiled over. He exploded. In the blink of an eye he was on her, like a lion pouncing on a silly deer. He just wanted her to be quiet, to shut up. He had to stomp out the noise, the insults, and the pain.

He tossed Tamara to the floor. He ripped off her pants. Time stopped. He was in the room and could see what was happening, but it was as if he wasn't there. He was on the sidelines, directing a movie. If it was a dream, he couldn't wake up.

Tamara screamed for him to stop. He could hear her, and the weaker side of him wanted to stop. But the stronger Andre wanted her to know that he was in control, not her. She wasn't so special. He wasn't special, and she wasn't, either. He wanted her to feel common, like less than a real person, as he had for years. With each thrust of rage, he wanted her to know that nobody could protect her. He wanted her to hurt as much as he had for most of his life. Satisfaction briefly crept in as his hatred for the Mitchell family fell upon Tamara. Dave, Madeline, and Sherry had planted the seed the day he walked out of their house and into Gateway. Their precious Tamara was reaping the harvest.

The noise, her screams were deafening. Finally, she was quiet. When his thoughts settled and he realized what he'd done, Andre rolled off of her and clutched his chest, letting out a guttural roar. Shame and disbelief gripped him. He didn't know what to do.

Don came tearing up the stairs. "Who's screaming like that?" he said, running into Andre's room. He stood in the doorway, unable to process the scene. Tamara was lying on the floor in a pool of blood, with her pants and underwear down. Andre was sitting on the floor with his back against the bed. His pants were unzipped, and he had a blank stare.

"What happened?" Don shouted at Andre. He didn't want to dare believe what it looked like. There was no way. It wasn't possible. "Tamara!" he yelled.

She didn't move.

He shook her frantically. "Tamara, wake up! It's Don."

She moaned faintly.

He dove onto Andre. "What did you do to her?" he screamed, spit flying. "What did you do?" He pounded on his brother. It didn't matter that Andre was much bigger. He had to protect his sister.

"I don't know what I did," Andre wailed and didn't fight back.

"What did you do?" Don cried out, this time barely hitting Andre. He was too shaken to fight. "I have to call Mom! I have to call the ambulance!" He charged out of the room.

Andre didn't move. Besides, he had nowhere to go, especially now. He knew it. His fate was sealed, and he didn't attempt to resist. The few brief years of joy he'd experienced had died many years ago with his mother. The happiness he'd managed to hang on to died with his father. There was nothing else worthwhile for him to hang on to. What came next had to be better than the ache of his past. He was ready for his punishment, actually welcomed it.

Chapter 63

Madeline and Dave waited in the emergency room.

"Not in my worst dreams could I have painted this scenario. We knew Andre had problems, but never like this. Dave, what have we done to our children?" Madeline said, crying on his shoulder.

"I don't know what to say. This is a nightmare. I'm going to the chapel to pray," Dave said.

Madeline pulled away from Dave. "You prayed every day when we were married, and where did it get us? Really Dave, what has prayer done for us?"

"You can't think that way."

"Why shouldn't I? You can't honestly say that our family has benefited from your years of praying and believing in some special favor. Our problems are real, and I have to blame it on someone or something. I just have to.

"I'll take my share," Dave told her.

"And I'll take mine," she said gently laying her hand across her chest.

"Fair enough, as long we don't use my beliefs as the escape goat. We all contributed to this situation."

"Including Tamara?" Madeline hurled at him.

"No, of course I'm not saying this is her fault."
"Then what *are* you saying, because you're confusing the heck out of me."

"We have been hanging on by a thread. We've walked around with anger and bitterness for years. Wherever there is bitterness and anger, peace and joy can't exist. It's like night and day can't exist simultaneously. You can only have one at a time. Face it. You, Sherry, and I are the primary people to blame because we are the adults. We allowed our family to be at odds and did nothing."

"Hmmm," Madeline moaned.

"We let our emotions go unchecked, and unfortunately, that cancer spilled onto the kids. They don't like Sherry. They don't like Joel."

"Well . . . ," was Madeline's full response.

"Well, look where those seeds of discord have landed us."

"Sherry doesn't like my children. So they don't like her, and I will never make them get along with her. She dug her claws into a married man. What did she expect?"

"Right. I see," Dave said. "And like I said, we're the problem, Madeline, you and me. I need to repent for my part in this. You might not want to hear this, but you need to do the same."

"Don't go there with the faith speech, Dave. Look around here, man. You're waiting in the emergency room. This is real. Your only daughter is undergoing surgery because her brother damaged her uterus; so much for your prayers of faith and protection over our family. Madeline crossed her legs and patted her hair into place. She turned away from Dave.

He got the hint and left, probably going to the chapel, anyway. She couldn't be bothered with options that didn't work. Madeline wasn't saying prayer was irrelevant altogether. She acknowledged God; who He was; and what He could do. Her complaint was purely with Dave in thinking God was interested in treating their family special. He hadn't and their suffering seemed endless. She was frustrated beyond reason and felt helpless with no solution on how to fix her branch of the Mitchell family. Her family had crashed to the ground on her watch. She wanted meaningful answers. She didn't have any at the moment, and Dave didn't, either. What a pitiful pair of parents they made, she thought.

It dawned on Madeline that nobody had called Sam to tell him the news. She fretted about whether or not to call him. He deserved to know. On the other hand, what could he do nearly three hundred miles away? She didn't want to disrupt his studies. She fretted a bit longer and decided he'd want to know. She found a secluded pay phone past the cafeteria, poured in a ton of change, and got him on the line.

"Sam, I know it's late."

"Not really," he said. "We just had a late study break."

"What's that?" she asked, giving herself time to get composed. She couldn't just rush to deliver such devastating news.

"It's when they give out snacks in our dorms, usually around midterms."

"Do you have a test tomorrow?" she asked.

"No, no, it was a random break. Honestly, I'm not sure why we had the break, but you know students don't ask questions when they're giving us extra food," he said, laughing.

She was saddened, realizing the laughter would soon end. "Sam, I'm calling to tell you something important." She dreaded having to tell him, knowing how he was going to react about his sister.

"What?"

"Tamara is in the hospital."

"For what?"

"Well, I don't want to get into the details over the phone, but I will tell you that she was raped."

"W-w-what!" he yelled. "Mom, tell me you're not sure!"

"I wish I could, Sam, but it's true. She was brutally raped."

"Who did it?" he asked, with a piercing sound of rage.

The most painful words she'd ever spoken followed. Nothing spoken before could be more devastating. "It was Andre."

"Andre who?"

"Your brother."

She heard the phone receiver on the other end banging against something and Sam screaming.

"Sam, Sam!" she called out.

"I'm going to kill him."

"Don't talk like that! You don't mean it."

"I do, Mom. I really do."

"We have to deal with your sister and your brother's situation."

"He's not my brother. He's nobody to me. He's dead to me."

She didn't think the night could get any worse. She was wrong. "We have to think clearly, Sam."

"I'm coming home."

"Why don't you wait? Let us find out how she's doing first."

"You can't stop me."

Sam was a rational young man. She knew three hundred miles would give him plenty of time to calm down. She wasn't overly concerned about his initial reaction. It was understood. Sam had been Tamara's protector from the moment she came home from the hospital as a baby, when he was a toddler. Their relationship hadn't changed.

"How are you getting here? Are you flying or taking the train?"

"Not sure, but I'll probably drive."

"I don't want you driving home tonight. It's too late, and you're too upset."

"I'm coming tonight, Mom."

"I said no, Sam. I don't want another child getting into trouble because none of us took time to think about the outcome of our actions. Now, I'm not stopping you from coming home, not at all. But I am begging you to wait until the morning. Please fly or take the train. I can wire money if you need it."

"No, I have plenty of money left over from what you gave me at the beginning of the year. I'm good with cash. I'll get a ticket home in the morning. See you tomorrow, Mom."

"Get home safely, Sam."

Madeline eased the pay phone receiver on the hook and wept into her hands. Her misery was stuck on replay.

Chapter 64

Dave stayed at the hospital most of the night, until her doctors decided to admit Tamara for a few days. Between the physical trauma she'd undergone and the psychological damage that was sure to follow, Dave and Madeline were relieved that she would have medical care around the clock.

Sherry was awake as Dave finished his quick shower and shave. "Are you going into the office?" she asked.

"For a few hours, I guess. There are a few urgent matters I have to tend to today, and then I'm going to the hospital to relieve Madeline. She's been there since Tamara went in last night."

"This is just awful," Sherry said, bending her knees and resting her elbows on top. "I hate to say this, but I knew something bad was going to happen with Andre around."

Dave wasn't up for this conversation. In the last ten hours, he'd heard enough and seen too much. Even he was tired.

"This is exactly why I didn't want him here."

Dave was pulling the shoehorn out of one of his leather shoes as he peered up at Sherry, hoping she'd read the expression of exhaustion on his face and give him a break.

"He's trouble, Dave. I hate to say this, but he is."

"Sherry, please stop."

"I know it's bad to say, but you know I'm right."

"Sherry, please stop," he said again, this time giving her a long drawn-out stare. He slipped on the other shoe.

Sherry kept going. "If he'd hurt Joel, I don't know what I would have done to him."

She just wasn't going to let Dave take the easy way out. What was with his family? Why did each discussion have to result in an argument or violence? The seeds of hatred had been planted deeper than he'd realized before last night.

"Sherry, why can't you shut the heck up?"

She was stunned. He was too, but she was quiet.

"I apologize," he said to her. "I'm tired, and we had a rough night. Unless you're going to speak a word of encouragement, I'm asking you not to weigh me down with any more negativity. Trust me when I tell you there's plenty to go around in this family without any additions." He straightened his tie. "I'll be at DMI if you need me," he said, kissing her cheek.

"Dave, I'm sorry. I wasn't thinking about how you must be feeling. I know Tamara is special to you.

"Andre too," he said.

"For what it's worth, I am truly sorry for the way this has turned out."

He lifted his gaze to Sherry. "Thanks. I needed that," he said and walked out.

Today was going to be long and arduous. He ached for mercy on both his daughter and his son. Both needed a miracle that only the hand of God could extend. He'd pray for both equally, as his fatherly touch was far too inadequate to come close to providing what either needed. His heart wept.

***

Dave took the same route to and from work over two hundred mornings and evenings out of the year. He knew each bump in the road, every curve. He could drive the route without thinking about it, which was practically what Dave was doing this morning. The car might as well have been on autopilot. His mind wasn't on I-75, but it was torn between the hospital and the county jail. The situation threatened to take him down. Dave called on the only source of strength he had.

On his happiest day, he believed God was there. In his greatest sorrow, he believed God was with him. He wholeheartedly believed in destiny. God had a plan for Dave and his family. Even though a storm was raging in their lives, God was still there. Dave cried out, "You see me. You see my anguish. You see my shredded heart. Yet I also know that your mercy, your grace, and your everlasting love will sustain my family." Tears beaded on Dave's eyelids. "Please heal my daughter's body and my son's mind. Please don't let the guilt slash away at him like a knife. Father, my heart is heavy, but your mercy is light," Dave said, letting both index fingers simultaneously swipe across his eyelids. There was a time to cry. He had, and it was done. As he drove into the parking lot, he heaved a deep sigh. It was time to stand up for his family and do what had to be done.

He popped up to his office. Thank goodness no one was on the executive floor yet. He didn't know who had heard what, and he just didn't want to hear from his staff about the devastating events. He dropped off his briefcase and hustled down the stairs to Frank's office. He took a quick glance at the wall clock in the hallway and saw that it was 7:15 A.M. Frank was generally in by 7:00. Dave hoped today was one of those days. He approached his brother's office and entered. There he was. Dave was relieved, closing the door behind him.

"Good morning," Frank said. "I'm not used to seeing you on this floor. Are you slumming down here, where the real work gets done?" Frank said, good-humored.

Dave should have laughed, but the joy buried inside couldn't reach the surface. It had to climb over too much sorrow. It was futile. He walked to the windows and leaned against the sill with his arms folded, causing Frank to swing his chair around.

"What's got you acting stiff this morning?"

"Let's just say I had the worst night of my life."

"Okay, you got my curiosity. What happened, or is it something you'd rather not say?"

"No, you're family. You'll find out, anyway. So will everyone else at DMI."

Frank slid his chair back and clasped his hands. "Now, you really got my curiosity up. What is it?" Dave directed his gaze out the window, at the wide outdoors. "Tamara is in the hospital."

"For what? Is it serious?" Frank said.

"Pretty serious, although it's not life threatening. She was attacked."

"What?"

"Actually, she was raped." Dave couldn't face Frank and say the words.

"Oh no!" Frank said. Nah, nah. I don't know what to say, little brother. I'm at a loss for words." He paused for a moment. "What animal could do such a thing?" he asked with his voice raised.

Each bit of this ordeal was difficult for Dave to share. Madeline had laid into him, and Sherry had too. He knew how Frank could be, but he had to tell his brother. There was no one else he could trust who didn't already know the painful details intimately. He was hoping Frank would deal him a break. He desperately needed a friend, not another judge.

"It was Andre."

"Who? Your son Andre?"

Dave nodded in confirmation, unable to say his son's name again without wailing in agony.

"Wow," was all Frank could say while his head shook from side to side.

Minutes passed, and so too did Dave's doubt that God would help them through this nightmare.

"I'm going to need your help," Dave told his brother.

"You have it. Anything I can do, name it." Frank's reaction made it feel like old times between them. Maybe the mutual support and respect hadn't died, which was a dab of encouragement to Dave at a time when he needed it most.

"I have to get an attorney for Andre."

Frank looked perplexed. "Getting a lawyer is no problem. I can do that with a simple phone call, but I have to ask, is that what you want to do?"

"Yes," Dave answered without hesitation.

"But let's think about this. The only reason I'm adding my two cents is that you came to me for help. As your brother, who cares about you and your family, I'm going to tell you the truth. You know me. I always have and always will be straight with you. Andre deserves whatever punishment is coming to him. The court will appoint a lawyer to represent him. You don't have to get involved."

Dave had anticipated Frank's reaction. He expected most people to have the same opinion. They weren't going to understand why he was willing to help his son, the rapist. He was certain many believed Andre was a worthless criminal and deserved to be right where he was, behind bars. Dave's heart couldn't shut the door on Andre, no matter what he did. God hadn't cast Dave aside when he sinned and fell from grace. Dave wouldn't cast Andre aside, either.

"He's my son, Frank, and I will not abandon him again. I've done it three times already, as Madeline has bitterly pointed out to me. I won't let him down again."

"Fair, but how are you going to live with getting your daughter's rapist legal representation?"

"I am crushed by what my son did, but I have to forgive him. Who am I not to?"

"How can you forgive something like that, Dave?"

"Not easily, but I'm commanded to forgive. Trust me, it's not easy, but I choose to forgive. I have to. Otherwise, anger, revenge, and a boatload of negativity would have plenty of room to grow in my heart."

Frank shook his head. "You are definitely more of a man than I am if you can forgive that easily."

"I don't feel great about any of this, but this is the situation I find myself in. I have two kids who are in crisis. They both desperately need a strong father to be there for them, and I will be there for both."

"This may be a silly question, but where is Andre going to stay when he gets out? I hope you're not going to ask me if he can stay with me."

"No, I wasn't going to ask. It hadn't crossed my mind."

"Good. Because I want to support you, but I have my limits."

"You do raise a good question, though," Dave acknowledged. "I guess I hadn't really thought about it. When he gets out on bail, he can't stay at my house. I'll probably get him a place at the Westin and stay there with him until his court date."

"You know how slowly the legal system moves. He could be out on bail for a year before his trial," Frank said.

Dave raised his eyebrows and hunched his shoulders. "Then we'll be at the Westin together for a year."

"And Sherry's going to be okay with you moving out?"

"What choice do I have?"

"Well, I can tell you flat out, I couldn't get him out on bail if he were my kid. And if I did, it would be to kick his tail."

"Honestly, I don't hate my son. Actually, it's just the opposite. Andre needs help, not a jail cell. My heart cries for him. To do what he did speaks to the hell he's been drowning in for years. We just didn't realize he was this far gone. I've been so caught up with the back and forth between Madeline and Sherry for the past ten years that I lost touch with my kids and what they've been dealing with. For that I'm truly sorry," Dave said, pounding his chest with his fist. "I will get him some intense therapy as soon as his feet hit the ground. I should have done it years ago, but this is where we are. I can't dwell on past mistakes, which are too many to count. I'll have to do what I can for him now and make it count."

"Well, I'll have the name of an attorney for you in about an hour."

"I appreciate that," Dave said.

Surprisingly, Frank stood and drew Dave in for a solid hug. He didn't pull away from Dave for several seconds. Dave was grateful for the embrace and the support.

Dave walked to the door and placed his hand on the handle. "Oh, and I'm going to need your help around here for a few days . . . maybe even a week or two."

"Whatever you need," Frank said, flicking his hand in the air, his fingers pointed toward the door.

"I'll have Sharon come down this morning and walk through my calendar with you." Dave twisted the knob and then released it, remembering one more thing. "Oh, and I suspect it's going to be a frenzy around here when the media gets wind of the story," he said in a solemn tone.

"You're right. It's wise for you to stay away from here for a while. Let the dust settle."

"I hate to leave you here alone to clean up this mess."

"Don't you worry. I'll take care of it. You just go home and take care of your business. Your family needs you. Go, and don't worry about DMI or the media. I got you covered."

Dave wanted to weep. The support was overwhelming from someone he loved and trusted. Dave acknowledged that one decision a long time ago had set in motion years of anguish for those he loved. Yet he wasn't going to live with regrets. What was done was done. Frank's actions were a hearty reminder to him that family restoration was possible, even when it was least expected and most desired.

He entered the empty hallway and found a safe haven. It might appear dark at the moment for the Mitchell family, but there was hope. Dave clung to the notion that somehow, someway, his family would be united. It was that hope that allowed him to keep moving forward.

Chapter 65

A week later . . .

The newspaper was sprawled across the kitchen table. Madeline's grip was so tight on the paper that the sides were torn. Perhaps if she read the story a ninth time, it would be different.

"Madeline, come on. Let me have the paper," Dave said as he attempted to pry it from her hands.

"Quit it!" she yelled out. "We did this," Madeline wailed at Dave and Sherry, who was standing next to him. "All of us killed my sons!" She pointed her finger at Dave and Sherry, reserving nothing.

Sherry gasped. "You can't say that."

"Oh yes, I can!" Madeline said shaking the paper at Sherry as a stream of tears ran down her face. Madeline had no idea she could be in such agony. The pain hurt deep inside. Pain pills hadn't helped. Sleeping pills hadn't worked. In her wildest dreams she couldn't have imagined this day happening.

She brushed aside the tears and read the article again, aloud this time. "Tragedy strikes prominent Detroit family. Late Friday evening Dave Mitchell, CEO and founder of DMI, discovered the bodies of his two oldest sons, twenty-two-year-old Andre Mitchell and nineteen-year-old Sam Mitchell, in a suite the family had reserved at the Detroit Westin. The younger son was a freshman at Perdue University and was only a few weeks from his nineteenth birthday. Details are

sketchy, but it appears to be a murder-suicide. Report-
edly, there was a note left by one of the sons. The con-
tents of the note have not been disclosed. The family
spokesman, Frank Mitchell, chief financial officer of
DMI Enterprises, said, "The family is distraught and is
asking for privacy at this devastating time."

The tears wouldn't let her continue reading. "Where's
the note, Dave?" Madeline asked.

"The police have the note."

"I want my son's note," Madeline pleaded.

"We can't have the note until the police complete
their investigation."

"What is there to investigate? Sam and Andre are
dead. Why are they wasting time with an investigation?
Can't they let me have my note before I bury my sons?"

"I'll see what I can do," Dave told her.

Madeline's head ached around her temples. She
massaged them fruitlessly. "Sam told me he was going
to kill Andre."

"When?" Dave asked, grabbing her hand. She jerked
it away from him. She didn't want his comfort.

"The night I told him about Tamara. He told me, but
I didn't take him seriously. I just thought he was upset
and was blowing off steam."

"Madeline, you can't blame yourself for this. None of
us knew."

"But I'm his mother," she blurted out. "I should have
known. One of us should have known, Dave!" she cried
out, resting the side of her face on the table and sob-
bing uncontrollably. Dave wrapped his arms around
her shoulders, laid his head next to hers, and sobbed
too. She was too weak to push him away. When she
finally mustered the strength, she said, "This is too
much for a person to bear."

"We'll get through this, I promise you," Dave said.

"No, Dave, don't do that," Madeline wailed. "Don't promise me more than you can deliver." She lifted her head and stared at Dave and Sherry. "I can't help but think that your selfishness all those years ago has brought us here," Madeline said, spewing her words. "The two of you have brought shame and sorrow on my entire household. Our lives will never be the same, and much of the blame falls on the two of you." She sobbed again.

"Madeline, my heart goes out to you. I've lost a child before and know how much it hurts," Sherry said, placing her hand on Madeline's shoulder. "You've lost two children, which is unimaginable." Sherry bent down closer to Madeline and whispered, "As one mother to another, I'm so sorry, so sorry." Madeline could hear Sherry's voice cracking. It was evident that Sherry was sincere. After all, she had lost a child. The gesture was nice, but nothing could soothe Madeline's hurt.

Dave leaned over and put his arms on the shoulders of both Sherry and Madeline. "We have to put our differences aside and pull together. Tamara is going to need our support."

"My baby girl! Oh, God, how could this be?" Madeline said, feeling a fresh gush of emotion rising. How could there be any tears left? She'd cried on and off for the past day. There wasn't much left, no fight, no tears, and no reason to continue. "I might as well be dead too."

"Stop talking like that," Sherry said forcefully, which caught Madeline by surprise. "You have two other children who need you." She paused and then added, "Dave needs you at DMI, which means I need you at DMI."

The weight of the loss was heavy, especially since it came in a double dose, but much to her astonishment, Sherry's word brought some comfort. Madeline didn't plan to become best friends with her ex-husband's wife, but clearly Sherry was no stranger to tragedy and might be a source of strength during this tough time. Madeline gladly accepted the comforting words.

"Dave," Madeline called out, "we have to band together around Tamara and get her through this."

He bent down next to Madeline as Sherry stood and put a little space between them, allowing Dave to get closer. "Whatever she needs, it's done."

"Right now she needs counseling and space."

"Done," Dave replied. "What about you, Madeline? What do you need?"

"Peace," she said without hesitation. "And an end to our fighting. The children can't take it anymore, and I can't, either."

"Done," Dave said again.

Madeline felt a small infusion of calm. Most likely, it would be fleeting, given the history of the three adults in the room, but for now, right at this moment, there was harmony. Madeline gobbled up the peace among them, recognizing that as the days passed so too might their truce. Maybe next week or next month the war would be rekindled, but that left at least six or seven good days to be normal. She'd take it.

"Thanks for being here," she said, grabbing both Sherry's and Dave's hands and giving them a firm squeeze before letting go. The burning question she'd had right after the divorce had finally been answered. Leaving Dave hadn't been the best decision for her children in the long term. She had to admit that Dave wasn't the only one who'd made a critical mistake. Back then her pride led the charge to kick him out regardless of how she felt. Her emotions had gotten the best of her over a decade ago, and it was too late to rewind. From this day forward, she'd put her energy into building a new life now that the old one was dead.

Madeline reached out for Don, refusing to let him be swallowed alive into the pit of doom they'd each created. She would guard him and his future with every breath in her body. That was Madeline's solemn promise, and she aimed to keep it.

Reading Guide

MAKES YOU GO "HMMM!"

Now that you have read *Betrayed,* consider the following discussion questions.

1. Madeline refused to reconcile with Dave and insisted on the divorce. Yet she felt betrayed when he married Sherry. Why? Did she have a right to be upset?

2. How do you feel about Sherry living with Dave in Madeline's former house? Is that an issue for you or not?

3. Given the death of Andre's birth parents, did Dave and Madeline's divorce contribute to his breakdown? Were there any other steps Dave or Madeline could have taken to help Andre before he snapped?

4. Dave prayed about and repented for his affair with Sherry. He believed God had forgiven him. So why did he continue experiencing one disaster after another in his family (e.g., rape, murder, suicide, a stillborn birth, the loss of clients, and estrangement from his children)?

5. How would you describe Madeline and Dave's relationship? Was it primarily based on love, hate, friendship, their children, and/or a business partnership? Should Sherry have been concerned about Madeline and Dave spending time together at DMI?

6. Why was Frank mad at his brother? Did he have a legitimate reason?

7. When Dave asked Sherry to leave DMI early in the pregnancy, was it to protect her and the baby, or was he looking out for Madeline?

8. When Andre came home from Gateway Prep, was Sherry correct in wanting him to leave the second time, or did she overact when he shoved Joel?

9. What went on between Frank and Madeline? Do you see Madeline getting remarried?

10. DMI was always at the center of Dave's priorities. Frank attributed the incredible success of the company to the favor Dave had from God. After his personal life crumbled, Dave's professional life did too. Do you feel the company's clients were justified in questioning Dave's ability to lead DMI after failing in his marriage? Are the two connected? If yes, how? If no, why not?

11. The Mitchell family was in shambles. Each adult contributed to the family's demise in some way. Pick a character, and state how he or she contributed to the destruction of a family that was once prominent and highly successful.

12. Did Dave treat each of his kids the same, or did he have favorites? And Madeline?

13. Not counting Andre and Don, which character do you like the least, and why?

14. Initially Madeline blamed Dave's infidelity and Sherry's lack of morals for breaking up their family and ultimately shoving her children into one crisis after the next. Do you agree? Why do you think she softened on this later, taking some of the blame?

15. Dave was quick to forgive Andre, despite the terrible deed his son committed. Could you forgive someone under such extreme circumstances? Forgiveness is powerful and enables the offended to release pain, hurt, rage, disappointment, and bitterness, opening the space for peace, happiness, and love. Forgiveness isn't easy to do, depending on the offense, but it is necessary in order for us to move forward in a healthy state. It is a gift to yourself. Is there anyone you need to forgive?

Note:
The Mitchell family drama is loosely based on the story of a mighty biblical warrior, King David, who had God's unprecedented favor and a profound purpose. However, King David was also plagued with family problems, personal failures, and sinful mistakes. Because he was able to forgive those who had wronged him and went the extra step of forgetting (letting go of) the pain, the anguish, and the bitterness associated with mistakes of the past, he was at peace regardless of what was going on around him.

Acknowledgments

This section is the most difficult part of the book to write for me, because there's no way I can do this justice. Even though it is my heart's desire to thank all those who encouraged, supported, challenged, or prayed for me during the creation of *Betrayed* (and the entire Mitchell family drama series), I know it's impossible to list everyone here. So I ask that you accept my heartfelt appreciation up front, even if I miss calling out your name. I pray the Lord will shower you with blessings for your kindness.

As I begin the personal thanks, I have to start with my loyal readers. It is always my hope that every book the Lord allows me to write, including *Betrayed,* will both entertain and inspire you to fulfill God's purpose in your life.

There are those who have abundantly blessed me, such as my incredible husband and best friend, Jeffrey Glass; our beautiful daughter, "Sweetie Pie"; my parents—Fannie, Deacon Earl Rome, and Jeraldine Glass; big brother Rev. Fred & Gloria Haley, little brother Freddy Deon & Christal Haley, Bob Thomas, Lorena Skelton, Frances Walker, Kimberla Lawson Roby, Bethany, and nieces: Azhalaun, Kamryn, Shantel, Asia, Michelle, and Ashley. Much love to the rest of my relatives (Haley, Glass, Tennin, and Moorman), my friends, my sorority sisters, my fellow believers, my sisters-in-law, my brother-in-law, my god sisters/

brothers, my goddaughters, and my dearest Martin family (Eddie, Regina, Sierra, and Mariah). I honor my dad ("Luck"), my brother (Erick), and my father-in-law (Walter), whose memories are always with me.

Much love to Emma Foots, Laurel Robinson, Tammy Lenzy, Dorothy Robinson, and Renee Lenzy for always providing incredible editorial feedback. Special thanks to Joylynn Jossel-Ross for being an exceptional editor. You have truly been a blessing and a joy to work with. I'm grateful for the literary partnership with the entire Urban Christian team. I also have to thank Shirley Brockenborough, Dear Washington, Maleta Wilson, Regina Carlisle-Williams, Beverly Cooley, Audrey Williams, Linda Gurrant, Don/Mary Bartel, and the late Helen Leonard (my junior high English teacher) for always encouraging me. Special thanks to my prayer warriors: Dorothea/Ravi Kalra, Ann/Michael Jarvis, Pop Ron/Mom Dottie Fisher, Emira/Leroy Bryant, Pastor Gus/Carolyn Howell, and Pastor Jim/Joni Di-Palma.

Thank you to my Delta Sigma Theta Sorority sisters, especially my chapter Schaumburg-Hoffman Estates (IL), Rockford (IL), Valley Forge (PA), Milwaukee (WI), Madison (WI), Louisville (KY), Greater Cleveland (OH) Alumnae Chapters, and Omicron Chi (Stanford, CA). Many thanks to my church families at World Overcomers Church (IL), Beulah Grove (GA), New Covenant (PA), Church of Acts (PA), and Trowbridge (CA). I'm grateful to a long list of book clubs, media venues, booksellers, and ministries who continuously bless me: First African-Sharon Hill (PA), Circle of Hope-Jones Memorial (PA) with Dale Lee-Sharpe and Mother Wright, Sistas Empowered and Making a Difference (DE), St. James (IL), Sherry Zabikow at B&N (IL), CLC Book Center (PA), Trappe Book Center (PA),

Acknowledgments

Dana Campbell at B&N (IL), and Rockford Public Library (Staci and Faye).

Congratulations to my goddaughter, Roslind Burks, on her college graduation, and to Tobia Thomas and Sierra Martin on their high school graduations. May each of you always have the blessings of the Lord upon you. Love to Mrs. Minnie Hamilton at St. James AME (IL) as she celebrates ninety-one wonderful years of life. You're not only one of the oldest readers of my series, you're undoubtedly one of the most supportive and encouraging too.

Thanks to you all with lots of love from me.

Author's Note

Dear Readers:

Thank you for reading *Betrayed*. I hope you continue finding the Mitchell family drama to be an entertaining read. Look for the other books in the series. The saga kicks off with *Anointed*, followed by *Betrayed*, then *Chosen, Destined, Broken,* and more to follow.

I look forward to you joining my mailing list, dropping me a note, or posting a message on my Web site. You can also friend me on Facebook, at Patricia Haley-Glass, or "like" my Author Patricia Haley fan page.

As always, thank you for the support. Keep reading, and be blessed.

www.patriciahaley.com

Notes

6724
Notes